SUMMER SUNDAES AT GOLDEN SANDS BAY

THE GOLDEN SANDS BAY SERIES - BOOK ONE

GEORGINA TROY

Boldwood

First published in 2017. This edition first published in Great Britain in 2023 by Boldwood Books Ltd.

Copyright © Georgina Troy, 2017

Cover Design by Alexandra Allden

Cover Photography: Shutterstock

A CIP catalogue record for this book is available from the British Library.

Paperback ISBN 978-1-80426-047-0

Large Print ISBN 978-1-80426-048-7

Hardback ISBN 978-1-80426-049-4

Ebook ISBN 978-1-80426-045-6

Kindle ISBN 978-1-80426-046-3

Audio CD ISBN 978-1-80426-054-8

MP3 CD ISBN 978-1-80426-053-1

Digital audio download ISBN 978-1-80426-051-7

Boldwood Books Ltd
23 Bowerdean Street
London SW6 3TN
www.boldwoodbooks.com

To my daughter Saskia, with love

1

JUNE – ROME

'You've what?' Sacha asked, only half listening to her aunt. She stared out at the terracotta rooftops from her balcony, finding it hard to believe that only eight hours ago she'd been mesmerised by the gentle waves breaking on the golden sand below her bedroom window, hundreds of miles from here.

Right now, she longed to be there, breathing in the warm, salty sea air and preparing to begin another day in her Summer Sundaes Café. She loved living on the boardwalk, overlooking the small sandy bay enclosed on both sides by cliffs and rocks. A cosy feeling rushed through her. She missed her café. It was noisy at times and often busy, but its beach location always had a calming effect, which was more than she could say about being on holiday with her Aunt Rosie.

'It hurts to raise my voice,' her aunt said, her voice straining as if she was about to expire. 'Come inside.'

'Sorry,' Sacha said, doing as she was asked and going back into the cool of her aunt's room. 'You were saying?' She hoped her voice gave away her annoyance, as she almost dared her aunt to repeat her earlier announcement.

'I've arranged for someone to show you around Rome. It's a glorious city and you can't sit inside with me for the next couple of days.' Her aunt moaned, resting her perfectly manicured right hand over the cooling eye mask covering her eyes as she reclined on the large hotel bed.

'I don't need a tour guide.' Sacha's reaction sounded harsh, even to her own ears. She took a deep breath to try and calm down.

Her aunt lifted one side of the eye mask and gave her niece a determined look that Sacha recognised only too well.

'I know from experience how this damn migraine works,' Aunt Rosie murmured, lowering her eye mask. 'I'm going to be incapacitated for the next couple of days and I don't want to have to fret about you.' Before Sacha could argue, her aunt added, 'It's a big city and rather a complicated one. How will I know where to find you if you get lost?'

Sacha forced a smile. She could see her aunt was in pain and didn't want to add to it by arguing. She gave it one last try. 'I'm twenty-nine, Aunt Rosie, and I've travelled all over the world, usually by myself.' She hesitated for emphasis, to let this reminder settle into her aunt's mind. 'I think I can find my way around a European city. I really don't need an annoying boy joining me while I go sight-seeing.'

'I never said he was a boy, did I? Anyway, you must go,' her aunt said, sounding more determined. 'He's expecting you.' She gave a pained sigh. 'If nothing else, you can take the opportunity to visit some of the gelaterias, maybe pick up a few tips for your ice cream café back in Jersey.'

Sacha had to admit, her aunt did have a point. Taking over the running of her dad's smallest café, almost two years ago, had been more challenging than she'd imagined. She was always looking for ways to improve the business and keep ahead of other local cafés.

'That's a good idea,' she said, relenting slightly.

Aunt Rosie lifted the eye mask again. 'You look very pretty.' She raised an eyebrow as she spoke. 'It never ceases to amaze me how fair you and your brother are when your father is so dark.' Sacha could tell she was trying to distract her from being annoyed, and didn't need to be told that Jack was tall and muscular like their father, while she took after their small, fine-boned mother; though they'd both inherited her sun-kissed blonde hair and blue eyes.

'I don't see what that's got to do with what we were saying about today,' Sacha said.

'Indulge me, just this once,' Aunt Rosie said. 'Go with Alessandro. You never know, you might agree with me that he's rather dishy.'

Sacha sighed, suspecting her mother and aunt were in cahoots. Neither understood why she was reluctant to date anyone, since her ex had decided he had more in common with a woman he'd met during a friend's stag weekend than he did with Sacha. No, she was happily single and the last thing on her mind right now was flirting with someone she didn't know and would probably never see again. She picked up her sunglasses, straw Panama hat and small bag, checking her purse was inside. She felt a little guilty for being irritated by her aunt's interference, but knew how Aunt Rosie took over any situation given half a chance. Sacha's life was finally how she liked it and she had no intention of changing anything. She opened her mouth to speak when there was a sharp knock on their bedroom door.

'That'll be him now,' her aunt said, sitting up gingerly and smoothing her hair.

Sacha might have felt sorry for her, but she couldn't miss

her aunt's self-satisfied smile as she marched past her to the bedroom door.

'I won't forget this, you know,' Sacha grumbled, her irritation refuelled by her aunt's reaction. She pushed down the handle and pulled back the heavy wooden door, only vaguely aware of her aunt saying, 'I don't expect you will,' as she came face to face with a quizzical look from a deliciously handsome man.

'I am too early?' he asked, in a beautifully musical accent. He peered over her shoulder at her aunt and gave a forced smile. 'I believe I am to be your tour guide of the city.' He looked from Sacha, to Aunt Rosie and back again.

Sacha stared at the tanned, muscular Adonis, who looked to be at least six feet two in height. She thought she recognised him from somewhere, although she couldn't place him. She opened her mouth to speak but no sound came out. Sacha didn't like to admit defeat, and couldn't remember the last time she had, but maybe this guidance business her aunt had arranged behind her back wasn't going to be nearly as tiresome as she'd expected.

Sacha cleared her throat. 'I'm Sacha Collins, pleased to meet you.'

'I am Alessandro Salvatore,' he said, smiling at her as he shook her proffered hand. 'You are ready to leave now?'

'Yes, all ready.' She turned to her aunt to say goodbye and didn't miss the hint of a smile on her lips. 'Have fun.'

Switching her gaze back, she saw that Alessandro's smile had slipped. He didn't look much happier than she suspected she did. She assumed he must have been forced into taking her out and wondered if his relatives were as bossy as her own.

As she stepped out to join him in the hallway, he pulled a

black peaked cap onto his head. 'Are there any places you wish to see, or would you rather I choose where we go first?'

Sacha thought of the list she'd written back in her room, trying to recall the places she'd looked up on the Internet. 'The Trevi Fountain has to be one of the places I'd like to see, also the Spanish Steps,' she said. 'That is, if you don't mind?'

He shook his head. 'No, they are perfect places to see.'

They walked out of the air-conditioned hotel foyer and into the harsh bright sunshine. Sacha quickly put on her sunglasses and shoved her hat down on her head. The heat had already taken out any bounce that she'd managed to get into her straight hair earlier that day. At least the hat would hide how hideously flat it looked.

'The Trevi Fountain, it is this way,' Alessandro said, indicating that they turn left.

He hadn't smiled once, she noticed. She wondered whether he was bored already.

'This really is very kind of you,' she said as they walked along the pavement, and when he didn't answer, she couldn't help feeling irritated. 'This wasn't my idea, Alessandro. My aunt arranged this tour without me knowing, I'm afraid. If you'd rather be somewhere else, I'm perfectly capable of wandering around Rome without your help.'

She stopped walking, leaving him to continue for a couple of steps before he realised she wasn't next to him.

He turned and frowned at her. 'You have forgotten something at the hotel?'

'No,' she said. 'But I don't want you to feel you have to come with me today. You can go and do whatever it was you were planning to do before my aunt poked her nose in.'

His black eyebrows knitted together in confusion. 'Poked her nose?'

'What?' She realised what she'd said. 'No, I mean. Um. Poking her nose into business where it's not wanted.'

He mused over her words before shaking his head. 'This is something in England that you say?'

She laughed. 'Yes, sorry. It means, you know, getting involved in something when no one wants you to.'

'Ah, like my uncle. They have been talking, I think.' Alessandro's annoyance appeared to dissipate and he smiled, displaying perfect white teeth. 'I am sorry. I have been rude. I am happy to show you the beautiful places here.'

'If you're sure you don't mind.' Now she came to think of it, Sacha did rather like the idea of not wasting time wandering around the labyrinth of streets alone and maybe missing the best bits of the city. And Alessandro seemed nice enough, at least now that he'd cheered up a bit.

'Please,' he said, a glint in his blue-grey eyes. 'I do not mind. Your aunt stays at my uncle's hotel whenever she is in Rome, they tell me. I have met her also several years ago, when I travelled with my aunt and uncle to the naming ceremony of the ship, Queen Victoria.'

'We're going on a cruise on that ship in a couple of days,' Sacha said, noticing that the dark grey rings around his irises seemed to make his eyes even more piercing. 'It's why we're spending a little time in Rome first. I didn't know my aunt knew your family.'

'They met at the ceremony, but I have not seen her since.' He laughed. 'She is a strong lady, one that enjoys life very much, I think.'

'You're not kidding,' Sacha said, picturing her aunt in her red sports car, the roof down as she raced around their home island of Jersey on her way to a lunch, cocktail party, or rendezvous with her latest boyfriend.

Alessandro narrowed his eyes. 'Your mothers are sisters?'

'They are, but very different to each other.' She stared at him briefly and couldn't resist asking, 'Have we ever met? You seem a little familiar, but I can't think why.'

He pulled his cap down slightly, looking uncomfortable under her scrutiny. 'I do not think we have met before.'

They walked on in silence, stopping every so often for Sacha to look in a shop window.

'I want to buy a few gifts for my parents, brother and three closest girlfriends,' she said, unsure whether to buy the presents now, or wait to see if she came across better items during the cruise.

He didn't seem to mind that she kept stopping to take photos of buildings. There was something intriguing about the city's architecture that fascinated her. Sacha wished she could remember everything about Rome. She savoured the sweet fragrance of the flowers growing in wooden containers sectioning off the seating area outside one of the trattorias. She was relieved to have remembered her hat and sunglasses to shield her eyes from the brightness of the summer sunshine.

'This is the Trevi Fountain,' he said a while later. He was stating the obvious, but it was impressive enough to deserve the announcement. Sacha gazed in awe at the display of elaborately carved marble she'd seen many times in photographs over the years. 'It is named after this district and was designed by Nicola Salvi and completed by Guiseppe Pannini.' He frowned briefly, rubbing his chin. 'They began building it in 1732, but it wasn't opened until thirty years later.'

She was impressed with the fountain and Alessandro's knowledge. She had to move slightly to get a good view, due to the crowd of people milling around them, trying to take photos with their selfie-sticks. 'Did you know those dates already, or did you have to look them up?'

'I looked them up.' He took her left hand. 'Hold your bag with the other hand,' he said, drawing her through the throngs of people until she'd reached the edge of the pool of water, glistening between them and the magnificent statues of the fountain. 'There are many pickpockets here and you must be careful with your belongings.'

The pushing and jostling was a little tiring, but it was worth walking through the heat to see it and she decided to come back to view the fountain at night when it was lit up.

'You wish me to take a photo of you?' Alessandro asked.

She handed him her mobile. 'It's the button on the front there.' As soon as she'd shown him, she could tell he was being polite and doing his best to hide his amusement. How stupid of her, of course he knew how to work her phone.

He waved for her to step back and, bending his knees slightly, took a few pictures of her smiling like a typical tourist. Thanking him, she took back her phone and fanned herself with her hat.

'Phew, how do you stand this heat?'

'Not as easily as you might think,' he laughed. An excited voice called out his name and Alessandro and Sacha turned to see who it was. 'Your friends?' she asked, spotting two beaming girls Sacha assumed to be about sixteen or seventeen hurrying towards them.

'Shall we go for an iced coffee?' he said, taking hold of her hand and pulling her along with him without waiting for an answer. 'There is a café over there, I have been there many times and they serve the best coffees.'

She glanced over her shoulder to see the two girls disappearing into the throng of tourists, as she let him take her towards the white-fronted café he'd indicated.

Ordering two iced coffees, they found a spare table just inside the building to make the most of the air-conditioning blowing down from the unit over the door.

'Thank heavens for that,' she said, forgetting about her hair and taking off her hat, placing it over her bag on the vacant seat beside her. 'Do you know those girls?'

He puffed out his cheeks and shook his head slowly. 'No. I am sorry, it was rude of me to pull you away.'

She looked out to see if she could spot the girls, but they were nowhere. 'Why were they chasing you?'

He waved the waitress over. 'They think they know me,' he said.

She didn't like to add that she'd thought the same as them. 'Why would they?' she asked, hoping it would help her to try and place where she knew him from.

'I do not know,' he hesitated. 'I did a little modelling, maybe they recognise me from those pictures,' he said, as if it was something he didn't want to discuss.

Taking the hint, Sacha changed the subject, but unable to come up with anything more original said, 'I'm used to British summers and I don't think they ever get as hot as this.'

'Where in England do you live?' Alessandro asked, relaxing once more.

'On the island of Jersey,' Sacha said, taking a breath to explain exactly where the island she'd spent most of her life could be found, but he smiled knowingly. 'You know it?' she asked, curious if maybe that's where she might have seen him before.

'No,' he said, his voice quiet as he peered out of the door. 'I've never visited, but my father worked there in the sixties and

I will be visiting for a couple of months this summer. Next month in fact.'

Sacha couldn't believe it. 'Seriously? You've booked to go there?'

Their coffees were delivered and he thanked the waitress, who, Sacha noticed, reddened when Alessandro spoke to her.

'My father still has friends there. He arranged for me to spend time getting to know the place.'

She was intrigued. 'Why Jersey?'

He laughed. 'You have your famous Jersey milk, no?'

She wasn't sure what that could have to do with his visit, but assumed he must be staying with one of the farming families on the island. 'We do, and Jersey Royal new potatoes. They're creamy and taste like they have butter on them, but without butter being added, if you see what I mean?'

'I will have to sample those,' he said, widening his eyes.

Sacha giggled. 'They're delicious and so is the milk. If you haven't tasted it already then you're in for a treat.'

They fell silent and stared at each other for a few seconds before Sacha focused her attention on her coffee. She wasn't sure if she should offer to meet up with him and show him around when he got to the island. After all, the poor guy had been forced into showing her around Rome. It wasn't as if they were friends though, or if he'd even been the one to instigate their afternoon together. She didn't want him to feel obliged to spend time with her back home as well as here, so kept her thoughts to herself.

Both drank their coffees and Sacha checked the photos on her phone for something to do. 'These are great, thanks,' she said, relieved to be able to fill the awkward silence between them. 'I hate having my photo taken, so it's not often that I have pictures of myself and when I do, I usually don't like them.'

He leant over and looked at the screen on her phone as she scrolled through several images. 'You look very pretty. Bellisima. Very natural, it is good.'

'Thank you,' she said, feeling a little awkward under his scrutiny. She hoped she wasn't blushing, but suspected he could probably tell her reddening cheeks were down to embarrassment rather than the heat. 'My friend, Bella, is very clever with adding filters and things to her photos, but I can't be bothered. To be honest, it's not often I take photos of myself, I'd rather take them of my surroundings.'

'Surroundings?'

'Yes,' she said. 'Like the little beach that my flat overlooks. Essentially the view is the same; sand, sea and rocks on each side. But the sky changes colour depending on the weather and the tide comes almost up to the sea wall twice every twenty-four hours. Even the plants growing on the cliff top and headland change all the time, sometimes they're pink with the heather, at other times white with clusters of daisies, or yellow when the daffodils are in bloom. There are never two days when the view is truly the same.'

'I like that idea. My, er,' he hesitated, 'friend, she is always taking pictures of herself. Selfies.' He glanced outside at a group of tourists smiling up at their mobiles as they held up selfie sticks.

Sacha laughed. 'Yes, some people like to take them,' she said. 'Though it isn't my idea of fun. I rarely remember to look at photos once I've taken them, how about you?'

Without answering, he stood up and so Sacha did the same. She was a little taken aback when he went to the counter and, producing a few Euro notes, paid for their coffees. She went to join him.

'No, please. I should be getting these,' she insisted. 'After all, you're here to show me around the city, not pay for things.'

'I am happy to buy you a coffee,' he said, his shoulders less hunched than when they'd arrived at the café.

Sacha frowned. 'I'll pay for the next drinks then,' she said, immediately wondering whether that sounded like an invitation.

'Now, to the Scalina Spagna.'

Sacha didn't like to disagree, but was desperately hoping to visit the Spanish Steps before heading back to check up on Aunt Rosie. 'Um, I was rather hoping to see the Spanish Steps next.'

'Si,' he nodded, amused. 'La Scalina Spagna, the Spanish Steps.'

Sacha followed him out of the door. She couldn't help being amused, despite feeling a little foolish, at having used the English version of the Italian landmark. She followed him down a passageway and after about ten minutes they arrived at the wide steps, again with many tourists milling about taking photos, or sitting on the steps, staring at the view of the skyline below.

'Wow,' she murmured. 'This is stunning.'

'There are one hundred and thirty-eight steps connecting the lower Piazza di Spagna with the upper piazza, Trinita dei Monti.'

'And when were they built?' she asked, unable to help teasing him.

He laughed. 'Ah, I know this also, I have looked it up on the way here. They were built in 1723 to 1725 to link the Trinità dei Monti with the Spanish square below.' He held his hands up and bowed his head.

Sacha clapped. 'Very clever,' she said.

She tried to memorise everything he was saying then, spotting him checking his mobile discreetly, realised she could simply look it all up later, like he was doing, when she was back at the hotel.

'That is the Fontana della Barcaccia,' he said, indicating a stone fountain surrounded by a circular pond. 'And there, where you begin climbing the steps, is where your English poet, John Keats, lived and died in 1821.'

'That house?' she asked, excited at the unexpected discovery.

'Yes. It is a museum and filled with, um, mementos.'

'I'd love to go and see it, if you think we have time?'

'We can make the time,' he said.

Delighted for the opportunity to investigate such an exciting place, Sacha ran over, stopping to gaze up at the marble sign above the door. 'Keats Shelley Memorial House,' she said, in awe. 'How didn't I know this was here?' Sacha couldn't believe she'd travelled to Rome and stumbled upon this museum honouring the Romantic poets. She pictured Keats, seeing this house for the first time when he came to stay, ill with tuberculosis.

She walked through the rooms, relishing the scent of old books neatly displayed in the library, gazing at the flower motifs on the high ceiling, and marvelled that she was in the building where Keats had once lived.

She'd forgotten about Alessandro waiting for her outside. Hurrying out, she spotted him sitting on one of the steps. He was leaning back, his elbows resting on a higher step, his long legs stretching out in front of him. His face was tilted up to the sun, his eyes closed and his long black lashes rested on his tanned cheeks. She watched him for a moment, studying his roman nose and perfectly shaped mouth, enjoying the opportunity to study his beautiful features. She wondered what he would be doing if he hadn't been persuaded to traipse around with her this afternoon. Poor man, he was being very decent about having his time hijacked. She realised he'd opened his eyes and quickly looked away.

Sacha suspected he'd spotted her staring at him. Mortified, she went to join him further up the steps, tripping on one of the edges, only just managing to right herself before landing on him. She could see him struggling not to smile.

'You enjoyed the museum?' he asked, kindly changing the subject. 'I have seen it many times, but it is a place I like to visit.' They began walking. 'You like poetry?'

Recovering from her humiliation, she thought she'd better be polite and answer his question. 'I love the English Romantics, which is why I was so excited to go inside. I don't write poetry though, I've tried to and I'm dreadful at it.'

'You might not be as bad as you think,' he said, stepping aside to let her walk between two groups of people.

Her steps faltered. 'You write poetry?'

His face reddened slightly under the tan. 'A little.'

She didn't want to embarrass him further, so didn't ask him to quote some for her. It dawned on her that her feet were getting sore in the heat.

'I should have worn more sensible sandals,' she said, stopping to take one foot out of her espadrilles and wriggling her toes to get some feeling back into them. 'Or worn these in before coming away.'

He looked baffled. She wondered if it was because of the language barrier, or whether he just didn't realise how women sometimes wore shoes because they looked nice rather than for comfort.

Sacha smiled. 'I'm a bit parched. Shall we get an ice cream? This time, I'll pay.'

He considered her suggestion and nodded. 'I will take you to the best gelateria in Rome.'

'I'd like that,' she said, happy to be able to tick off another item in her 'Rome: To Do List'.

'We have to walk for a few minutes. You don't mind?' He narrowed his eyes and glanced down at her feet.

She didn't want to be a bore so agreed, instantly regretting it after only a few steps. This had better be worth it, she mused, not wishing to make a fuss. He led her down various roads and passageways, and she was beginning to lose her determination not to give up when he stopped in front of a marble fronted building. It didn't look like any gelateria she'd seen so far.

She peered inside when he waited for her to pass him. 'Where are the glass fronted freezers displaying the flavours?'

He gave her a knowing smile. 'They are none. The gelato is in there.' He pointed.

Sacha could only see about ten metal bins. 'There isn't much choice, is there?' she asked, hoping that there was indeed some choice. From where they stood it was hard to tell.

'There are the flavours everyone likes, chocolate, vanilla, mint, but also those of the fruits that are in, um, season? Maybe now would be peach.'

She thought about it and decided she liked the idea of natural fruits being used in the ice creams. 'I think I'll try a peach one, then. You?'

He put his index finger up to his chin and gazed heavenward, considering his choices. 'I will choose the peach also.'

'I don't see how this works if they're not displaying the stock to the passers-by.'

He shrugged one shoulder. 'This gelateria is known for its

excellence and so visitors don't need to see the product first.' He placed their order and continued. 'It is a different way to sell the gelato, but it is working well and people seem to feel like they're buying into a secret.'

Sacha mulled over his words and decided there might be something in them.

She watched as the assistant took one of the crunchy cones in a napkin, and with the other hand lifted the lid from one of the metal bins and scooped out two large dollops of the pale pinkish ice cream, pushing each one down into the cone. Her mouth watered at the light, fruity scent as the assistant handed her cone over.

Barely able to resist, Sacha breathed in the delicious aroma as Alessandro patiently waited for his to be prepared. Once he'd been handed his cone, she gave the assistant several euros and they sat down in silence at one of three small metal tables in the tiny parlour.

Sacha took a lick, closing her eyes in bliss as the enchanting flavour hit her taste buds, cooling her throat. 'Heaven,' she murmured, taking another mouthful. Neither of them spoke as they devoured their gelatos. The sheer pleasure was worth every second it had taken to get there on sore feet.

'I would walk miles to have this again,' she said.

'Si, and me,' Alessandro said, smiling at her. 'Is very good, no?'

'Oh, yes. Its texture is a little different to the ice creams at home,' she said thoughtfully. 'I wonder why that is?'

He smiled. 'It is because they are made in a slightly different way.'

Fascinated, she asked. 'How though?'

'The gelato is um, churned at a much slower rate. This way

less air is brought into it and leaves the gelato denser than your ice cream would be.'

'I didn't know that.' She thought back to the taste and how the gelato had felt in her mouth. 'It was silkier and softer, somehow.'

'It is because gelato is served at a slightly warmer temperature than ice cream. It softens the texture. There is also a lower um, percentage of fat than in ice cream, so that the main flavour that's added to the mixture, like maybe strawberries, comes across slightly stronger.'

'Wow, I never knew that.' She'd learnt so much about ice cream since taking over her father's café, especially the sundaes that she specialised in, but hadn't realised there were different ways to make it. 'I simply thought that gelato was the Italian word for ice cream,' she said, aware she probably sounded rather silly. Giles, her ex, had never resisted an opportunity to mock her when she got something wrong. She knew he was in the past and that her confidence was slowly building again, but sometimes found it hard to believe in herself.

'I don't think many people know the difference.'

She laughed. 'You do, though.'

He winked at her. 'Maybe it is because I eat gelato most days.'

Her stomach did a little flip. There was something intriguing about him and it wasn't only his gorgeous looks. Maybe Aunt Rosie had done her a favour, after all. She glanced at him from under her eyelashes. He was still lost in his own world of bliss as he continued eating his gelato. He'd been funny and kind, despite having to bring her here, and to the other places she had wanted to see, under duress. She decided to be as generous to him when he visited the Channel Islands. It was the very least she could do.

They finished and wiped their hands, then strolled back towards the hotel. Their slow pace gave her feet a chance to adjust to the heat.

Sacha had to concentrate on navigating the cobbles while taking in the splendour of the buildings and trattorias as they walked. She pointed up at an abundant display of flowers on a stone balcony just as her foot slipped on one of the cobbles. Alessandro grabbed her left arm a split second later, stopping her from falling over, and then bent to retrieve her hat from the ground.

'That was close,' she said, smiling at him and taking her hat. 'It's difficult to focus on where you're walking when there are so many intriguing sights to enjoy.' She replaced her hat on her head and they began walking again.

'The cobbles are not easy for women wearing their heeled shoes.'

'I'm wearing flats, so don't really have an excuse for my clumsiness,' she said, giggling as she pictured how silly she must have looked when she stumbled. 'There's so much to take in,' she added. 'I don't want to miss anything.' She watched an elderly couple cross the road holding hands as the man whispered something to his partner, making her laugh.

'They remind me of my grandparents,' Alessandro said.

'Do you get forced to show many tourists like me around the city?' She hoped he didn't mind her question.

To her relief, he laughed. 'Am I a good guide, do you think?' he asked, smiling at her, his blue-grey eyes twinkling in a rather flirtatious way.

She couldn't help being amused by him. 'You are.'

He shrugged. 'You are the only person I have agreed to show around. Because your aunt is unwell and my aunt and uncle asked me to help you enjoy your first time visiting Rome.'

'Well, it's very kind of you.'

'No.' He pushed his hands deep into his chino pockets. 'I do not mind. I have enjoyed this afternoon very much.'

She was glad to hear it, a little more than she expected. 'Thank you, so have I.'

They reached the entrance to the hotel and Alessandro stopped. 'If your aunt is no better tonight, will you come with me for dinner? I can take you to a small restaurant with views I think you'll appreciate.'

She didn't have to think for more than a second before replying. 'I'd like that very much. How will I let you know?' she asked, delving into her bag for her room key card.

'Er, I can wait for you outside the hotel, here at half past seven? If you do not come I will know that you are with your aunt.'

'Okay, thank you,' she said, excited to have plans instead of spending the evening alone in her room. If she was travelling alone she'd think nothing of setting off to see everything by herself, but she knew how Aunt Rosie fretted about her and didn't want to give her any cause to do so while she was suffering so badly. 'I'll probably see you later, then.'

She gave him a wave and stepped into the hotel lobby where she was instantly surrounded by cold air, and hurried over to the elevator. As she waited, she slipped the espadrille off her right foot, and rested the sole of her foot on the cold floor tile. It was utter bliss. Forgetting others could possibly see her, she stepped out of the other shoe and stood, eyes closed, unaware that the lift had reached her floor.

'Ahem.'

She opened her eyes, horrified to see another guest glaring at her with distain. She quickly pushed her feet back into her shoes, wincing as the pain in her toes jolted through her, just as the lift doors drew back, and stepped aside. 'Sorry. Hot feet.'

The man pressed the button for the second floor and raised his eyebrows in question.

'Oh, third floor for me, please.'

He pressed the third button and glowered at her and then down to her sore feet, before emitting a deep breath to show his disgust. The lift stopped at the second floor and as the doors drew back he stepped forward and without bothering to look back, said. 'This is a hotel, not a hostel.'

'It must be nice to be so cheerful,' she said as the doors closed, eager to go back down to find him and give him a piece of her mind.

It dawned on her as she walked along the corridor that maybe he had a point. Her aunt would have said the same thing, or certainly commented on it to her when they were alone. By the time Sacha reached their room she was embarrassed that she'd been caught without her shoes on.

She listened at the door for any sound then, hearing none, carefully pushed her key card into the slot and slowly pushed down the door handle. Opening the heavy door, she walked inside the darkened bedroom and saw the shape of her aunt lying on the bed.

'It's all right,' Aunt Rosie whispered. 'You don't have to be afraid to move. This migraine isn't nearly as bad as I'd dreaded.'

Sacha kicked off her shoes and sat down on the brocade chair at the side of the bed. 'Do you think you'll be well enough to come downstairs for some supper?' she asked doubtfully. 'Or we could have a bite to eat up here, if you'd prefer.'

'No, darling. I'll just stay put and keep my eyes closed for now. If you'd rather go out somewhere though, do so. I don't want to hold you back from enjoying this incredible place.'

They sat in silence. Sacha didn't like to disturb her aunt and it was a relief not to be wearing her shoes.

'Did you have a lovely time with that delicious looking man?'

Sacha smiled, glad the heavy curtains were keeping out most of the light, and that her aunt's eyes were still closed. 'Yes, thank you. He was very kind.'

'Kind? Tell me where he took you and what you saw.'

Sacha told her everything, leaving out the bit about the man in the lift telling her off about her shoes. 'It's a stunning place. I love Rome, I can't believe I've never made the effort to come here before now.'

'Nor can I,' her aunt said. 'It's where I had my first holiday romance. I was twenty-one and travelling on my own for the first time without my parents.'

Sacha hadn't heard about this before. Rosie was her aunt, but also her godmother. She was sixty and very young at heart, as well as glamorous, with a charm and charisma that intrigued men of all ages. Sacha hoped she could learn a few things from her aunt during this holiday. How to be a bit more self-confident, for a start.

'If you don't need me to stay with you this evening, Alessandro has asked me out to dinner. He's going to show me more of the sights.'

'I'm so relieved,' her aunt said. Sacha could tell she was smiling as she spoke and knew she'd approve. 'I have only met him once before, several years ago, he was charming then. I can imagine he's great company. He's an interesting young man, you know.'

She wasn't sure how her aunt could know such a thing if she'd only met him once, several years ago. 'He was,' Sacha admitted.

'Good. You go and enjoy yourself. You're not even thirty. You should be having an exciting time. I keep telling your father you work too hard in that café.'

'I don't, not really,' Sacha said, not wishing to go over their usual argument. 'Working in finance all those years was far harder for me. At least running the café, I get to walk about in the sun if it's quiet, and I enjoy meeting the customers and seeing them enjoy their sundaes.'

She thought of Betty, the oldest resident on the boardwalk at ninety-three. She was also the local heroine, having helped a young French man desperately trying to get back to his family in 1941 to escape the Nazis. Sacha had grown up seeing the stone monument, placed at one end of the boardwalk in the seventies to honour Betty's bravery. She recalled asking her father when she was a teenager why it had taken so long to honour the lady, and been surprised to discover that Betty had never told anyone what she had done. It was only when the Frenchman returned to the island to find her in the late sixties, and reported her actions, that anyone found out.

Sacha enjoyed chatting to Betty on the mornings when she came in for her chai latte and Jersey Wonder. Betty loved the local doughnut, so different to the ones on the mainland that were coated in sugar and filled with jam. These plain dough-nuts were typical to the island, and delicious. Sacha always had to resist temptation when a fresh warm batch was delivered to the café by Mrs Joliff.

Then there were the retired statesmen. They were well known on the island, their decades long differences in politics causing many a front page headline over the years. Sacha found it amusing how they met up at her café each morning and put the world to rights over a couple of coffees. She was grateful to have such a pleasant job.

'When it's quiet, I get to go out to the boardwalk,' she continued. 'I can make the most of the sea air, rather than spending my day cooped up in an air-conditioned office, sitting at a desk with my head in some files.' She shuddered at the memory. 'I know some people enjoy their office jobs, but it's just not for me.'

'Personally, I always thought it must be wonderful to dress up in a suit and go to meetings with clients. Being a florist was fun, but there wasn't much call for me to spend time in a boardroom.' Her aunt moved slightly and winced in pain. 'I can't wait for this to pass,' she said, her forearm over her eyes.

'The novelty of working in finance wears off, or it did with me. You probably like the thought if it because you've never done it.' Sacha thought of the bags of suits, blouses and court shoes she'd donated to the Salvation Army clothes bins the day after she'd left her office job. Her mother had been sure she'd need them again, but she was determined to make the café work, and saw the donations as the closing of an era of working in finance that she never imagined repeating.

'And you don't mind living in that tiny box flat above the café? After all, you were used to that large apartment in town when you were with The Little Shit.'

Sacha shivered. Hating to be reminded of The Little Shit. It was a name her aunt had always used to refer to her ex, Giles. Although Giles, being six-feet-one and a part time rugby player, was hardly little.

'I love my flat. It's cosy, and the view of the boardwalk, and the sound of waves rolling onto the beach couldn't be better. Really, I'm very happy now, and Giles has moved on. I heard he was getting married to the estate agent who sold our apartment. Good luck to them, I say.'

'Rubbish, he's a pig and deserves someone doing to him

what he did to you. It wasn't as if he stayed with that girl he dumped you for either, moving on to the next one within weeks of leaving you. He thought he was so clever, and it never occurred to him that someone as nice as you wouldn't put up with his philandering and might just dump him.'

Sacha pushed away the memory of the one occasion he'd come round to her tiny flat, a bottle of red wine in his hand as he tried his best to persuade her that they'd enjoyed something magical, and she should give him another chance.

'Can we change the subject, please?' she said, feeling that familiar pang of humiliation whenever the subject of Giles and what he'd done to her was brought up. 'We're in a beautiful city and we're going on a cruise in two days. That's if you're well enough to go,' she added, when it occurred to her that maybe they'd have to cancel their time on the ship.

'I'll be fine. I always am. Don't start worrying about me. Worse things than a ruddy migraine have failed to hold me back from having fun. Right, you can top up my glass of water from that jug if you don't mind and then you'd better freshen up for your date with the lovely Alessandro.'

Relieved by this change in the conversation, Sacha laughed. 'Fine.' She filled up her aunt's glass, then walked over to the wardrobe and selected one of her new sundresses; a raspberry and green cotton shift. She carried it into the small shower room to get ready.

2

'Seriously, I want to know,' Sacha insisted, as Alessandro shook his head.

'No, I do not sing opera, or anything else.' Alessandro laughed. 'Why do you think that I sing?'

She was enjoying teasing him and he appeared to be enjoying it, too. 'Because you must do something. You said you don't work at the hotel as a guide, so what *do* you do?'

He looked at her as if he wasn't sure whether she was joking or not, then said. 'I have been travelling.' He held his hands up in resignation. 'You really wish to know? I am an archaeologist.'

She hadn't expected him to say that. She glanced at his hands. They appeared too unmarked to have been working on digs. 'You said you'd done modelling, though.' She thought of the girls who'd followed them. She didn't like to be nosy, but was intrigued. He certainly had the height and looks to be a model.

'I was offered modelling work and accepted it to help pay for my studies. My father was angry when I didn't immediately join his business and refused to help me pay for my studies in Cagliari.'

'Where's that then?'

'Sardinia. Is a beautiful place, I loved my time there.'

Excited, she said, 'My aunt and I are visiting Sardinia on our cruise. I've always wanted to go and it's a shame it's only for the day, but cruises are a bit like taster menus. You get to try out places, and if you like them you can go back later and stay for longer.'

'Good idea. You will like Sardinia, I am sure.'

'Would you go back?'

He looked surprised by her question. 'I've been back many times and will hopefully visit the friends I've made there, soon.'

'Why did you give up the modelling though, isn't it easy money if you do well?'

He studied her for a moment. 'It can be very hard work. I was lucky enough to be offered several well-known campaigns, but as soon as I was qualified I gave it up. I am an archaeologist, it's what I love doing. It's what I trained for.'

'I understand,' she said. 'Don't you ever model now?'

'I only do it for charity and not very often.'

She could see he didn't like referring to that part of his life. 'What are you doing now?'

'I have been working in Spain for several months, but my father became ill and asked me to return to Italy and help him in his business.'

'That's kind of you.'

He shook his head. Something told her that talking about his father upset him a little and she wondered quite how ill he must be. 'What work do you do?'

She told him about leaving her old job in finance after ten years. 'I became tired of the intensity of it all. I left university with a lot of ambition, but I lost that over the next few years and wanted to venture out in a different direction.' She hesitated, not wishing to divulge any information about Giles. 'My circumstances changed,' she said simply. 'When one of my father's managers moved away, I offered to step in and now I run the café.'

'Café?' He hesitated and seemed surprised, but she wasn't sure why.

'Yes, I love it there. It's long hours, and in the summer I might work seven days a week at times. I can honestly say I never dread going to work and that's got to be a massive bonus.'

He narrowed his eyes. 'It helps if you love what you do,' he said, rubbing his chin slowly.

The waiter brought over their plates of fresh tomato salsa on toasted bread. The smell of the tomatoes, basil, garlic and oregano filled the air and Sacha's stomach rumbled noisily.

'Sorry,' she said, reddening. He pretended not to notice and she continued. 'Life is much too short to spend it doing something that doesn't fulfil you. Do you agree?'

'I do,' he said. 'This food smells very good.'

It was delicious and Sacha finished her bruschetta unsure how she would manage to eat the following course. A short time later bowls of pasta were placed in front of them. Tempted by the delicious smell of the pesto sauce covering her pasta, she picked up her fork and stabbed it into her penne. After savouring a few mouthfuls, she said, 'There have been quite a few archaeological digs on the island where I live.'

He put down his fork and stared at her. 'There have?'

'Yes. Some men found a load of coins a couple of years ago with their metal detectors.'

'Ah, yes, I have heard of it.' He thought for a moment. 'The

Celtic hoard? Found in a field and worth maybe ten million pounds?'

She nodded. 'That's the one. The coins were estimated to be about two thousand years old and were exhibited at the museum for a while. I went to see them during my lunch hour once when I worked at my previous job. I was so engrossed that I was late back to work. It was fascinating to think that two men had found them locally.' She laughed. 'My father wanted to go out and buy a metal detector. You see quite a few of them on the beaches, sometimes.'

'Your father is interested in archaeology?'

'I'm not sure. I think we all were when the coins were found.' She couldn't help being amused by the memory. 'They've also found Neanderthal teeth, mammoth and woolly rhinoceros' teeth at La Cotte. That's in one of the southerly parishes, called St Brelade. That dig was years ago though. King Charles came over to help with the dig. I'm not sure if he was still at university then?'

Alessandro's eyes widened at this information. 'I think I will enjoy visiting your island. It seems there is much that goes on there.'

'Yes, I suppose there is. In fact, I recently heard someone mention a new find somewhere on the island.' She tried to recall the details, but failed. 'It sounds like a quiet back water and seems like that sometimes, but an awful lot has happened in such a small place. I must admit I love it there.'

'You have travelled much?'

'Yes, my father always took us away each year and after I left school, I took a gap year and travelled extensively doing the usual, Cambodia, Thailand, Vietnam. Now I'm enjoying running the café and staying close to the boardwalk.'

'Boardwalk?'

Sacha pictured the boardwalk, recently built along the promenade overlooking the beach. It was the first thing she looked at every morning, and she couldn't imagine ever wanting to live anywhere else.

'It's actually a village, known locally as, The Boardwalk by the Sea. Even the holidaymakers call it that. There's a row of buildings, cottages mainly, but some are shops, and my café. We've got a second-hand book shop, which is run by my friend, Jools. It's her mother's really, but she's less and less mobile and Jools lives with her now and helps run the place. Jools is an artist and I sell some of her paintings in my café, as does our friend, Bella, who has an antique shop on the boardwalk. All our homes overlook the beach. There's a small pier on one side, and cliffs on the other. We love it there.'

'It sounds interesting and very beautiful.'

It was. Sacha smiled at the thought. 'I've only lived there for a couple of years, but I've lived on the island my whole life.'

After dinner, Alessandro suggested they walk off some of their bruschetta al pomodoro and pasta meal.

'I will show you more of this city,' he said. 'There is much to see and although you won't be able to view everything in the time you have here, I can take you past the Colosseum and St Peter's Basilica.'

Sacha couldn't help taking photos. She was torn between taking in the sights by gazing at them and trying to memorise them, and holding up her mobile to record them for posterity. 'I love this city,' she exclaimed, taking in the golden light and shadows cast by the ancient monuments. 'It is truly breath-taking.'

Stopping by the Spanish Steps once more, she covered her mouth, unable to help yawning.

'You are tired,' Alessandro said, sounding guilty.

'No, I think it's stopping, after working so hard the last week before I came away. I wasn't planning to go on holiday, especially as the season at home is almost at its height, but my aunt had a falling out with her partner and refused to let him come with her. When she asked me to join her, my mother decided it would do me and my aunt good if I accompanied her.'

She thought back to her argument with her mother, about leaving the café at such a busy time, but her mother was determined Sacha should have a break, even if only for ten days.

'My aunt and I get along really well, but I worry about leaving the business during the busiest time.'

They began walking in the direction of the hotel.

'Who is looking after it now?'

'My twin brother, Jack.' Sacha grinned as she pictured Jack in an apron, wiping tables and making ice cream sundaes. 'He was guilt-tripped into taking two week's leave from his job in London. He's left his girlfriend behind because she couldn't get the time off from her job. So, he travelled over to the island without her. I think he secretly liked the idea, but he made a bit of a fuss before agreeing to do it, to save face.'

Alessandro laughed. 'Ah, guilt-tripped? It's what parents do to us to make us do as they wish, no?'

'That's the one.' Sacha giggled, picturing her mother's face as she spoke to Jack, thinking he couldn't see through her reasoning for getting him to come and look after the café. 'Jack is usually very independent of our family, or likes to make out that he is. I think my mum doesn't particularly like his present girlfriend and is hoping that time away from her will make him see that she's not the right woman for him.'

Alessandro frowned, his eyes twinkling. Sacha suspected he might have experienced something similar from his own mother. 'You think this will work?'

'Not for a second. Jack's far too strong-minded to be influenced by our mum, but if it keeps Mum happy for a while, then I don't mind.'

* * *

Back at the hotel, Sacha thanked Alessandro for a wonderful evening and was surprised when he offered to take her out again the following afternoon.

'I'd like that, thank you,' she said. 'But only if you don't have anything else that you'd rather do?'

'No,' he said.

Again, that sadness, thought Sacha, wondering what had happened to give him a fleeting, haunted look every so often, when he thought no one was watching.

'It will be my pleasure.'

Mine too, she thought. 'Good night then. I'll see you tomorrow. Same time?'

'Yes, I will be here.' He bent his head down and kissed her on both cheeks. 'Ciao, Sacha.'

She enjoyed the way he said her name and rather liking being kissed on both cheeks.

She went to thank him again for a wonderful evening but before she managed to say anything, he bent his head and kissed her hard on her mouth. Sacha's eyes widened. He faltered, and when she didn't pull away, he closed his eyes, his firm lips pressing against hers, taking her breath away. He pulled her against him and for a few blissful seconds all the sounds around them disappeared. Alessandro let go of her and moved back and from the look on his face, Sacha suspected he hadn't planned to kiss her. She wasn't sure which of them must look more surprised. They stared at each other in silence.

'Ciao, Sacha.'

Not sure what to do next, she forced a smile and went into the hotel. Looking over her shoulder, she could see he was waiting for her to enter before he left. Once inside, she ran up the stone staircase, stopping before entering the bedroom to rummage for her key card. She didn't want to disturb her aunt so as soon as she was inside, Sacha took off her make-up as quietly as possible, changed and got into bed. She lay in the darkness, her fingers resting against her lips where only minutes before, Alessandro's had been. She fell asleep almost instantly and dreamt about a tall Italian with dark green eyes.

* * *

The next afternoon and evening with Alessandro were as much as fun as the first day. Sacha couldn't help feeling guilty that she was having such a wonderful time while Aunt Rosie suffered in their room. She decided to buy her a gift, so her aunt would at least have a keep-sake to take home.

Sacha yearned to bring up the subject of their kiss, but couldn't find the right moment and suspected Alessandro was keeping the conversations going so that they couldn't address it. Eventually, he brought it up as they sat outside a café, drinking iced coffee.

'I kissed you,' he said suddenly.

'You did.'

He looked away from her, staring at a couple with a small dog on a lead, before adding. 'You did not mind?'

She put her hand on his arm, waiting for him to turn his attention back to her. 'Not at all,' she admitted. 'It was a bit unexpected, though.'

'I didn't mean to kiss you,' he said, hesitating before continuing. 'But you are so pretty and I was enjoying your company very much. It just happened.'

Sacha was flattered. 'Thank you. I had a lovely evening with you, too.'

'I wish you were staying here for a few more days,' he said, picking up his glass and drinking some of the coffee. 'I would like to spend more time with you.'

'Then we'll have to make sure that we go out together when you come to Jersey.'

Alessandro put down his glass. Leaning forward, he kissed Sacha lightly on her mouth. 'I am looking forward to my visit already.'

So was she.

They sat in silence for a few minutes, each lost in their own thoughts.

'What would you like to go and see tonight?' he asked, before finishing his drink.

'I'm not sure.'

Alessandro smiled and took her hand in his. 'Then I will take you to a few places that I know on our way to a bar over-looking the Colosseum. As the sun goes down the ruins are lit, and I believe it is one of the views you should see.'

She nodded. 'That sounds perfect. Let's go.'

* * *

After saying goodbye to Alessandro later that evening, it cheered Sacha up to discover her aunt showered, sitting on the bed in a pair of shorts and a T-shirt. 'You're feeling better,' she said. 'I'm so relieved.'

'I knew it wouldn't last too long,' she said, raking her hands through her hair. 'Now, tell me about your day and that gorgeous man you've been spending so much time with.'

Sacha shook her head. 'I have to admit you were right to arrange for me to go out with Alessandro,' she said. 'He's great company and knows so much about the city. He's an archaeologist, you know.'

Aunt Rosie's perfect eyebrows moved up as much as they could with her Botox-injected forehead. 'I had no idea. I just thought he was related to the Salvatores who run this hotel.'

'He is.' Pulling the small present she'd bought her aunt from her bag, Sacha held it out to her. 'I got you this,' she said. 'It's only a little something, I hope you like it.'

Aunt Rosie opened the top of the bag and peeked inside. 'Oh, it's beautiful. Is it hand-painted?'

'Yes,' Sacha said, relieved her choice had been right. 'The cover of the notepad is all hand-painted. Alessandro suggested the shop when I told him I wanted to buy you something beautiful to keep, but also use.'

'Clever, as well as handsome then?'

Sacha tilted her head to one side. She sensed where this was going. 'Stop it.'

'Well, you could do worse than become involved with the very beautiful Alessandro.'

Sacha knew this was coming so wasn't surprised by her aunt's attempt at matchmaking. 'What am I?' she teased.

'Happily single,' her aunt mocked, mimicking Sacha's voice. 'I sometimes think you protest too much. And although I'm sure you are,' she said, raising her hand when Sacha went to speak. 'I suspect you're only trying to protect yourself after The Little Shit did the dirty on you. You're young, you have the sort of fresh-faced beauty that wouldn't look out of place in *Sports Illus-*

trated, and, quite frankly, I don't think you know what you're missing.'

Sacha wanted to argue, but her aunt had hit a nerve when she'd mentioned Sacha not wanting to be hurt again. 'I just think life is easier without the distraction of a man,' she said, wondering if she'd think quite the same way if she was in a relationship with Alessandro.

Her aunt took the notepad from the paper bag and studied it thoughtfully. 'I don't know why you younger generation are always so unadventurous.'

'We're not,' Sacha said, trying not to sound as indignant as she felt. 'We just have other things on our minds apart from sex.'

'Dull, that's what it is.'

'No,' Sacha giggled. 'It's called being ambitious, and not needing another person in our lives to make us feel whole.'

She'd had this conversation with her aunt many times. Her mother had been an ambitious woman until she'd had her and Jack, she'd said so many times. Then she discovered motherhood and realised that her ambitions lay with bringing up her children to the best of her ability. Sacha didn't see anything wrong with that at all, it just wasn't for her.

'Maybe he's not ready yet either for the next relationship in his life,' her aunt said, thoughtfully.

'What do you mean?' Sacha hated herself for asking, but couldn't let a comment like that go by without finding out more about the man with whom she'd spent the last few days.

'I shouldn't say anything more,' her aunt said, mysteriously, sipping her glass of water and staring out of the window. 'If he'd wanted you to know, he would have told you.'

'Why can't you tell me?'

'No, it's not for me to say.'

Not wishing to ask again, Sacha stood up. 'We'd better get packed for boarding the ship tomorrow. I'll be back shortly, after I've sorted a few of my things out.'

Sacha went to her room next door. She loved her aunt, but wasn't going to press the matter. Sacha enjoyed her company, but was looking forward to being able to spend time alone on the ship and catch up with reading some of the many books she'd loaded onto her tablet. She'd become very used to her own space when she wasn't working, and from what her aunt had told her, she should be able to spend time, quietly enjoying a cocktail, while reading a good book and lying in the sunshine. It was what she envisioned for herself for the next week. That, interspersed with trips to new places each time they docked somewhere.

She went into the shower room and gathered her hand washed underwear. As she folded the dress she wore for dinner with Alessandro the night before, she couldn't help reminiscing about their evening together. Tonight had been more of the same, and as much as she'd forced a smile on to her face when she had to leave him, she couldn't help feeling that she was missing his company already, which was ridiculous as she hardly knew him.

Returning to her aunt's room, she asked, 'Do you want me to pack your things?'

'Not necessary, darling,' her aunt said. 'I've barely taken anything out of my suitcase. It's the first time in months that I've gone a couple of days without putting on any make up, and I have to admit it's been quite a treat not to have to take it all off again before going to sleep.'

She stood up and opened the balcony doors. A rush of heat swept into the room.

'Are you looking forward to the cruise?' Sacha asked, breathing in the warm jasmine filled air. 'I know I am.'

Her aunt turned around and walked over to her, giving her a hug. 'I'm delighted you've come along with me and I know you'll enjoy yourself. Cruises are the best fun. Arriving at a different destination each day without having to cart your case through a packed airport. It's so tedious, all that hurrying, and the endless waiting to be called for flights. With a cruise, someone else does everything while you relax, drink and eat. Bliss.'

Sacha laughed. 'I can't wait to get going,' she said. It was a bit of a fib. She was looking forward to seeing what it was like to be on a beautiful and massive cruise ship, but she'd enjoyed Rome and meeting Alessandro far more than she'd expected. Not seeing him again for a month was going to be a little hard.

She focused on the matter in hand. 'I'd honestly never considered a cruise before. I thought it was for families or older people, but knowing you'll be on the ship I'm sure it must be quite sparkly.'

'Sparkly? In what way?' Rosie walked past her, making her way to the shower room. 'Time for me to freshen up.'

'You know, like dazzling,' Sacha said, picturing the photos of the ship she'd seen online. 'All the chandeliers, and everyone dressed up in ballgowns.'

Her aunt closed the door, laughing. 'Yes, I suppose it is like that, but it's also very informal during the day time and not as imposing as you're probably imagining. I'm sure you'll love it once you get on board.' The door opened and she poked her head round. 'I know you were pretty much forced to come along with me by your mother, darling, but I do think the break away from everything will do you a lot of good. It seems to be working so far, I haven't seen you looking so bonny in months.'

She disappeared behind the door again, closing it and leaving Sacha to wonder what she meant. Why did her family always assume that the drastic change in her lifestyle had been a problem for her? Her mother always hinted that she was being brave earning less money and not travelling for work to conferences and business meetings most weeks. It didn't feel brave at all; more like tasting freedom for the first time since leaving university.

Sacha walked onto the balcony and stared out over the city. No, she was perfectly happy as she was. She might earn very little and now live in a tiny flat, but it was her business, sort of, and her flat. Sort of. Either way, there was nothing about her life that she intended changing. Or so she'd believed until today, when she'd said goodbye to Alessandro and had to remember that if she did see him again when he visited Jersey, their time together would never be quite as isolated as it had been when he was showing her around this beautiful, historic city. The thought saddened her.

* * *

Sacha stared up at the navy and white ship with its red and black funnel.

It looked massive from where she stood on the dock. Magnificent, too. *Queen Victoria*, in all her glory. She'd heard of Cunard before being booked on this trip, but she'd never thought about the ship's height, or connected it with anything she might wish to do.

She'd been disappointed to receive a message from Alessandro that morning, letting her know that he wouldn't be able to make it to the hotel to see them off, but now she was here and about to board, Sacha couldn't help being excited.

She only hoped she'd packed the right clothes and enough of them. Thankfully, she still had a lot of her clothes from her former life, and just hoped they were suitable for wearing on the ship.

A short while later, she and her aunt were walking along the lengthy, blue-carpeted corridor, looking for their stateroom.

'4150,' said Rosie. 'This is us.'

Sacha grinned. Their door was open and they walked into the luxurious bedroom with twin beds, which Rosie insisted were the most comfortable beds she would ever sleep in, to find their cases lying on protective mats on their bedspreads.

'This is stunning,' Sacha gasped. Just inside the door was another one, to the left. Sacha peeked in and found a shower room, complete with small bottles of shampoo, conditioner and various other complementary gifts. In the main area of the stateroom was a small sofa, a coffee table and dressing table, and a television on top of a built-in fridge. Sacha walked to the other end of the room and stepped out onto a glass-fronted balcony.

She couldn't decide where she was most excited about visiting; the Gaudi park and La Sagrada Familia by Gaudí in Barcelona, the Ponte Vecchio bridge in Florence, or anything in Sardinia before returning to Civitavecchia and flying home from Rome.

'You will see for yourself why I love this mode of travel best,' Aunt Rosie said, coming out to join her on the balcony. 'I'm going to show you all those amazing places I've been telling you about. You'll have experiences you'll never forget,' she insisted, her arms held wide and a smile on her face.

Sacha believed her.

'But now, we need to get freshened up and ready for the sail away party.'

'The what?' Sacha couldn't mistake her aunt's delight at the thought of the party. Her excitement was infectious.

Twenty minutes later they were standing by the rails in the sunshine, a floppy straw hat with a scarlet ribbon around it on Aunt Rosie's head and a Panama hat that she'd bought in Rome on Sacha's to keep the heat of the afternoon off her head.

The waiter brought over the cocktails they'd ordered in tall glasses. 'The Sundowner?' he asked, handing it to her aunt when she nodded. 'The Mojito,' he said, smiling at Sacha. 'Is very good, you will enjoy this, I think.'

Sacha thought so too. She took a sip, unable to resist, and closed her eyes in bliss. 'Oh yes, this is heavenly,' she said, promising herself not to overdo it.

'If you get brain freeze from that thing,' her aunt said, presumably speaking from experience, 'rest your tongue against the roof of your mouth. These things are too damn delicious for our own good.'

Sacha knew all about brain freeze from the many times she'd hurriedly eaten an ice cream, and more recently those delicious gelatos Alessandro had taken her to sample. She thought back to Alessandro kissing her and how much she was going to miss spending time with him.

'Isn't this fun?' her aunt asked, breaking into her thoughts.

They were standing on deck nine at the back of the ship. Passengers were arriving to join the party. Some were already tipsy and dancing to the live band, who were entertaining them with summery songs that everyone recognised, including 'Under the Boardwalk' and 'Walking on Sunshine'.

'When do we set sail?' Sacha asked, looking down as the huge ropes were lifted from the iron hooks holding the ship against the side of the dock.

'Very soon, by the looks of things,' her aunt replied, taking another sip of her drink and swaying her hips.

Sacha was relieved to see her finally enjoying herself, now that her migraine had gone. It had concerned her that she'd been the only one enjoying the trip, up until now.

She realised the ship was slowly moving away from the dockside and stood with her arms resting on the varnished wooden rail, looking back at the quayside and wondering what Alessandro was doing now. No point in doing that, she admonished herself. She would just have to wait until she met him again in Jersey.

'Brace yourself,' her aunt said, interrupting her thoughts.

Sacha narrowed her eyes, unsure what she meant and opened her mouth to ask, when the captain sounded the horn, making her jump. 'Bugger,' she moaned, noticing that she'd spilt a little of her drink down her summer dress. 'What the hell was that?'

Her aunt laughed so hard she had to place her cocktail on a nearby table. 'Sorry, but your face, it was a picture.' She bent over and held her stomach. 'I did tell you to brace yourself,' she added apologetically, after a while.

Sacha puffed out her cheeks, her heart slowly returning to its usual steady beat. 'Yes, but you didn't say why, did you?'

She rested back on the rails once more and watched as the land became more distant. The cerulean blue of the sea, where spangles of light hit the peaks of tiny waves, and the heat of the sun on her face soon calmed her. Her aunt was right, this was the perfect antidote to hard work and she intended to enjoy every second.

'So,' Sacha said, nudging her aunt, gently. 'First stop Barcelona. I've travelled a lot, but it always seemed to be to distant places,' she said, thoughtfully. 'I've never really seen much of the Mediterranean.'

'You will now, my darling,' her aunt said, waving over the waiter. 'Let's order another couple of these delicious cocktails. Or, would you rather try different ones?'

It was going to be a blissful evening, Sacha realised. Her aunt was feeling better and by the looks of things was intending on catching up on all the time she'd spent in the darkened hotel room in Rome.

* * *

They were half way through their trip, enjoying afternoon tea served by white-gloved waiters in the Queens Room, where themed balls would be held on several evenings during the cruise. Sacha had enjoyed a pleasant few hours walking through the town of Ajaccio. Her aunt had insisted they visit a museum filled with magnificent eighteenth-century furniture and documents that had belonged to Napoleon, and Sacha had enjoyed learning a little about the history of the Bonaparte family.

She waited for the tea to be poured and had just picked up her cup when her aunt startled her by saying, 'I was thinking about Alessandro today. I saw this young couple, obviously very much in love, and it made me think that you were right not to take any notice of my encouragement between the two of you.'

Sacha took a sip of her Earl Grey tea. 'Why?'

'Well, when I saw this couple walking along, hand in hand, it made me think of what Alessandro's aunt told me about him and Livia.'

Sacha's heart pounded. She didn't like the way this conversation was going, but was unable to stop herself from asking, 'Who is Livia?'

Aunt Rosie leant towards her across the small, highly polished table between them. She checked that no one was listening to their conversation, which was a little out of character and alarmed Sacha further. 'She was his fiancée, and he was desperately in love with her.'

'Was?' Sacha's heart pounded.

'She died, darling. It was too tragic. His aunt was only telling me about it the morning we left Rome.'

Sacha couldn't believe what she was hearing. Poor Alessandro, no wonder he'd had that haunted look that she kept noticing. 'When did she die?' she whispered. 'What happened to her?'

The waiter came up to their table, holding a silver salver displaying tiny pastries. Her aunt pointed at a chocolate éclair and a small jam and cream sponge. The waiter smiled at Sacha. 'No, thank you,' she said, desperate for him to move on to the next table so her aunt would continue telling her about Alessandro's tragic past.

'Oh, um, it must be two years ago now,' her aunt said, taking a small bite from her éclair. 'This is heavenly, darling, you should try one.'

'No thanks. What happened to her?'

'It was heart-breaking,' Rosie said, popping the rest of the cake into her mouth and eating it. 'She was hit by a car, in Paris, I believe. The poor boy was broken with grief.'

Sacha's heart contracted at the thought of what he must have gone through. 'Poor Alessandro.'

'Yes, the poor chap, such a waste. I gather there's been no one since.'

'Too heartbroken, I suppose. It's understandable.' Sacha

took a sip of her tea and looked out of the window at the beautiful port of Ajaccio's pale stone buildings, with their terracotta roofs gleaming in the strong Mediterranean sunlight. So much beauty in the world, yet so much tragedy. 'I don't suppose he'll ever feel he can replace what they had together.'

'No.' Her aunt waved the waiter over to top up her tea. 'She was incredibly beautiful, too.'

Sacha wasn't surprised by this information. Someone as handsome as Alessandro would never have a problem finding stunning women to date, should he so wish.

'You met her?' she asked.

'No darling, but I've seen her picture in the magazines over the years. You must remember her?'

What was her aunt going on about? 'When would I have seen her?'

'I suppose you don't treat yourself to editions of *Vogue* and *Harpers*, do you darling? Not now you have to be so cautious with money.'

Sacha hadn't ever bought those magazines, but couldn't see what that had to do with Alessandro's girlfriend. Then it dawned on her. She trembled with shock, spilling her tea all over her navy Capri pants. 'She was a model?' So that's why her aunt had been concerned that someone might overhear their conversation. Alessandro's fiancée had been famous.

'Yes, darling. I thought I said, Livia Bianchi. You must have heard of her, surely?'

She had, vaguely. Sacha thought for a moment and then it came to her. The stunning model who had died so tragically, she remembered now. Sacha recalled seeing photos of the beautiful woman, with her equally tall, beautiful and attentive boyfriend, in *Hello!* magazine when she'd last visited the hairdressers, several months before. She'd remarked to the woman cutting her hair how fabulous the couple had looked, and was upset to discover that the magazine was months old and that the woman had been killed. That's where she'd seen Alessandro before.

She cleared her throat, not wishing to show how much this information had shocked her. A waiter came over to their table to refill their cups, but her aunt waved him away with an apologetic smile.

'Are you alright, Sacha? You look rather upset.'

She forced a smile. 'I'm fine. It's such a sad story, that's all. I had no idea Alessandro had gone through something that devastating.'

'I know. Poor chap. I'm not sure how anyone recovers from such an unbearable loss.'

'Neither am I.' She couldn't help wondering what he must have been thinking when he kissed her. Was it his way of trying to move forward from his heartbreak, or something else? Whatever it was, any woman would need to be incredibly special to compete with someone as glamorous as Livia Bianchi.

3

HOME

Sacha stood on the boardwalk and watched several oystercatchers darting above the sea, while others strutted along the beach, their long orange beaks stabbing the wet sand, looking for food. She stared out to sea. Every day the colour seemed different. Today it was a pale, jade green, the colour it always became during stormy days. So different to the navy blue of the Mediterranean that she'd been used to for the past week.

Sacha rested her palms on the cool, newly painted railings, sticky to the touch with salt from the waves that had washed over them during high tide earlier. She'd enjoyed her cruise with Aunt Rosie. It had been more fun than she'd expected, despite her discovery about Alessandro, and she'd pushed away any fleeting fantasies she'd had of them together. Why would he ever look at anyone as ordinary as her, when he'd been engaged to a supermodel?

She had enjoyed visiting the beautiful and inspiring places where they'd docked, but it was good to be home and standing on her beloved boardwalk. Sacha turned to face the Summer Sundae Café. She loved the pale blue of the shopfront, shining in the weak sun that was forcing its way through grey clouds. A warm, cosy feeling rushed through her; she'd missed this place.

She looked up at the two windows above the café; the living room window to the left and her bedroom on the right. There was a strange mark on the shopfront, next to the door handle, and she was about to go and inspect it when a drop of rain landed on her forehead. Sacha laughed; she was certainly home. She bent to grab her suitcase just as the café door opened. Her brother stood frowning and waved her inside.

'What are you doing standing out there?' he shouted. 'Get your bum in here before you get soaked.' He pointed out to the bay behind her. 'Didn't you see that shower coming towards us from Guernsey, while you were gawping at the sea?'

Yes, she was home and by the looks of things, Jack was glad she was back so he could return to his high-powered girlfriend. She'd already received twelve messages on her phone from her mother since her plane landed three quarters of an hour ago, moaning about Nikki's constant phone calls to Jack while he was supposed to be looking after the café. Despite trying to explain to her mum that Jack was twenty-nine and had long ago stopped accepting her advice about girlfriends, her mother continued to fret about his relationship.

The rain began falling more heavily and Jack ran across the road to her, grabbed her case without waiting for her to say anything, and waved for her to follow him inside.

'You've spent too much time with Aunt Rosie, she's always daydreaming, too,' he said, carrying her suitcase upstairs to her flat with a few loud groans. 'What the hell have you got in here, pebbles from all the beaches you've visited? Or is it bottles of booze to cope with having to share a cabin?'

Sacha could hear him continue to grumble as she walked into the café. She was pleased she'd returned after closing time. She looked around the familiar room, which she'd had updated eighteen months ago. The walls were painted Vanilla Dream, and she'd had a local carpenter make some tables using reclaimed wood. Straightening a large piece of driftwood propped up in a corner with fisherman's nets strung above it, she couldn't help giggling at Jack's comment. He was right. Aunt Rosie was a little eccentric and could be a bit exhausting, but she was also great fun and when Jack came back downstairs to join her, Sacha admitted that she'd happily go away with her on another cruise.

She couldn't miss the smell of burnt toast. 'Again?'

'It's that bloody toaster,' he grumbled. 'Damn thing doesn't work properly.'

'It works just fine,' she said, wondering how many times this had happened while she'd been away. 'You just need to remember when you put something in it to toast.'

'So, how was it?'

'I knew you weren't listening. I had a fun time, thanks.'

He pulled a face. 'Seriously? I thought you'd both be at each other's throats. The ballsy Sacha I remember so well wouldn't let Aunt Rosie get away with any of her annoying games. Although, I must say you do seem to be getting some of your old confidence back. Slowly.' He glowered at her. 'It's a good thing I was away when everything happened with that arse, Giles, you know.'

'It is.' Jack had always been protective of her, and would probably have enjoyed punching Giles. 'I'm glad you weren't around,' she said.

He put his arms around her and pulled her into a bear hug. 'I liked it when my sister was Miss Independent and it's good to see to see her coming back.' He let her go. 'Still though, I find it hard to imagine you spending so much time with Her Ladyship.'

'I did imagine it would be harder than it was. I expected us to fall out.' Sacha tilted her head. 'To be honest, there were a couple of moments, but it was great fun overall.'

Jack nodded.

'How did you get on while I was away?' She took one of the large latte glasses from the shelf and made herself a drink. 'Want one?' she asked.

'Nah, you go ahead. I had one a while ago with some toasted cabbage loaf. It's so tasty, I wish we could get it on the mainland.' He turned the sign on the door to CLOSED and sat down at one of the tables nearest the window. 'Mum has nearly driven me nuts though, and Nikki hasn't stopped phoning, texting and emailing me the entire time I've been here. I don't know who's been more annoying.'

Sacha sympathised. 'Mum does have a tendency to try and over-protect you sometimes.' Which always seemed very odd to her. He wasn't shy in standing up for himself and it never ceased to amaze her that her mother always assumed he was pretending to be tough and was actually very sensitive on the inside. 'Thankfully, she doesn't really do it with me.'

He stared out of the window at the rain rapping against the glass. 'Nikki has gone from being really chilled about everything to crying and threatening to dump me if I don't go back to the mainland as soon as you're home.'

Sacha blew on her drink in a vain attempt to cool it. 'She's obviously worried that you might decide to stay here. Anyway, I'm back now, so there's no reason for you not to return to her as soon as you like.' She took a sip of her latte and waited for him to reply with his usual quick retort. When he didn't, Sacha was taken aback. 'What's wrong?'

He rubbed his face with his hands. 'I'm not sure I want to go back, Sis.' He closed his eyes and shook his head thoughtfully. 'I didn't realise she was such a control freak.'

'Who, Mum?' Sacha asked.

'No, Nikki. She's been a right pain. She knows why I was here and to be honest, I've loved doing it.' He smiled for the first time since her return. 'The locals are characters, aren't they?'

She agreed, always grateful for those who continued to visit the café even in the depths of winter.

'And the holidaymakers are usually cheerful.'

'It's that sort of place,' she said. It had been something that she'd never considered before working here, how coming to a place where you served ice cream sundaes was an activity that made everyone happy. Why wouldn't it? It was part of why she loved this job so much. 'You want to stay working here, with me?'

He nodded slowly. 'Yes, I think so. If you need me, that is?'

She and Jack got along for the most part and she liked the idea of him working with her, but wasn't sure if there was enough to do through the winter. She didn't want to have to give her assistant, Lucy, or Milo, the teenager who sometimes helped her out after school and during the holidays, the push.

She'd met Milo when he'd come to the café to have an ice cream with his father. She'd been frantically busy and had dropped the ice cream she was preparing for him.

'I'll do my own, if you like,' Milo had said, jumping up to join her behind the counter before she had a chance to argue.

Too busy to mind, Sacha had let him get on with it, and, later, when he'd asked her about a holiday job, she'd been delighted to offer him work. She shared her thoughts with Jack, then drank the rest of her coffee while he mulled it over.

'Good point,' he said at last. 'Maybe I could help you out

through the summer and find something else to do at the end of the holiday season?'

'Would you make enough money to live on, though?' she asked. 'And where would you sleep? I've only got one bedroom upstairs in the flat.' She didn't have the heart to tell him outright that she would rather not share the flat with him. She loved her twin, but despite sharing the same colouring, almost everything else about them was different. He seemed to take up so much room, which she suspected had more to do with his enthusiasm for life rather than him being tall. He also believed that tidying up after himself was a waste of good kayaking time, and that there was nothing wrong with eating a microwavable meal straight out of the pack without transferring it into a bowl or onto a plate, which he probably exaggerated to irritate her. Which it did.

He laughed. 'I might get on okay with you, Sis, but I wouldn't want to be your flatmate. You take too long faffing about in the bathroom, I seem to recall. I remember only too well having to fight my way through jars of make-up stuff and knocking over boxes of horrible things when I went to the loo in the middle of the night.' He shuddered. 'Still haunts me.'

'Don't be so dramatic. Anyway, it's something you have to think about.'

'Boxes of... things?' He looked horrified.

'No, of course not,' she said, wondering why men seemed so horrified by tampons. 'Where you'll live if you stay on the island. I can't imagine you wanting to move back home again, Mum would never let you leave a second time.'

They laughed. It was true. She thought back to her mother feigning the risk of a heart attack from devastation when he'd initially moved away from home. That she ever thought her dramatic threats would be believed by him amused them both.

After a lifetime of being on the receiving end of their mother's adoration, Jack was used to taking little notice of his mother fretting about all the terrible things that could befall him should he move away from the island.

'I wanted to ask you if you'd noticed that strange symbol on the front of the shop?' Jack asked.

So, he didn't know what it was either. 'I was going to ask you about that.'

He opened his mouth to add something, when the left pocket in his shorts vibrated. Jack closed his eyes briefly in irritation and pulled out his phone to gaze at the screen. 'Shit. It's Nikki, with another ultimatum, no doubt.'

'You chat to her,' Sacha said, taking her glass over to the dishwasher and placing it inside. 'I'm going upstairs to unpack and get my clothes ready for tomorrow. Thanks though, Jack, for looking after this place. I owe you.'

'You do,' he said, giving her a wink as he pressed his phone to take the call. 'Nikki, babes...'

Sacha left him to pacify his girlfriend and wondered if he really would return to the island and come to work at the café. There would have to be rules, she decided as ran upstairs to the flat. She was going to have to make sure Jack realised that she was in charge now she was back. It wasn't going to be as easy for him, once the novelty had faded. He always used to say, 'You turn either left or right out of the driveway and wherever you go to on this island, you soon arrive back home again'.

Sacha walked into her cosy bedroom, with the high headboard made from driftwood, and a gale lantern on the pine stripped floor. It would soon be time to replace the candle inside. She flung open the lid of her suitcase, which Jack had left on her blue and white quilted bedspread. She had left the clean clothes on the top, not that there were that many, and now dumped her worn clothes in her wicker laundry basket. She'd take them to the laundrette later in the week, when she had a bit of time.

She wondered how Lucy had coped with Jack taking over. A petite girl in her early twenties, Lucy had come to Jersey from Ireland last season, looking for work. She was always on time, didn't mind working late if necessary and she and Sacha worked well together.

Sacha closed her suitcase and lifted it up onto the top of her ancient walnut wardrobe to make the most of the space in the small bedroom. She walked over to the window, stared out at the rain, and hoped Jack hadn't annoyed Lucy while she'd been away. She noticed he hadn't mentioned her at all.

Sacha changed into her favourite shorts and slippers. Bliss. She would dress like this all the time if she could. Years of having to wear make-up, style her hair to perfection, and truss herself into a suit and heels for the corporate world had taken their toll, and Sacha rarely wore anything smarter than a sundress and sandals these days.

She would catch up with Lucy when she arrived for work in the morning. Maybe Lucy would give her some idea why Jack had been so quiet about their time working together in the café.

The next morning, Sacha was up earlier than usual and dressed by six. The moaning of the wind and the sound of waves crashing against the sea wall had woken her several hours earlier and she'd been unable to get back to sleep. She lay in bed, curtains left slightly open, which she did every night so that she could wake up naturally as the dawn broke, rather than be shocked awake by a noisy alarm.

This morning though, she lay in the dark, thinking about Alessandro until the sun came up. Spending time with him had been the highlight of her trip, and she wondered if he really would end up coming to the island this summer. She would have to be a friend to him and show him around. After all, hadn't he gone out of his way to do the same for her? She felt a pang of regret at what she might never share with him. His kiss had been magical – the thought of his lips pressed against hers as he pulled her against him still made her legs feel like jelly. But now she knew about him and Livia and that he'd been planning to marry her. Maybe the kiss had been a momentary lapse for him. Or even a kindness he thought she needed. Whatever it was, she now knew what she was missing.

Not wishing to dwell on her thoughts, and unable to resist a sunny dawn, she got up, showered, dressed, and went downstairs for her first cup of tea. She crossed the road, the cup warming her hands, and stood on the boardwalk looking out at the sea. It was so much calmer today with small waves flopping over the rocks on the beach. Breathing in the familiar salty air, Sacha sighed happily. This place always cheered her up.

Spotting Lucy arriving for work, Sacha ran across the narrow roadway back to the café.

'Hi, Lucy,' she said as she entered the room. 'How are you?'

'Fine, thanks,' Lucy said, carrying her small rucksack through to one of the small rooms at the back of the café where staff stored their bags and coats while they were working.

'Everything here okay while I was away?' She joined Lucy behind the counter and began counting the petty cash. Satisfied there was a decent amount of till roll in the machine, she closed the lid and went to wash her hands.

'Yes, er, it was fine,' Lucy answered, eventually.

Sacha sensed something was wrong. 'Are you sure?' she

asked as she came back out to join her, watching Lucy pull on one of the pastel aprons they wore to protect their shorts and T-shirts. 'You would tell me if there was something wrong, I hope.'

Lucy's pale cheeks reddened, making her look even younger than her twenty years. She turned her back on Sacha, pulling the band from her curly auburn hair and redoing her ponytail. 'I'd better check that we have enough ice cream in the bunker.'

Not wishing to hound her, Sacha let Lucy go into the largest storeroom in peace. The room was housed in a couple of tiny bunkers dug deep into the hill behind the café. It was perfect for storing food because the temperature never rose. Sacha had wondered many times what had been kept in there during the Occupation, when the Nazis had taken over the island, and when the bunkers had been built. She supposed it must have been ammunition, or maybe even food for the soldiers stationed down at the boardwalk, keeping watch over the bay.

Lucy returned to stand in front of Sacha, her hands clasped in front of her. 'I'm sorry,' she said, her voice barely above a whisper. 'It's Jack.'

Concern coursed through Sacha. She'd only been gone ten days. She hoped he hadn't been too distracted by Nikki to keep a proper eye on things here.

'What has he done?' she asked, trying not to show how annoyed she was with her brother. Jack was a charmer, but could be oblivious to the effect he had on women.

Lucy stared at her pink plimsoll-encased feet for a few seconds. 'He hasn't done anything wrong,' she said. 'But you're back now and he doesn't have any reason to stay here.'

Sacha frowned. 'Sorry, what?' If he hadn't done anything wrong then what was the matter with Lucy?

'He is going to be leaving Jersey again, isn't he?'

So that's what was upsetting her. Jack changing his mind

and not going back to his girlfriend. She smiled and sat Lucy down at the nearest table. She noticed how tired Lucy seemed, and that she had dark shadows under her eyes.

'You're going to have a cup of tea and one of the low calorie chocolate brownies you like so much and gather yourself. We'll have our regulars coming here, in,' she glanced at the retro clock above the door. 'Four minutes. They come here to cheer themselves up and expect us to have smiles on our faces.'

'Sorry,' Lucy said, resting her chin on her palm. 'It's just that I know he's your brother and he seemed to love working here. He sounded like he was having a hard time with his girlfriend, too, and I'm worried that if he stays you won't need me working here any more.'

Sacha was relieved. When Lucy had first mentioned his name, she'd been concerned that her assistant might have a bit of a crush on Jack. Sacha had spent so much of her teenage years having to put up with besotted friends of hers hanging around her home, waiting for Jack to come back after being out with his friends. She made Lucy a mug of tea and gave her one of her favourite double chocolate brownies in an attempt to give her a bit of a boost.

'You don't need to worry,' Sacha said. 'We'll be busy enough for you to stay if Jack decides he doesn't want to go back.'

'But the winter time? It's so much quieter then.'

Sacha pushed the plate with the brownie on it towards Lucy. 'Eat that, and stop worrying. Jack knows the score and you have nothing to worry about. Anyway, he'll probably go home soon, whatever he says now.'

Lucy's head bobbed up. Her mood had lifted for some reason. 'Probably?'

'What?'

'I don't want you to think I don't like him, I do, but I need this job more than he does.'

Sacha could see their first customers walking hurriedly towards the café. She didn't have time to go over what Jack had said. 'Look, you finish your tea and brownie, and I'll serve.'

'Thank you, but I'll have these around the back,' Lucy said, picking up her mug and plate.

Sacha walked to the door and turned the sign to OPEN, smiling as her first customers of the day walked in. She welcomed the fisherman and his two children as they noisily entered the café behind him.

'You have two minutes,' she whispered over her shoulder, as Lucy practically skipped to the storeroom.

The fisherman, whose wife had died a couple of years before, brought his young son and daughter in to the café several times a week for their breakfast and Sacha always gave them a discount. She loved seeing the two blonde, angelic looking children, who always seemed happy to be in her café. It was the perfect way to start the day. She grabbed three menus, despite being aware that the three of them must know everything on it by heart.

'Good to see you all,' she said, as they sat down at their favourite table near the counter. Sacha wished that when the handsome man in front of her smiled it would one day reach his eyes. He must have loved his wife very much to still be so sad at her loss. Seeing him acting so cheerful in front of his children always gave Sacha's heart a bit of a tug.

'Good morning,' the family sang in unison, taking their menus to study, before ordering the same thing they all had every day.

Sacha smiled. 'Coming right up,' she said, taking the menus back and going into the kitchen to cook a fry-up of two eggs, bacon, sausages and hash browns for the father, and one egg and two rashers of bacon for the children.

'Bad storm last night,' she said, serving them each a mug of tea as she waited for the bacon and sausages to cook. 'Woke me up and I couldn't get back to sleep.'

'I slept like a baby,' the fisherman said. 'Always do in a storm. Love them.'

Mrs Joliff arrived, wearing her usual straw hat and baggy linens. She seemed to have a wardrobe full of linens, Sacha thought, smiling at her and waiting for her to exchange pleasantries with the small family before taking a seat at a nearby table. Sacha served her a pot of English Breakfast tea and two slices of cabbage loaf toast with fresh raspberry jam, bought from the farm shop up the road.

'This is my favourite bread and the best jam I've tasted,' Mrs Joliff said. 'You're a good girl, Sacha. You always make sure you serve the best ingredients.'

'She buys my fish too, when she's doing her summer suppers here,' the fisherman said. 'You should make sure you attend the next one, you'll be in for a treat.'

'I will, thank you.'

'Did you notice they've painted the railings above the beach?' Mrs Joliff asked.

'I had,' Sacha said. 'I didn't realise they were going to be painted, but they look good.'

'Trouble is,' Mrs Joliff said. 'No one seems to know who did it.'

Sacha found that hard to believe. 'What, no one saw them being painted? It must have taken hours.'

'There were two men,' the fisherman said. 'But no one knows who arranged for them to do the work and when asked, they said it was booked and paid for online.'

'Strange,' Sacha glanced out of the window at the smart blue railings. 'It's not as if something like that is cheap.'

As the morning wore on, Sacha and Lucy served one customer after another. It was non-stop and the café was full most of the time. Lucy's mood had lifted so much that one of the customers asked her if it was her birthday. Several people asked after Jack and Sacha was asked if he was still going to be working at the café. She was pleased to be able to say that he might be staying a little longer than initially planned.

It wasn't until about two-thirty that she had a chance to take a proper break and sit down to eat a couple of toasted sandwiches with Lucy.

'I'm grateful to you and Jack for looking after the café so well while I was away,' she said, when Lucy was blowing on the sandwich she was holding. 'I know he's easy to get along with but it can be difficult working with someone you haven't worked with before.'

Lucy's eyebrows knitted together. 'Not really, he was lovely.'

Sacha looked at the young girl in front of her. She worked hard, but there was a fragility about her and she suspected Lucy thought she was tougher than she was.

'You don't need to worry,' Lucy said, catching Sacha looking at her. 'Jack was nice to everyone and we got on very well. I only said what I did before because I was worried you'd get rid of me if he decided to stay.'

Sacha studied her. She was pretty, with curly auburn hair and dark blue eyes. 'It's fine,' she said. 'I know you did.'

The door opened with such force that the handle hit the wall behind it. 'Lazing around, are you?' joked Jack. 'What have you two done with all the customers? Scared them off?'

'Careful,' Sacha shouted, relieved no one was in the café for the time being, and that his noisiness had alerted them to his arrival before he caught them chatting about him. 'We've been flat out all morning,' she said. 'This is the first chance we've had for a sit down, and you're disturbing our peace.'

'How's my brilliant workmate today?' he asked, taking no notice of Sacha's reply. He patted Lucy lightly on her shoulder. 'We worked well together, didn't we, Lucy? I hope you've told her she can go away whenever she likes from now on and we'll keep everything running.'

'Where have you been, anyway?' Sacha asked. 'I thought you might come and help out here this morning.'

He sat down at the table and Sacha noticed Lucy stop eating and gaze at him from under her long eyelashes. So, she did have a bit of a crush on him. Jack, of course, was blissfully unaware of the effect he was having on the poor girl.

'Well?' Sacha kicked him lightly under the table.

'I've been carrying out a few errands for Mum.'

'What did Nikki have to say?' she asked, noticing Lucy stiffened slightly at the mention of his girlfriend's name.

He shook his head. 'We argued, again. I'm not sure what to do. I need to give this a bit more thought.'

Lucy got up from the table, taking hers and Sacha's plates and cups to the small kitchen. She was only gone a couple of seconds when she reappeared. 'I don't know why you don't just stay here for the summer and take it from there,' she said, before disappearing back into the kitchen again.

Sacha and Jack stared at the empty doorway, stunned by the girl's uncharacteristic outburst.

'She has a point,' he said. 'Maybe I should tell Nikki we're on a break for the summer and we can both see how we feel being apart for a couple of months?'

Sacha groaned.

'What's the matter?' he asked. 'I think it's a great idea.'

She just hoped it wouldn't result in him and Nikki making up mid-summer and him leaving the island, and her, in the lurch. Thinking about it, she wasn't sure what would be worse – not having enough staff to cover the customers, or Lucy's devastation if she got used to working with him for a few months, and her reaction if he suddenly left.

'It's a great idea, only if you commit to it.' She shared her concerns, leaving out any mention of Lucy. 'You must be sure though, Jack. If you're going to stay here for the summer then you have to commit to it. I don't want Nikki enticing you back when the café is at its busiest.'

'Hey, Sis, I wouldn't do that to you.'

'Probably not,' she admitted. 'But don't tell me you're going to stay here and then change your mind. Give yourself a couple of days to decide. Then, tell your girlfriend and after that we'll talk about your shifts. We open on Friday and Saturday nights, in July and August, because a lot of the parents like to have something to do with the children for supper during the holidays. I'll need you to work those shifts sometimes, too.'

'Sounds fine to me.' Sacha went to speak, but he raised his hand to stop her. 'But I'll do as you suggest and give it a few days to be certain. I'll let you know when I've spoken to Nikki.'

'And work out where you're going to live while you're here.'

'Yeah, that too.' He stared at her thoughtfully. 'You don't happen to know of anyone around here with a spare room going, do you? I really don't want to move back home with the parents.'

She did. 'Maybe, but I'll have to speak to her before I tell you about it.'

'Great.' He clapped his hands. 'We're going to have a brilliant summer together, Sis.'

She closed her eyes to still her rising temper. 'You just said you'd think about it...'

'Teasing. Stop being such a misery.'

She gave him a playful punch to his right shoulder. 'You're a pain, do you know that?'

'How can I forget, when you're always reminding me?'

Sacha saw a couple of ladies making their way to the café. 'Break over. I need to get back to work. And you,' she said, pushing him towards the door, 'need to sort out your love life. I'll find out about that room and let you know.'

She watched him open the door with a flourish and greet the two women. 'Ladies, it's good to see you again,' he said. 'Your usual table, I presume?'

Flattered by his attention, the two women, who Sacha had never served before, sat down and began chatting to him. Well, if nothing else, it looked like business would be busier with Jack working here.

She left him to it and went to find Lucy in the kitchen.

'He's staying then?' Lucy asked, before she'd completely entered the room.

'He doesn't know yet, but I think he probably will be joining us for the summer season, yes.'

Lucy beamed at her. 'He's brilliant with the customers, you know. You'll be glad if he does stay.'

'So I gather,' Sacha couldn't help being amused by the mystical whirlwind Jack always managed to cause. It was as if he lived in a haze of light and cheeriness, inducing everyone around him to feel the same way. 'I'll leave you to it,' she said, happy to see Lucy happy again.

4

Sacha closed the café, having tidied everything ready for opening the following morning. She ran upstairs to her flat and changed into a fresh sundress. Then, taking a bottle of prosecco she'd let cool in the fridge, she walked along the boardwalk to a small blue cottage. She stopped in front of the wooden sign with gold lettering displaying the name of Bella's antique shop, The Bee Hive. Bella was one of her three closest friends, and she couldn't wait to see her and have a natter.

The brass bell jangled, announcing her arrival as she walked in.

'Hello, stranger,' Bella grinned, popping up from behind her counter. 'I saw your light on last night when I was out walking, but didn't want to bother you. Have fun on your trip with your eccentric aunt?'

Sacha smiled. 'It was brilliant, thanks. I've got so much to tell you. I thought we could catch up over a glass or two of this?' she suggested, lifting the frosted bottle, looking forward to sharing a glass or two of their favourite tipple. It was always a pleasure spending time with Bella.

'Perfect,' Bella beamed, waving a loose curl away from her face with the back of a gloved hand.

'I see we're sporting the pink floral look today.' Sacha said, raising her eyebrows, unable to resist teasing her friend.

Bella waved her hands in the air. 'My jazz hands,' she pulled a face. 'If one more person asks me why I'm wearing gloves on a warm summer's day, I'll slap them.'

'Better not,' Sacha said, feigning horror. 'Think how hysterical you'd be if you broke a nail.'

Bella visibly shuddered, and Sacha felt mean, teasing her. Being a hand model had sounded glamorous to her when she first discovered what her neighbour did part-time. As they got to know each other better, she learned how careful Bella needed to be to keep her hands pristine in case she was lucky enough to get a gig.

'It's a nightmare.' Bella tilted her head to indicate her cottage. 'Why I ever thought this would be a fun job, I don't know. I'm thinking of giving up the modelling and sticking to selling my antiques.'

Sacha was stunned. 'But you love going to London for shoots, you always say so when you come back.'

'That's probably because I've been paid, or at least am about to be.' She shrugged. 'I love going to London, but taking care of my hands is constant hard work. The shoots are exhausting, trying to reach around a rude celebrity and leaning at awkward angles for hours until the photographers get the picture they want.'

'I see what you mean,' Sacha said, glancing down at her tanned scrubbed hands with their short varnish-free nails. 'I didn't know there was such a thing as a hand model until I met you,' she admitted, making Bella laugh. 'That's probably because it's an odd job to have and no-one boasts about doing it for a living.'

Sacha spotted a convex brass mirror with candle holders on each side, hanging on the wall across the room. She'd tried not to like the mirror too much, but sometimes she forgot she didn't have as much spare cash as she did when she worked in finance. She was tempted to buy it though. 'You'd miss it, if you did give it up,' she said, trying not to look at the mirror.

'Yes, but I never know when I'm going to be booked for a campaign and it can be months in between them,' Bella said, taking off her gloves and inspecting her hands for what was probably the twentieth time that day. 'Being ridiculously careful about my hands is a pain, especially when I'm dealing with awkward items here.'

Sacha could see her point. 'Think about it before doing anything radical though, won't you? I'd hate you to regret giving up something you enjoy.'

'I will. How's that delicious brother of yours? I made a few unnecessary stops at your café while you were away, just to check on the place.' She winked at Sacha. 'I wish he lived over here permanently. We could do with a bit more eye candy down here. There's only that gorgeous fisherman, but he's too grief stricken to look at anyone.'

Sacha tapped the side of her nose. 'You never know. My brother might just end up moving back...'

Bella's large eyes widened. 'I do hope so.' She pulled her gloves back on and straightened them at the wrist. 'Has he finished with that dreadful girlfriend yet?'

Sacha thought of Nikki. She was different to any of Jack's previous girlfriends. Most of them had been fun-loving and pleasant, but Nikki was harsh and demanding. Secretly, Sacha wouldn't mind him moving on from her and finding someone friendlier and more fun to be around. Like Bella. Sacha mulled over the idea for a bit. No, she mustn't think that way. What about poor Lucy? She wished her young assistant didn't have a crush on him. It could lead to so much unnecessary upset.

'Don't get your hopes up,' Sacha smiled. 'Knowing Jack, he'll go back to Nikki and carry on with his life. I think being here has given him a taste of freedom that he didn't expect to enjoy quite so much, which is probably why he doesn't want to leave. That and being able to get to the beach in a matter of seconds if he chooses to go kayaking.' She noticed Bella chewing her lower lip thoughtfully. 'I think he must love her though, otherwise it wouldn't be such a difficult decision to make, would it?'

'Shame. I'll just have to hope for the best then, won't I?'

'How about this prosecco?' Sacha said, changing the subject and trying to remember what it was that she'd been meaning to ask Bella. 'I'll pop through to the back and grab us a couple of glasses.'

Bella locked away two silver salvers. 'A new customer was looking at these earlier,' she mused. 'Sadly, he didn't think to buy either of them, but promised to come back again.'

'Shall we go out and sit on the boardwalk?' Sacha suggested.

'How about the beach? We can sit there and natter until the tide comes up.'

'Perfect, I'll leave you to lock up the shop and grab a towel,' Sasha said, going through to Bella's tiny kitchen for the glasses. 'I'll meet you down there.'

Sacha looked down at the golden sand from the boardwalk, marvelling as she always did at the beauty of the place. She wasn't surprised that on a warm evening like this there were groups of families and friends cooking their supper on disposable barbecues. Children kicked footballs, and because it was after six, people were allowed to bring their dogs onto the beach without them having to be on leads. She spotted a quiet place in between two large rocks and decided to see if it was free for her and Bella to settle down there.

As she walked down the granite steps to the sand, Sacha thought about how meeting Bella had helped her settle into life in the small village. Bella was a little eccentric, and very different to her, but they'd connected immediately. It was easy to be friends with Bella, and everyone in the area loved her. She was a great friend, as was Jools from the second-hand book shop, and Lexi who lived in one of the three fisherman's cottages on the hill that she ran as holiday homes for her artist father. They'd helped Sacha through several difficult times after her breakup with Giles and she looked forward to catching up with the other two soon.

She was happy to find that the sandy area she'd chosen from the boardwalk was indeed free, and pushed the bottle into the damp sand shaded by one of the rocks to keep it cool. Resting her bum on a smooth part of the stone, Sacha watched people making the most of the long summer evening. She thought back to her trip and how much she'd enjoyed being on the ship, and the places she'd visited. Rome. A picture of Alessandro's handsome face appeared in her mind. Was it possible to miss someone you'd only spent a couple of days and magical evenings with, breathing in the warm, herb-scented Italian air? She recalled their walks, taking in the exotic vistas, the sights of the Villa Borghese park, and the dramatic sunsets from Gianicolo above the Trastevere district. It seemed so long ago. She sighed, wishing she could keep her emotions in check a little better.

'What's that for?' Bella asked, appearing around the rock, two towels and a large packet of nachos in her hands.

'What?' she said, embarrassed to have been caught thinking about him.

'That sigh,' Bella raised an eyebrow. 'I'm going to want to know what caused it, you know that, don't you?'

'I think we need to open that bottle,' Sacha said. 'And quick.'

While Bella arranged the towels, Sacha unscrewed the bottle top, thinking how horrified her father would be to see her drinking something that came from a bottle without a cork. She poured them both a glass of the golden, fizzy liquid and handed her friend one.

It dawned on her what she had been meaning to ask Bella. 'Any lodgers at the moment?'

Bella made the most of her three-bedroomed cottage, not only by using her living room as a shop, but also by renting out her two spare rooms during the summer months, when local hotels or guest houses were full. It worked out well for both parties. The lodgers had to enter by the back door, so that they could reach their room without going through the shop, which was locked each night. Because Bella only offered lodgers tea and biscuits laid out on a pretty tray in each room, they usually made the most of Sacha's café by eating their breakfast and sometimes their supper with her.

'Only one, but she leaves tomorrow. She's a teacher and comes back to visit family each summer, but doesn't want to stay with them, so always books up with me.'

'It's not like you to have a spare room at this time of year, though.'

Bella scowled. 'I know. I turned down two couples who were hoping to book both rooms, because a young couple had booked one of them first. Then the bloke phoned me last night to let me know they'd split up, so wouldn't be coming over to the island on holiday now. Really bloody annoyed me, I can tell you. I could have done with the cash, too.'

Sacha thought of her brother and smiled. 'Jack might want to rent one of them,' she said, hoping he hadn't changed his mind when Bella's face lit up in delight. 'I don't know for certain yet, but I can let you know as soon as he's decided if he's going to stay.'

'That'll be brilliant,' Bella said.

'I'll chase him to make a decision. Anyway, I'm sure something will crop up for the other room,' she said, taking a sip of her drink. 'It always does.'

They drank in silence relishing the warm, lowering sun on their skin.

'So, tell me about this trip of yours,' Bella said. 'Meet anyone nice on that ship?'

Sacha thought of Alessandro. 'Yes, but the person I want to tell you about was the man Aunt Rosie hired to give me a tour around places in Rome.'

'You? Needing a tour guide?' Bella laughed. 'But you've travelled to all sorts of places by yourself, why would you need a tour guide in Rome?'

Sacha giggled, recalling her quarrel with her aunt. 'I thought so too, but I soon changed my mind when I met Alessandro.'

'Ah, I wondered if that heavy sigh before meant you'd met someone. I hoped you would. It's about time, you've been single for far too long.'

Sacha pulled a face. 'The words pot, kettle and black spring to mind. You've been single for as long as I've known you, almost.'

Bella nudged her and told her to shut up, so she told Bella all about her trip and how Alessandro had taken her to the best gelateria in the city. 'I've never tasted such delicious ice cream, apart from my dad's of course.'

'Did you arrange to keep in touch?'

Sacha admitted that she hadn't.

'Sacha, what's wrong with you?'

She tried to explain the situation. 'I'm glad I didn't. It wouldn't have been right for either of us.' She could see her friend was confused, but didn't want to elaborate. 'We only saw each other for a couple of days. Although we spent most of the time together, so I suppose it was like going on four or five ordinary dates.'

'Did you kiss him?'

'Only goodbye, but it was just the once and I don't think it meant anything.'

Bella groaned and pushed Sacha's shoulder. 'You're so annoying.'

Sacha was about to agree when she heard her brother's voice calling her. She glanced around but couldn't see him. Then noticed him paddling towards them in a kayak.

'Jack, hi,' Bella called out to him, waving. 'Come and join us.' She lowered her voice and speaking out of the side of her mouth, added to Sacha, 'You don't mind, do you?'

'Not at all,' Sacha said, happy to be able to ask Jack about whether or not he wanted to lodge in one of Bella's rooms.

Jack stepped out of his kayak and pulled it part of the way up the beach, placing the oar inside before jogging up to join them. He shook his head, his shoulder length hair spraying droplets of sea water all over Sacha. It was something he'd always loved to do, knowing it drove her nuts.

'Stop it, Jack,' she said. 'Sit down.' She was tempted not to mention Bella's room to him, but unable to resist helping her friend, she damped down her annoyance and told him about it.

'What do you think? It would be close to the café, so you wouldn't have to find your way here every morning, and I'm sure Bella wouldn't mind.'

She could tell Bella was trying hard not to show her enthusiasm for the idea. 'Yeah, sure,' Bella said, her tone nonchalant. 'It's a nice room, light and airy, you'll like it, and you can come and go as you please.'

Jack, of course, missed Bella's half concealed delight and sat down on the edge of her towel. 'Brilliant. I'd love that. If you're sure you don't mind, though.'

'She doesn't,' Sacha said, when all Bella did was gaze at Jack.

'Cool, how soon can I move in?'

'Tonight, if you like,' Bella said, managing to sound chilled.

'Right, I'll go and get my things from Mum and Dad's place and bring them over to yours. If you're not there, I'll come and find you.' He ruffled Sacha's hair and stood up, running back to his kayak and carrying it into the sea.

The girls stared after him as he got in and paddled away around the headland.

'He's exhausting,' Sacha said, wishing she had half of his energy.

'He's heavenly,' Bella smiled cheekily. 'Thanks, Sach.'

Sacha laughed. 'He's renting a room from you, Bella, he hasn't agreed to become your concubine.'

They fell back laughing, both spilling prosecco on themselves.

'What a waste,' Sacha giggled.

'What, Jack?'

'No, the prosecco.'

* * *

An hour later, Jack arrived, bag in hand and a wide smile on his face. Sacha hugged Bella and left them to it. She was glad she'd come up with a solution for both of them and hoped Jack and Bella didn't hit it off too well. She had enough on her hands where he was concerned, what with Lucy's crush and Nikki's constant phone calls trying to persuade him to go back to her.

As she walked back to the café, she spotted Betty resting on her walking stick as she unlocked her front door. Sacha called out to her and waved, but although Betty glanced in her direction, she didn't acknowledge her before stepping inside her cottage. Sacha supposed it was because the old lady's eyesight mustn't be as good as her own. Betty would have waved back if she had seen her.

Sacha thought of Bella's delight at the thought of Jack moving in to one of her rooms and then how disappointed Lucy might be hearing the same news. Once again, she was pleased not to be involved with anyone. At least with Alessandro living in Rome she could simply carry on with her life without being distracted by him.

She walked into the café and smiled. This place never failed to cheer her up. It was as familiar to her as the early family holiday photo of her, Jack and their parents she kept in a silver frame upstairs on the tiny sideboard in her living room. Even now, almost two years later, she still couldn't quite believe that her father had allowed her to take over the running of this place.

Sacha walked through the café and passed the counter, through the little corridor to the two bunkers at the back, to check that the old wooden door was firmly locked. It was where a previous waitress had snuck out for a cheeky cigarette, and she knew it was where Lucy went to make the odd phone call, although she never asked who it was that she contacted. As long as she only did it when she was on a break, or there was someone else looking after the café, she didn't mind.

Confident the doors were locked and everything was ready for the morning, Sacha took the takings from the till upstairs and poured herself a glass of rosé. It was back to reality and time for a little bookkeeping.

She was delighted to discover that the café had done well in her absence. Jack, Lucy and Milo had obviously worked very hard. Even though it did quite well for the most part, Sacha couldn't help experiencing a dip in her stomach every time she thought of going through the takings. It was still strange to her to think that this place gave her the only income she could rely on, as well as providing her with a home. That knowledge, and the fact that Summer Sundaes was the first of a chain of cafés her parents owned, and therefore special to them, made her more anxious and determined to succeed. The alternative was too terrifying to contemplate.

She loved running a business and being her own boss, not having to take instructions from superiors, or having to sit at a desk for hours each day. The thought of returning to that way of life, where every six minutes of her working day had to be accounted for on a time sheet, her feet throbbing in court shoes, was too awful.

Sacha thought about how she'd always hoped her father would see something in her that made him proud and now, running his pride and joy, she could prove to him that she was capable. She had a lot to live up to, and a lot to lose. Shaking the troubling thoughts from her head, she pulled a calculator from a nearby drawer and sat on the floor at the coffee table. Nothing was going to go wrong, she told herself, taking a sip of her cool rosé, as long as she worked hard, was careful with money, and carried on the way she was going, promoting her Summer

Sundae Specials, she should be fine. Soothed by her thoughts, she put down her glass and focused on her bookkeeping.

* * *

The following morning, Aunt Rosie arrived at the café before it had even opened. With a silk scarf over her hair, tied neatly underneath her chin, and large sunglasses covering her eyes, she looked like she'd stepped across time from another era.

'Aunt Rosie,' Sacha beamed, hugging her. 'You don't often come down this way. Can I make you a tea, or coffee,' she asked, knowing her aunt didn't eat breakfast.

'Capuccino please, darling,' Rosie said, taking off her scarf and sitting down on the chair nearest the window. 'I'm glad I caught you before anyone else arrived, I've got something incredibly exciting to tell you.'

Sacha went to make drinks for them, hoping that her aunt would carry on with what she'd come to tell her, but infuriatingly Aunt Rosie waited patiently for her to finish what she was doing. She rushed, spilling a little into one of the saucers, but keeping that one for herself, placed the drinks down on the table and sat opposite her aunt.

'You'll need to hurry, I'll have customers arriving at any moment.'

'Alessandro, darling,' Aunt Rosie said, looking, Sacha decided, very smug. 'He wants to come to Jersey for a few weeks. Some business project or other, I don't really know what it is.'

'He's an archaeologist,' Sacha said, wondering where he'd be working. 'He did mention something about coming here, but not about working.' She was a little taken aback at the thought of seeing him again. 'When is he arriving?'

'No idea. I phoned the hotel because I thought I'd left

behind one of my favourite bags and spoke to his aunt. I asked her how he was and she told me that his father had been unwell and that he would be coming over to the island soon. I'm not sure how the two work out together,' she said. 'I'd expect him to stay at home if his father was sick, but who knows? Exciting that he's coming here, don't you think?'

Sacha agreed, it didn't make much sense, but then again, her aunt could have got things mixed up. She tended to get a little carried away when retelling stories and ended up embellishing them a little too much so that they veered off in a different direction to the facts.

Surprised at her aunt's enthusiasm after what she'd told her on the ship about Alessandro's past, and not wishing to encourage her, Sacha told her aunt about Jack contemplating staying on the island and that he'd moved into Bella's cottage.

'How wonderful,' she said. 'Bella is a dream of a girl and I adore that cottage of hers. I've bought a few treasures from there over the years.' She checked her watch. 'I might just pop over now and see what she's got hidden.'

'She won't be open yet,' Sacha said. 'It's early, so you'll probably be better off coming back later.'

'Hmm, maybe.' Aunt Rosie finished her coffee and stood up. 'Thank you, darling girl. I'll see you very soon.'

'Okay,' said Sacha. 'And thanks once again for taking me on that incredible cruise. I had a brilliant time.'

'As did I. Thank you for accompanying me. You were the perfect travelling companion and I'll be asking you to come with me again, but only if you're free.' She put her sunglasses back on and tied her scarf around her head. 'Bye bye, darling.'

Sacha couldn't help smiling as she watched her aunt walking out of the café, her kitten heels click-clacking on the tiled floor.

No sooner had her aunt left than Mrs Joliff arrived.

'Good morning,' she said.

Sacha liked most of her regulars, but she especially liked Mrs Joliff. She was always happy and ready to help anyone. This morning her cheeks were flushed and she seemed excited about something. She went up to the counter where Sacha was opening a box of cones and refilling the holder.

'I didn't know someone had taken over the lease of Mrs Le Breton's little wool shop at the other end of the boardwalk,' she said.

Neither did Sacha. 'Why, is someone moving in?'

Mrs Joliff shook her head. 'Not yet, but I saw a couple of people measuring up inside.' She lowered her voice even though she was the only person in the café other than Sacha, and added. 'I hope it's something a little different that doesn't clash with any of the other businesses around here.'

'Me, too,' Sacha said, wishing it wasn't Lucy's day off. She'd have to wait for Jack to arrive, if he decided to, or Milo after he finished school, if she wanted to pop out and have a snoop.

Mrs Joliff sat down and Sacha made her a latte with vanilla syrup. She carried it over to her, putting it down on the table, and said, 'Are you glad Milo suggested you try these now?'

Mrs Joliff closed her eyes and smiled. 'That little chap is so clever. For years, all I've drunk is tea, believing I didn't like coffee, and when he insisted that I should at least have one latte to try it, how could I refuse?'

Sacha laughed. 'He shouldn't have really, but he's right, they are delicious.'

'They are. Such a treat,' the older woman said, taking a tentative sip. 'I can make as many teas as I like at home, can't I?'

'You can.' She noticed Mrs Joliff glance over at the glass dome covering a fresh batch of chocolate brownies. 'They're low calorie if you'd like to try one. They're the first low calorie brownies I've tasted,' she said. 'I usually like mine full fat, as it were, but these are delicious.'

'Go on then, why not?'

As the day wore on the temperature rose. It was mid-June, and in a few weeks the schools would be breaking up for the summer holidays. Sacha looked forward to the days when Milo worked with her. He was cheeky and very funny, always telling her and Lucy silly jokes that made them, and any nearby customers, laugh.

Milo arrived after he'd been home to change out of his school uniform. 'Did you know someone is doing something at that place further along the boardwalk?' he said. 'You know the one where that old lady had her shop before she died.'

'Yes,' said Sacha, as she passed him and took a toasted tea cake to a customer.

He opened his mouth to say something else and she added, 'And, no, I don't know who it is. But I do know that we're busy, so can you go and clear a couple of those tables at the back for me please?'

He did as she'd asked, humming a tune she didn't recognise.

She picked up a load of crockery and turned to take it to the kitchen when she heard the café door open.

'I won't be a moment,' she said, going through to the kitchen. It was typical of people to arrive so close to closing time, especially on such a sunny day. They usually wanted to eat an early supper so that they didn't have to cook when they got home. She didn't blame them, she'd probably do the same, given the choice. She washed her hands to rid them of a dollop of ketchup and dried them hurriedly, finishing off the job on her apron as she hurried back to serve the new customer.

'Hello, Sacha. It is good to see you again,' said a deep voice she recognised.

She glanced up and stared into a pair of blue-grey eyes she'd been trying hard to recall. 'Alessandro? You're here?' she asked, aware how stupid her question must sound.

Her heart pounded and she forced a smile, willing her brain to work through this surreal moment of seeing him in her café. She opened her mouth to say something, but the words vanished.

A customer walked up to the counter, his bill in his hand. Glad of the momentary distraction to give her a chance to collect her thoughts, Sacha smiled at Alessandro. 'Please, take a seat,' she said, indicating the recently vacated table. 'I'll come over to chat to you after I've served this gentleman.'

She couldn't believe he was here already. Her aunt had only mentioned that he was coming this morning. She took the customer's bill and cash, her mind racing. She'd imagined Alessandro coming to the café, but in her dreams she'd pictured herself freshly showered and nonchalant, maybe sitting outside on one of the tables, reading a book and drinking a latte. He might not be hers, emotionally or otherwise, but wearing a top smeared with strawberry sauce, and with her flyaway blonde hair needing a good brush, wasn't how she'd hoped he'd see her for the first time since they'd said their goodbyes in Rome.

'Thank you,' she said, handing the customer his change. 'Enjoy the rest of the afternoon.'

She smoothed down her apron and walked over to where Alessandro was sitting. He immediately stood up and grinned. 'It is good to see you again, Sacha. This is your café?'

'Yes,' she said, giving him a kiss on each cheek, and sat opposite him, perching on the edge of her chair so her customers didn't think she was too comfortable to serve them, should the need arise. 'My aunt mentioned you were coming over to the island, but I hadn't expected to see you here so soon.'

'My father, he asks me to come here on an, er, errand. I have much to do and will be busy, but wanted to visit you as soon as possible.'

She couldn't help smiling. 'Is your father here with you?' She glanced over his shoulder out of the window to see if the older man might be waiting for Alessandro outside.

'No, he is at home in Italy. I am here on his behalf.' He checked his watch and stood up. 'I must leave now, but would love to see you again, soon.'

A lady cleared her throat behind Sacha. She stood up. 'Maybe I could show you around the island?' She saw the woman becoming impatient. 'I'm sorry, will you excuse me for a moment?'

She took the lady's payment, bid her good day, and turned to see that Alessandro was standing next to her.

'Where are you staying?' she asked, thinking of Bella's spare room. 'I could contact you there and we could arrange something, if you like?'

'I would like that very much,' he said, his eyes twinkling, reminding her of their last evening in Rome when he'd kissed her lightly on the lips, leaving her wanting more, but too shy to do anything about it. 'I am staying at Bella's blue cottage along your beautiful boardwalk. You know it?'

She laughed. 'I do, how did you know about her place?'

'Your aunt,' he said, amused. 'She spoke to Bella for me and reserved a room.'

Sacha was delighted he'd be so near to her flat, it would help her find time to see him even if her days were busy, which they usually were at this time of year. 'Bella is one of my closest friends and I was only there last night. When did you arrive?'

'One hour, maybe?' he said, checking his watch. 'I phoned your aunt and she suggested your friend's cottage.' She noticed him glancing at the wall clock. 'I'll call there later this evening, if that's okay. We can arrange something then.'

'Perfect.' He leant forward and kissed her on both cheeks. 'Ciao, Sacha. I will look forward to speaking to you later.'

She watched him leave, wondering if the smile on her face would ever go. She knew she shouldn't be so happy to see him here, but couldn't help herself. She'd just have to keep a check on her emotions, and keep reminding herself that she had managed to survive Giles humiliating her with that woman. She was not the same trusting person she had been back then. Anyway, Alessandro was mourning someone he had lost and she doubted he would intentionally hurt her. He was her newest friend, nothing more. He waved at her before closing the door behind him.

'Oh, my, God, who was he?' asked a teenage girl, sitting with one of her friends at a nearby table. 'I haven't seen him around here before.'

'His name is Alessandro.' The girl gave Sacha a knowing look. 'And he's a good friend,' she added, spotting the girls' empty coffee glasses in front of them. 'Is there anything else I can get you both?'

'Only a date with him, and if not we'll have a couple of those low calorie chocolate brownies,' said the cheekier one of the two. 'If he's going to be coming in here, you'll be seeing more of us,' she added, nudging her friend.

'I'll look forward to it,' Sacha responded, trying to hide her amusement. She pointed to a brightly coloured poster on her wall, displaying the different types of old-fashioned sundaes she'd begun selling at the weekends. 'These are on special this summer, but only while the season lasts. Tell your friends about them.'

'Even more reason to come in here, then,' she giggled.

It was a long day, but a fruitful one. Sacha estimated that her takings were higher than ever, and wondered if it was because of the leaflets that Milo had been handing out in St Helier while she'd been on holiday. She was certainly seeing more of the locals in the café, and was relieved the States had relented and allowed the cafés to place a few tables and chairs outside this year. She wondered if she should consider having a retractable sunshade fixed to the front of the shop, for those days that were still warm, but a little drizzly.

Later, freshly showered and dressed, Sacha locked up the café and headed out to Bella's cottage. She still found it hard to believe that Alessandro was on the island. Excitement welled up inside her. Now it was her turn to show him around. She tried to think of all the places he might be interested in visiting. She reached the little shop that had been vacant until recently and noticed that there was a sign above the window. Unfortunately, it was covered, so she couldn't get an idea of what the new tenants would be using it for, and the wooden shutters she'd remembered only being used for stormy nights, were now closed. She'd just have to be patient like everyone else and wait to discover what this place was going to be.

She arrived in front of Bella's cottage and raised her hand to knock on the door, just as Alessandro opened it.

He smiled. 'I was coming to escort you here,' he said.

She laughed and handed him a bottle of prosecco. 'You don't need to act as my tour guide on this island,' she teased. 'I know my way around this place. Here,' she handed him the bottle. 'This is for Bella to open for us all.'

'I will enjoy this,' he said.

'Have you met Jack yet?' she asked, following him into the main living room, which was directly inside the front door. Sacha could see that Bella had changed the furniture around a bit, which usually happened when she sold a large sideboard or table. This cottage was a treasure trove for antique hunters like Aunt Rosie, and also somewhere Sacha could spend hours delving into drawers and the items on display. She never understood how Bella fitted so many things into one room, while still managing to keep it as a living area that she and her guests could enjoy.

'You know Jack?' He seemed surprised that she might. He had a lot to get used to in this small place, where all the locals knew each other, and most of the strangers didn't stay strangers for very long. He raised his eyebrows. 'Ah, he is the brother you mentioned?'

'Yes, that's right, my twin,' she said, walking into the cottage and taking off her sunglasses. 'Can't you see the resemblance?'

He narrowed his eyes. 'It is a possibility,' he said, sounding unsure.

Bella laughed as she walked up to them. 'Stop teasing him, Sach. You and Jack are opposites in many ways.'

'You're not kidding,' Sacha laughed 'He's muscly from all that kayaking,' she raised an arched eyebrow and went on. 'I'm not really into exercise, apart from running around at the café.' Alessandro's eyes swept her body, and she felt her face flush.

'So, how are you settling in here?' she asked him, recovering her composure. 'It's a bit chaotic at times but I've been assured that Bella is a brilliant landlady.'

'You lived here?' he asked, as Bella took them through the cottage to her small yard at the back, where she'd hung Chinese lanterns and displayed several pots of brightly coloured plants to make the most of the space.

'She lived here for a few months before moving into the flat above the café,' Bella answered, indicating they should sit down.

'And now your brother lives here,' he said, just as Jack appeared at the door.

'Room for a little one?' he asked, his hair wet, Sacha presumed, from being in the sea.

Bella indicated the spare chair next to hers. 'I'll fetch you a glass, you can have some of this delicious prosecco.'

Jack walked over and placed his hands on her tanned shoulders. 'No, you stay where you are. I'd rather have a lager.'

He began walking towards the kitchen, but hesitated and stopped. 'Hey, did any of you notice that odd sign that someone's etched into one of the planks on the boardwalk?'

Bella sat up straighter in her chair. 'You mean, the one like some sort of mathematical symbol, just before the steps?'

'I haven't seen anything,' Sacha said, trying to recall if anything unusual had caught her eye when she last went down onto the beach. 'What do you think it's for?'

'No idea,' Jack said, 'but it doesn't look like it was done by a kid. Odd.'

'It is strange,' Bella said. 'We can go and have a peek a little later. I can show you where it is, if you like, Sach.'

'Yes, please.'

Jack turned his attention to Alessandro. 'You want a glass of something other than that stuff, mate? Bottle of something from the fridge maybe?'

'That would be nice,' Alessandro said. 'Thank you.'

Sacha wasn't sure if Alessandro was being polite, agreeing to the beer, or if he simply wasn't enjoying the prosecco.

While they waited for Jack to come back, Sacha turned her attention to Alessandro.

Jack returned and handed Alessandro a frosted bottle of lager. 'Get that down your neck, it's good stuff.'

'Thank you.' Alessandro took a mouthful and closing his eyes, swallowed. 'Very good.' He grinned at Sacha. 'I will be busy tomorrow, but if you are free the next afternoon, maybe we can see some of the island then?'

'I'm sure Jack won't mind coming into the café to cover a shift for me.' She focused her attention on her brother. She knew he would stand in for her if she asked and wasn't surprised when he agreed straight away.

'I will come to the café at one?' Alessandro suggested.

'Perfect.'

Now all she needed to do was think of the most interesting places to show him. Places that would give them something to talk about. She hated being so tongue-tied, but seeing him again in her own surroundings made her less confident, somehow. She needed to find things to talk about to try and hide her shyness. She hadn't felt this awkward with a man before, but she hadn't ever met anyone quite as charismatic as Alessandro.

'Why don't I make us some supper?' Bella suggested.

'Great idea,' Jack said. 'We can take it down to the beach and eat it there.'

Sacha caught Bella watching her. She was wondering what her friend was thinking but before she could ask, Bella said,' Why don't you help me here, Jack? Sacha has been working at the café all day, she can take Alessandro down to the beach and we'll meet them there when we've rustled up some food for us all.'

Grateful for the chance to spend some time alone with Alessandro, Sacha stood up and took his hand in hers. 'Quick, let's get out of here before she changes her mind,' she said, only half joking. 'We can go and find that sign Jack was talking about.'

Alessandro finished his beer and handed the empty bottle to Bella, thanking her.

They stepped outside and Sacha could smell the heat emanating from the warm tarmac on the pavement outside the cottage. It was one of those rare summer evenings that wasn't much cooler than the day had been. She led Alessandro across to the boardwalk and to the first set of granite steps that would lead them down to the beach.

As she smiled at him, a red and blue beach ball hit her on the back of the head before bouncing along the roadway between the cottages and the boardwalk. A child cried out, and Alessandro withdrew his hand from Sacha's and ran after the ball, retrieving it for the little boy.

He brought it back to the railings above where Sacha was standing and, waving at the child, threw it down to him before re-joining Sacha. 'Your head, it is okay?'

'My head's fine, but I'm not so sure about my pride,' she laughed. 'Right, where's this symbol we're supposed to be looking for?'

They walked down several more steps, studying the ends of the boards underneath the railings.

'I do not know what I must find,' Alessandro said, running a finger along the wooden edges.

Neither was she. Sacha was about to give up when she spotted it.

'There, look.' She stared at the symbol. The circle with a horizontal crescent moon underneath reminded her of something, but she couldn't recall what it was. 'I'm not sure if it's an odd shape on purpose, or if it's because the person who did it found it difficult to keep their hand steady, carving into the wood.'

'It could be someone making a joke, no?'

The notion soothed Sacha. 'Yes, you're probably right. Come on, let's get our feet onto the sand.'

They took off their shoes and ran onto the beach.

'Is still hot.' He reached the water's edge and stepped forward to stand ankle deep in the sea. 'Jersey has very good weather, like Italy.'

She stopped at the water's edge and looked out at the small waves, the bright evening sunshine catching the tip of each one, making them appear silver. 'Not all the time, but I can think of no place I'd rather be than right here when the weather is this perfect.'

5

When Sacha woke the next morning, she didn't need to check the weather to know that it was going to be another hot day. She closed her eyes, just as a text pinged onto her mobile. She rubbed her eyes and, awake enough to read it, picked up her phone to see who it was from.

It was Bella:

Get your butt out here now!

Amused by her friend's urgency, she pulled on a pair of shorts and a bikini top and hurried out to meet her.

Bella was waiting and seeing Sacha, put her finger to her lips, indicating that Sacha shouldn't speak. She waved her over to where she was standing, next to the railings overlooking the beach.

'Sorry,' she whispered, 'but I couldn't risk you missing this.'

Sacha followed Bella's line of vision and spotted Alessandro swimming in the sea.

'I'm not sure what I'm supposed to be looking at?'

Bella grabbed her arm and pointed at him. 'Him, obviously.'

'He's swimming. Is there anything wrong with that, or unusual, maybe?'

Bella grinned. 'Just wait. Watch him. He'll soon get out again and then you'll see what I want you to see.'

Sacha tilted her head towards her friend and kept her voice low and her eyes on Alessandro. 'If we were two older men, you'd say we were a couple of old pervs.'

'True, but we're not. Now, shut the hell up and wait.'

Sacha gazed around her. Thankfully, the few other people out on the beach this early were mostly locals having their morning swim, or walking their dogs on the beach before work. None of them were interested in them and what they were doing.

She was about to go back into the café for her morning shower when Alessandro emerged from the water.

'Oh, I see what you mean,' Sacha said, her voice raspy.

As he stood, the water ran in rivulets from his muscular shoulders, down his pecs and past his pillar-box-red swimming shorts. The two friends stared in transfixed silence as he raked his fingers through his wet, wavy hair, and shook his head to get rid of the excess sea water.

'Isn't he gorgeous?' Bella breathed. 'Like something out of a movie.'

He was perfect, Sacha mused.

'You're thinking about licking that water off his stomach, aren't you?' Bella teased.

'What? Don't be ridiculous.' Sacha knew she was staring like someone obsessed, but didn't care.

'You are though, aren't you?'

She sighed. 'Oh, yes.'

A lady threw a tennis ball past Alessandro for her dog, but

the ball fell in the sea and the small Jack Russell refused to go in and fetch it, despite the woman calling for him to do so.

Alessandro turned and strode back into the water after the ball.

'Look at that peachy bum,' Sacha said.

'Told you he was something else, didn't I?'

He picked up the ball and threw it along the beach. The little dog raced after it, barking noisily.

Alessandro walked up the beach in their direction. Reaching the granite steps, he spotted them watching him. 'Ah, good morning, lovely ladies. You are not going for a swim this morning?'

They shook their heads. 'Not today,' Sacha said, trying to pretend she hadn't been staring. 'We were just having our morning natter.'

'Natter?' he frowned and ran up the steps to join them.

Sacha opened her mouth to explain, when Alessandro bent forward to give her a kiss on the cheek. Sea water dripped onto her face and he moved back.

'Sorry, I forgot to bring a towel with me.'

Bella gave Sacha a sideways glance and grinned. 'If you wait there I can throw one down to you,' she offered.

He shook his head. 'No, it is okay. I do not wish to disturb you. I will walk to the cottage, it is very close.'

They watched as he walked away, his wet shorts clinging to his firm bottom.

'He is proper sexy,' Bella said. 'Shame he's only got eyes for you.'

Sacha watched him go. 'If only,' she said, wondering if there ever could really be something long-term between them.

'That man is so damn hot,' Bella said. 'He should come with a warning sign strapped to his head.'

'Or his bum.' Sacha crossed her arms. 'What the hell is wrong with me this morning? We had a lovely evening with Alessandro. I like him, but he's been through a lot, and I'm not sure if he's as ready as I am to move things forward between us.'

'I'm so happy,' Bella smiled.

'Why? What did I say?'

'You sound like you're finally ready to move on from Giles and give love a second chance. Go, you.'

Sacha mulled over Bella's words. It had been far too long. She had a lot to lose, after spending the past two years working on her business and her self-esteem. She needed to know Alessandro a little better before really letting down the barriers she'd built up.

'I need to go and have a shower,' she said, crossing over to her front door.

'I think you'd better make it an extra cold one.' Bella shouted before waving and walking away.

* * *

Sacha's red Fiat 500 rounded the brow of Gorey Hill and Alessandro pointed when he saw Mont Orgueil Castle rising magnificently from the rocks ahead.

'Game of Thrones?' he said smiling. 'It is magical.'

'It is pretty splendid,' she agreed. 'We can go in there and have a look around if you like. But it's probably better for another day, when the weather isn't so good. I thought today I'd take you to see Le Dolmen du Couperon. I'll take you the long way so we can drive along the coast, past the castle and Archirondel beach. There's a Napoleon tower at Archirondel, it's painted with a large red stripe and has beautiful views of the sea. What do you think?'

He looked impressed at her knowledge and nodded enthusiastically. 'Yes, this sounds perfect. Very different from a busy city, no?'

Happy to have come up with an idea that suited him, as well as managing to fit in opportunities where he could hopefully take photos for his family back home, Sacha relaxed. As she drove, she gave him a brief history of the places they passed.

He asked her about the café and how long she'd worked there. She explained that it was initially her father's business, but that he was slowing down now and not wanting to look after so many small outlets, so she'd been delighted to take over the running of the place.

'When I broke up with my partner nearly two years ago, I decided that I'd had enough of working in finance and came back, after ten years in London. Dad suggested I take over the café and I'm slowly buying it off him. I didn't expect to enjoy the quieter life so much, especially after being desperate to get away when I was twenty. But I've loved being back here and especially living down by the boardwalk. I've been made to feel as if I've been there forever.'

'You didn't know these people before?'

She thought back to how strange it had initially felt to run the café, and how her relationships with the women she was used to seeing only a couple of times a year when visiting, had been so different when they were running businesses in the same area.

'They made me feel very welcome, especially Bella. My friends live and work around the area and we've become very close.'

Alessandro chatted and asked more questions while Sacha half-concentrated on checking road signs so she didn't miss her turnings. She generally kept to the main roads when she came this way and was usually in a hurry to get somewhere. It was a bit of a treat taking time to see so much of the country lanes and she found that she was enjoying herself.

Sacha spotted Rue des Pelles, turned right and kept going past green fields with horses grazing and the occasional Jersey farm house. Further along, she spotted Scez Street, almost missing the turning on the left that she needed to take. She knew that the notion of getting lost on this small island was amusing to those who'd never been there, but there were so many small lanes it was surprisingly easy to take a wrong turn and spend ages getting back to where you intended going.

The lane twisted and turned and continued for ages, becoming very narrow. Sacha was beginning to wonder if she should have turned off somewhere. She'd never been this way before and had only discovered it when researching places of archaeological interest for Alessandro.

'Ah,' she said, relieved to spot a small parking and turning area at the end, where a few bicycles and a lone car had been left. On one side was a narrow opening between hedgerows that she assumed led down to a small bay, and on the other was a pathway up to an old brick building.

'I think that must be the Le Couperon guardhouse,' she said when she'd parked, fumbling in her bag for her mobile, so she could tell him more via an internet search.

The two of them got out of the car and, remembering how well he'd described the places he had taken her to, Sacha began walking towards the guardhouse, saying. 'This place was built in 1689, apparently. It was a shelter for the Jersey militia who served the battery that commanded Rozel Bay but the guns have long gone.'

He looked fascinated. 'And the dolmen is just there,' he said, sprinting over to study the twenty-six-foot chamber, which was made up of large stones standing upright, and others resting on stones placed either side of the opening so that the chamber was covered.

She noticed Alessandro smiling and was pleased he was enjoying himself. 'You are doing well,' he said. 'You are a good tour guide.'

'I try my best. Right, it says here,' she said, pointing to a plaque, 'that these stones surrounding the actual stone covered chamber are known as peristaliths.' She got a bit tongue-tied as she wrestled with the word, but carried on. 'And that it's about five thousand years old.' Even to her that sounded impressive and she'd never even bothered to take note of these things before.

He crouched on his haunches to study it more closely, taking many photos. He seemed thoroughly in awe of the place.

'There are many more of these on the island?'

Delighted to have made the right decision in bringing him here, she said. 'Um, I'm not sure. There are loads, about fifteen maybe? They're dotted all over the place.'

'It is incredible that I haven't thought to come to this island before.'

Spurred on by his interest, she added. 'The biggest one is La Hougue Bie. That's up that way,' she said, pointing towards the north of the island. I can take you there if you like?'

'I would like that very much,' he said. 'But only if it interests you, too.'

Not minding what she did as long as she was spending some time getting to know him better, she said, 'Yes, it does, a little.'

'I may take a photo of you here?'

'What, in front the dolmen?' She stood in front of it with her back to the sea to give his photo the best background.

'Perfect,' he said, as she smiled and he took the picture.

She insisted of taking one of him and then they took a selfie with the sea behind them, the sun shining on its cornflower blue surface. 'We could quickly pop down to that tiny beach, if you like?' she said, wanting him to see as much of the island as she could possibly show him in the time he was on holiday.

They had to walk in single file down to the beach. Early blackberries were swelling in the sun and Sacha decided to come back in a couple of weeks and pick a few punnets to make some blackberry syrup for her sundaes.

'It is very beautiful here,' he said. 'And no one else is on this beach. We are alone. It is unexpected.'

She mulled over his strange turn of phrase, reminding herself that her Italian was non-existent and that she could learn a little of his language to be polite, if nothing else. 'There are so many small bays and coves here that the tourists tend to go to the bigger, more well-known bays, like the one at St Brelade, or Grouville Bay or St Ouen.'

'But the little beach by the boardwalk is always popular,' he said.

It was, she thought, relieved. 'Yes, it's much easier to get to.'

Sacha took off her sandals and waited while Alessandro removed his shoes. Then they walked down to the water's edge, where small waves ebbed and flowed onto the white gold sand.

'You are very lucky to live in such a beautiful place,' he said, picking up a handful of sand and letting the fine, pale grains flow between his fingertips.

'I agree. When I was younger I didn't appreciate it at all and couldn't wait to get away,' she said, thinking of the months she'd spent dreaming of a life in London with all the excitement and adventure she imagined waiting for her there. 'Now I'm glad to be back. I think I've had enough of trains, undergrounds and noise for the time being.'

'You don't like London? It is a great city,' he said. 'Very cosmopolitan.'

'No, I love it there,' she said. 'And I go back occasionally to have a wander about, go to the theatre and catch up with a few friends. I'm just enjoying being back here where everything is closer and I can walk out of my front door and onto the beach. I love feeling the sand between my toes.'

He looked down at her feet and laughed. 'I can see that you do.'

She followed his gaze, relieved she'd thought to redo her pedicure a few evenings before.

'Tell me more about your plans for your café, Sacha,' he said, as they walked along the water's edge, their feet cooled by the damp sand beneath their feet.

She liked that he was so interested in her work. It wasn't something she was used to. 'It used to look very different, but I gave it a makeover a while ago to bring it up to date.'

'Did you choose the name Summer Sundaes?'

'I did. It was known as The Café for years, but I wanted to make it mine with the focus on ice cream sundaes. Dad's cafés are all about feeding people, I want to do that, of course, but also give them an experience they'll remember and not just for the food. Does that sound odd?'

'No.' He thought for a moment, shielding his eyes against the bright sunshine reflecting off the sea. 'Your café is like a memory from a child.'

Buoyed by his understanding, she smiled. 'Yes, I want all my customers to feel that nostalgia that I have when I recall summer holidays visiting the seaside. The food and drinks are important and need to be perfect, but even on a cold, blustery day if families pop in to the café before school, or after work, I want them to feel like they're walking into a favourite childhood memory.'

'It is a clever idea and I see why it works well. I saw that your café was busy, is it always that way?'

'Mostly. I think it's all about making people feel special. The ones that live alone have someone to chat to and laugh with over a treat and the people with young families have a place to bring their children. I also like to offer the healthier options and sell home made fresh juices using what I can buy locally, so they're seasonal rather than something you can get all year round.'

'And the ice creams?' he asked, kicking the sand. 'Your sundaes?'

'Rather than me telling you about them, you'll have to come and sample one. We can stop off there on our way home after visiting La Hougue Bie.' She liked the idea of showing him how tasty her sundaes were.

She'd set up a couple of pages a year ago on social media and had been delighted by the response. She'd requested that anyone discovering her café via the internet let her know when they came in for a sundae, and she would give them a 10 per cent discount. It was an easy way to judge how well her posts were doing.

'I think we should get going if you want to visit La Hougue Bie today.'

Alessandro walked with her up the beach towards the narrow pathway back to the car. Half way up, she turned to him and said. 'It really is lovely having you here.'

She turned to carry on her way, when he took her hand and pulled her gently towards him.

'I am also very happy to see you again, Sacha.'

Saying her name with his lilting accent made her stomach

contract. She was about to reply, when Alessandro leant down and kissed her lightly on her mouth. She tried to speak, but was distracted by someone politely clearing their throat to let her and Alessandro know they were waiting to pass them.

They stood back against the bank to let the smiling man and his dog go down to the beach.

'Thank you,' the man said. 'Enjoy your day.'

They thanked him and hurried up to the car.

Her legs were a little wobbly after the surprise of being kissed. They got into the car without speaking. It took a few minutes to make it to the top of the lane, having reversed several times to let other vehicles go past.

'You really shouldn't do that, you know,' she said, mortified to have to confront him about his kiss.

'What?'

Sacha couldn't look at him. 'You shouldn't kiss me.'

'No?

'No.'

'You do not like me, Sacha?'

How could she answer without either lying, or embarrassing herself? 'It's not that I don't like you, Alessandro. It's just...'

'What is it? You have something to say to me, please, say it.'

She drove for a few more minutes, trying to find the right words, not wanting to spoil their afternoon.

'My aunt, she told me about your fiancée.'

'Livia.' His voice cracked with emotion as he said the three syllables. That one word spoke volumes to Sacha about his love for the woman he'd lost so tragically.

Neither spoke again for the next few minutes.

Forcing herself to focus on something else, she said. 'Finally, we're on our way to La Hougue Bie, or Hougue Bie, as we know it here. This is a much more impressive place than the one I've just shown you. At Easter, there's an Easter egg hunt for the children, which I think is rather nice.' Desperate to keep talking, and keep the conversation away from a subject that still obviously hurt him so much, Sacha tried to concentrate on what she'd read about the place. 'I think it's about six thousand years old and is one of the largest and best-preserved passage graves in Europe. They've found human remains here as well as the usual pottery, tools and that sort of thing.' He didn't respond.

They arrived and Sacha parked the car. 'There,' she said, pointing up at the hill with the stone chapel on top of it, but Alessandro had already spotted it. 'Impressive, isn't it?'

He looked miserable. 'Sacha, I need to tell you—'

'It's fine,' she said, not wanting to have to hear about the exquisite woman he'd lost. She held up her hand to stop him saying anything further. 'Another time, if that's okay? Please let's just enjoy our day out.'

He looked about to say something, then changed his mind. 'Yes, of course.'

She cleared her throat, hating that she'd been rude, but she wanted to make the most of these days out with him before he had to return to Italy. 'So, what do you think of this place then?'

He didn't say anything, but stared up at the stone chapel for a few moments, before they walked over to have a proper look.

'I don't know much about it,' she said, struggling to think of what to say next. She couldn't miss how sad he looked and wondered if he would ever recover from what had happened to Livia. 'Did you know that when the Nazis occupied the island during the Second World War, the German forces built a command bunker on the site?'

'My father told me about The Occupation. It was the same

for many people in Italy at that time. Here too, there is much history that people should not forget,' he whispered.

* * *

They arrived back at the café, after Sacha had parked in the small car park nearby. He looked happier than he had done earlier, and she was relieved that she'd managed to make his afternoon as interesting for him as he had done for her in Rome.

'The Gents is through there if you want to go and freshen up,' she said, pointing to a pale blue door with a small drift-wood handle. 'I'll do the same and then I can make you one of my special summer sundaes.'

He didn't respond.

Sacha left him in the café and ran up to her flat. After washing her hands and face, she quickly brushed her hair and went back downstairs to join him.

'Right, you're in for a treat now,' she laughed, cringing as it came out a little too forced. 'Or at least I hope you'll think it a treat. We did sample some incredibly tasty ice creams in Rome and I want to show you how delicious ours can be.'

'I'm looking forward to watching you create these sundaes.'

'Good.' She tied on her apron and stared at him for a moment, trying to gauge which particular sundae would suit his personality. 'I'm going to make the first one specifically for you.'

He smiled. 'This, I will enjoy.'

Deciding that he would enjoy something sweet, having seen the flavours of gelato he'd chosen in Italy, she took a few rasp-berries, blueberries and strawberries from the fridge and placed them into a bowl. Then taking some pistachios, she ground them up in her smaller blender. Bending down to take two scoops of her father's famous vanilla ice-cream – her favourite, made with fresh vanilla pods – she dropped them into a tall sundae glass, alternating them with two scoops of strawberry ice-cream and layers of fresh fruit. She smiled at him as she whipped up some fresh Jersey cream, dolloped it on the top, and scattered it with the roughly ground pistachios. Finally, she picked a fresh, dark red cherry from the cooler and popped it on top, adding a wafer.

'Okay, so far?' she asked, happy with the display in front of her.

'Of course,' he said, laughing. 'I am enjoying learning from you.'

Taking a long spoon, Sacha stuck it into the sundae and pushed the elaborate concoction towards him. 'Okay, let me know what you think.'

Alessandro stared at it in awe. 'This looks very impressive,' he said, studying the tall colourful creation.

Sacha waited silently as he dipped the spoon deep into the sundae and took a mouthful of strawberry ice cream and fruit. He savoured it, then went back for another, this time of vanilla and blueberries with a little of the cream and nuts.

She wished he'd give his verdict, but waited patiently for him to consider what he'd just eaten.

'It is delicious,' he said, his mouth pulling back into a wide smile. 'Like you said in Italy of the gelato – heaven in a glass.'

She clapped her hands. 'I'll make myself something a little less extravagant and come and join you over at that table by the window.' She handed him a napkin and turned to put a couple of scoops of vanilla into a bowl, showering them with grated dark chocolate.

Sacha ate her ice cream and enjoyed the silent companionship with this lovely man. She could imagine how delighted

Aunt Rosie would be to discover the two of them spending time together like this, and decided to give her a call later that evening. After all, it was thanks to her aunt's insistence that she had got to meet Alessandro in the first place.

'Very good,' he murmured, looking across and giving her a smile. He held up the cherry by its stalk. 'For you,' he said, smiling.

Happy to oblige, Sacha took the cherry from the stalk with her teeth, careful to chew slowly, and discreetly dropped the stone into her palm. 'I'm glad you enjoyed it so much,' she said, happier than she could remember being in years.

She finished her ice cream and glanced at him, noticing a sad expression cross his face briefly before vanishing.

'Is everything all right?' she asked, concerned that maybe something had reminded him of Livia. She hoped it wasn't something she'd said.

He shook his head and took her hand. 'It is nothing. I have enjoyed this afternoon with you very much, Sacha. I hope we will be able to do this again?'

He sounded so unsure. 'I'm sure we can,' she said, trying to cheer him up, wishing they could be more than just friends. 'I enjoy spending time with you. We can go out any time I'm not working. Just let me know when you're free and where you'd like to go next and I'll be happy to take you.'

He lifted her hand to his lips and opening her palm, kissed it lightly. 'You are a special woman.'

She felt as if her heart would burst. She was at risk of falling in love with Alessandro, but considering he was still caught up with his past, she was going to have to be very careful that her own emotions didn't get carried away.

'Thank you. And you're a very special man,' she said, smiling at him.

Alessandro leant forward just as the door crashed open and Jack marched into the café.

'Jack, I wish you wouldn't do that,' she snapped, getting a fright. 'One of these days you're going to smash that door or the wall behind it. Anyway, what are you doing?' She glared at him, furious at the noisy interruption.

Jack glared at Alessandro. 'I'd like a word with my sister, please.' His eyes narrowed. 'In private.'

Alessandro seemed confused and stepped away from the counter. He nodded at Sacha. 'I will come and see you tomorrow?'

'That would be lovely,' she said, watching as he gave Jack a brief glance and then left the café.

As soon as he'd closed the door behind him, Sacha rounded on her brother.

'What the hell was that all about?' she asked, not waiting for an answer. 'I presume it must be something that couldn't wait? You pretty much threw Alessandro out. It was rude, Jack.'

He scowled at her. 'Yes, well, sorry about that, but I needed to speak to you.'

She folded her arms and waited. 'Go on then.'

He seemed a little deflated. Then it dawned on her that he had something to share with her and was nervous about telling her what it was.

'Stop pacing and tell me what's happened. Hurry up, you're making me nervous.'

'Have you been to look at the new shop that's opening up where Mrs Le Breton's wool shop used to be?'

'Yes, last night, but it was boarded up and I couldn't see inside. Why?'

He took a deep breath. 'Did you notice the sign above the shop?'

'No, it was covered up.' She wished he'd just tell her what was bothering him.

He opened the door and peered out, first right then left, along the boardwalk. 'Right, it's quiet out here at the moment. Grab your keys and come with me.'

She didn't argue, and quickly locking the front door, ran after him. 'I really don't know what's got in to you tonight.'

Jack didn't speak for the short walk to the nearby shop, but when he reached it he stopped, stepped back and pointed up at the bright sign. 'Gelateria di Isola,' he said.

She said the words aloud too, her heart sinking as she realised what it meant and noticing in smaller writing the name on the bottom left hand corner. Salvatore. The name was familiar, but she couldn't place it for a moment. Then it hit her. Alessandro's last name was Salvatore. He'd said he was being sent here for his father, but she hadn't considered he would be on the island to set up a business that would be in direct competition to her own.

Stunned, she opened her mouth to speak. Looking up at Jack, she cleared her throat and said. 'I've been talking to him about Dad's ice creams all afternoon.' She recalled them both laughing over the sundaes she'd made only minutes before. 'I've just made him one of my favourite speciality sundaes.' She swallowed the lump forming in her throat as the enormity of his betrayal filtered into her brain. 'He's been lying to me.'

Jack put his right arm around her shoulders. 'He never said anything to you, nothing at all?'

She shook her head, trying to hold back the tears that were doing their best to make an appearance. Why hadn't he said something? He'd had more than enough opportunity to be honest with her. She felt stupid for chattering on and on about her café and the summer sundaes she specialised in. Now he could copy everything she was doing and only a few doors down.

Her business might be local, and somewhere people enjoyed visiting, but his was new and different. It was human nature to want to try out new things. She thought back to the delicious gelatos she'd enjoyed in Rome and it all began to make sense. Where she'd assumed he was just another ice cream lover, he'd known the business, and had probably been trying out the wares of his father's competitors. She'd been such a fool.

She gently pushed away from her brother. 'Thanks for telling me, Jack,' she said, motioning for him to follow her back to the café.

Once back inside and certain they couldn't be overheard, she said. 'I can't believe I didn't realise his connection before.' She still couldn't quite take it in that Alessandro hadn't told her. 'He took me out for gelato in Italy, but I didn't think for a second it was what his family did. I never actually asked him why he was coming to the island, either. I assumed it was to see the historical sites, as he's an archaeologist.'

'He's played you for a fool, Sis.'

She cringed. 'Don't say that,' she said, suspecting he might be right. 'What am I going to do now?'

'I know what I'm going to do,' Jack said, the muscle in his jaw working frantically. 'No one does something like this to my sister and gets away with it.'

He pulled open the door, but Sacha grabbed hold of his arm to stop him. 'No. Leave it.'

He shrugged. 'Why shouldn't I give him a piece of my mind?'

She thought quickly. She knew how hot-headed Jack could be, but wanted to sort this out her own way. 'Because you're both staying in Bella's home and it's not fair on her if you two have a go at each other.'

'He can leave then,' he said, shrugging her arm off and stepping outside.

'No, Jack,' she said, smiling at an elderly couple who happened to be passing by and looked rather shocked by the argument they were witnessing. Sacha lowered her voice. 'She needs the money. We'll have to think of something else. I won't have our issues affecting Bella, none of this is her fault.'

Jack's shoulders slumped. 'Fine, but he's not getting away with what he's done. What if he puts you out of business?'

That's all she needed to hear. 'I'd rather not think about that happening, if you don't mind. You go back to the cottage and I'll think about this overnight. Come in tomorrow morning before you go kayaking, so we can chat before Lucy arrives.'

He considered her suggestion. 'Fine, I'll keep my mouth shut for Bella's sake, but I'm warning you, Sach, that creep isn't going to get away with this.'

No, he wasn't, Sacha decided.

6

At three fifteen Sacha gave up trying to sleep. She thought she heard a noise out on the boardwalk, different to the usual sound of waves, and got up to have a look. She switched on her bedside lamp and got out of bed.

Peering through the gap in her curtains, she couldn't see anything but a cat ambling along the boardwalk. Nothing else seemed to be going on. She half turned away from the window and something caught her attention. Sacha looked back, but by the time her eyes had acclimatised to the darkness again there was nothing to see.

'Strange,' she murmured, lying back down on her bed and switching off the light.

She lay in the darkness, trying to get back to sleep, but her mind was racing too much. She stared at the shadows cast by the moonlight onto her bedroom wall, thinking about Alessandro. Disappointment oozed from every pore and she felt more miserable than she could ever remember.

She reasoned that maybe he hadn't been given any choice but to come here and start up a business for his father. After all, wasn't she doing the same thing? No, she argued. Her family had been established here since 1855. Alessandro's family had no connection to the area and anyway, if he felt the need to set up a business in competition with hers he had the entire island on which to do it.

Fed up with fretting, Sacha got up and pulled on her favourite shorts, a T-shirt and a light cotton jacket and went down to the beach. The sun was peeking over the horizon, casting a silvery glow on the sea as she walked down the steps and onto the sand. Apart from one other person at the opposite end of the beach, standing at the water's edge, staring out to sea, she was the only one there. She liked it that way.

She kept to her end of the beach and savoured the peace and the cool, wet sand on her bare feet. She took a deep breath, drawing in the salty, fresh air and filling her lungs before slowly exhaling. It helped, a little. Spotting a worn piece of pale green glass on the sand she picked it up, wondering where it might have come from and how old it could be.

'I thought it was you,' Alessandro said, surprising her so that she dropped the piece of glass.

'I couldn't sleep,' she said, her heart pounding as she thought about what he had done. He retrieved the glass, cleaning the sand off it with his thumb before passing it back to her. She noticed that his faded jeans and T-shirt were creased as if he'd slept in them. His hair, usually neat, was messy.

'No. I wanted to come here for some air.' His voice was sorrowful and she suspected that despite Jack's assurances to the contrary, he'd found a time to get Alessandro on his own and give him a piece of his mind. She didn't blame him, she'd have done the same if it was the other way around. They always stood up for each other, even if they had their own disagreements. She would have been surprised if Jack hadn't said something. He took his role as the bigger twin seriously.

'Sacha?'

She was at a loss as to what to say to Alessandro and kept staring at the small piece of opaque glass in her hand, rubbing it between her thumb and fingers.

'You saw the sign about the gelateria.' It was a statement rather than a question and despite the words sounding like music when he spoke them, she was angry.

She swung round to face him. The shock of seeing his handsome face, lit so perfectly by the moonlight, angered her even more. He might have lost the woman he loved but that didn't excuse him from not telling her the real reason he was in Jersey.

She glowered at him. 'Your gelateria?' she said, glad the light was behind her and he couldn't see the tears in her eyes. 'What about my café? What about being honest with me? It's not as if you didn't have the opportunity to let me know what you were planning.' She hesitated. 'That's why you're really here, isn't it?'

'Please, Sacha,' he said moving closer to her. 'I never lied to you and I can explain everything.'

She stepped away from him. 'I don't doubt that you can, but I'm not in the mood to listen.' She clenched her teeth together, trying to calm down. 'Not telling someone something is as bad as lying to them.'

'Yes, I know this,' he said quietly. 'I didn't think it was important.'

Stunned, she stepped back. 'Not bloody important? How do you figure that out?'

He tried to take her by the shoulders, but she pushed him away.

'No, that is not what I mean,' he said.

'Go on then, what were you going to do? Hope I wouldn't notice you selling gelateria a few doors down from my café?'

'No, I mean that I did not know that my gelateria was on the same boardwalk as your café. I did not think it would matter that I had a business on the island.'

Sacha took a deep breath, aware she'd been shouting and that it was still early. She didn't want to wake people and alert them to her humiliation. 'There is only one boardwalk on this side of the island, Alessandro.'

'I did not know this,' he shook his head. She wanted to believe him. 'I promise you,' he added, his eyes filled with sadness.

'How do I know you're telling the truth?' She began walking, the familiar coolness of the fine damp sand soothing her temper, slightly. 'You knew the first day you arrived here, didn't you? You could have told me then. Why didn't you?'

He moved to stand in front of her. His broad shoulders slumped and he stared down at the water's edge. 'I did not know how to.'

'So, you let me find out by accident, or rather let my brother be the one to tell me. Do you know how embarrassing that was? He's already waiting to find fault with you. Jack is extra protective after Giles made a fool out of me. And now you have. Bloody hell, Alessandro. I can't believe you've done this to me.'

'Sacha, please...'

'No, leave me alone. You've got nothing to say that I want to hear.'

She turned her back on him and almost ran up the beach, catching the tip of her big toe on one of the granite steps on her way back up to the boardwalk. Wincing, she squeezed her eyes shut for a few seconds to cope with the sick pain shooting through her toe. She tried to step forward to continue on her way home, but her toe was too painful and had already begun bleeding. The stinging brought more tears to her eyes as she hobbled slightly, determined to get into her flat before allowing herself to check how badly she'd hurt herself.

'Sacha, wait,' Alessandro said.

She hadn't realised he was behind her. 'No, don't.'

He stepped in front of her. 'You're hurt,' he said. 'Let me help you.'

Desperate to sit down and deal with her throbbing toe, and aware that she must have cut it quite badly as the sole of her foot was slippery with blood in her flip flop, she acquiesced.

Reaching down, he put his hand under the back of her knee and lifted her leg slightly to get a better look.

'One moment.' He carefully lowered her leg and, standing upright, pulled his T-shirt over his head, bending down again to wrap it around her cut foot.

Sacha groaned.

Alessandro looked up at her. 'I am sorry if I hurt you,' he said, mistaking her groan as one of pain.

'No, it's fine. Don't worry,' she said.

'You think you can walk?'

'Yes,' she said, stepping forward and grimacing.

Without another word, Alessandro put his arms under her and lifted her.

* * *

'Your keys?' he asked, waiting for her to unlock the door.

She fumbled for her front door keys, making him clear his throat when she inadvertently touched the outside of his shorts grazing his private parts.

'Sorry,' she said cringing with embarrassment. 'Wrong

pocket, I meant mine, pocket, that is.' Mortified, she rummaged with her other hand in the pocket on the other side of her shorts, relieved he was strong enough to keep holding her. Anyone would think she was wasting time until he had no choice but to put her down.

'Found them,' she cheered triumphantly, noticing several people on the boardwalk watching her antics. She realised her earlier annoyance had already evaporated. Maybe it was being in his arms, or the sight of his naked chest, but she couldn't seem to stay angry with him.

He held her closer to the door so she could put the key into the lock and let them in.

'I'm fine now,' she said, shy now that they were alone together. 'You can put me down.'

He didn't look convinced but did as she asked.

Sacha walked forward, slipping slightly on the bloodied tee shirt.

'I will carry you up to your flat,' he said, his tone not inviting any argument from her. Lifting her back into his toned arms, he carried her up the stairs and stopped. 'Which room?'

She pointed to the tiny room to the right. 'You go and take a seat,' she said, indicating the living room. 'I'll sort this out in the bathroom.'

Leaning over quickly, she closed her bedroom door. She didn't need him to see that her laundry was doing a good impression of a duvet on her bed. She really must sort out her clothes and get rid of some and put her holiday laundry away, she thought, before a shooting pain in her toe reminded her of what she'd done.

'Let me get some warm water to wash your foot,' he said. 'You sit and put it up.'

'No, I'll sort it out. You wait in here. Make yourself a drink if you like, while you're waiting for me.'

Some anger returned, but he had been very gallant, carrying her back. The least she could do was give him a chance to explain why he hadn't mentioned anything about coming here to set up a business.

She hopped carefully into her bathroom and sat on the lid of her lavatory. Closing her eyes for a second to brace herself, she unravelled his ruined tee shirt and peeled it back from her blood-soaked foot.

'Eugh,' she shivered, revolted by the painful mess she'd made of her toe. She was going to have to find a larger size of shoe to wear while it healed.

She could hear running water in the tiny kitchen at the back of her flat, the cupboard doors opening and closing and wondered whether Alessandro was making them both a cup of tea; she hoped so, she could do with one. A few moments later, he knocked.

'It's okay,' she said, a little calmer. 'You can come in.'

He entered the bathroom, doing a double take when he saw her seahorse taps and, before she could say anything, knelt down in front of her, a bowl of warm water in his hands and a kitchen roll tucked under one arm.

'You look very pale,' he said, frowning. 'You have had a shock.'

She did feel a little light-headed, but she'd always been squeamish whenever she'd cut her toes. 'I never wore shoes when I was smaller, not if I could help it, anyway,' she said, remembering her father shouting at her as she ran along the tarmac driveway, playing ball with Jack. The amount of times she'd cut the tips of her big toes was ridiculous, but like her father said, it never taught her to wear shoes like most people managed to do.

'You like the seahorses,' he said, putting the kitchen roll on the rim of the bath.

'I do. I found one once on holiday in Spain when I was little and I've never forgotten it. It was very beautiful, but alien-like.'

'You don't mind if I wash your foot?' Relieved not to have to look at the damage, she shook her head. 'Good. Then I can put this around it,' he said, holding up a bandage that she'd forgotten she had.

'Yes,' she said, feeling a little mean now for being so angry with him. 'Thank you, Alessandro. You're being very kind. I'm not so sure I'd be as charitable if I'd just had a row with someone.'

He took her foot and, dipping some kitchen roll into the warm water, squeezed out the excess liquid and began cleaning her toe. 'I believe you would, Sacha.'

He was so careful that she didn't notice it throbbing any more. Then again, she was watching him, and admiring his sexy back. She wanted to run her fingers through his black hair and push his fringe back from his face as he concentrated on cleaning her foot. She reached out, and realising in time what she was about to do, closed her eyes and tried to gather herself.

Oblivious to what she was doing, he took the plastic wrapper off the bandage and, placing a dressing that he must have also found in her rarely used first-aid kit, he deftly dressed her cleaned foot.

'It is done,' he said, slowly lowering it and gazing up at her.

She couldn't force her eyes away from his. Her heart pounding so loudly she was sure he could hear it, she opened her mouth to say something, when Alessandro rose slightly and, putting his hand behind her neck, brought his mouth up to hers and kissed her.

The sensation of his firm lips on hers dispersed any remaining anger she had towards him like bubbles in a champagne glass. She dropped his T-shirt on the floor and wrapped her arms around his neck and responded to him with all the pent-up emotion she'd been holding back. He put his other arm around her back and pulled her against his chest. Sacha lowered one hand down over his arm, desperate to feel the contours of his muscles.

'Er, what the hell?' Jack shouted, shocking Sacha and Alessandro so they broke away from each other.

Alessandro sat back on his haunches. 'I was—'

'I could see what you were doing, mate, but what I want to know is, why is my sister bleeding?'

Irritated with her brother for barging into her flat and interrupting their kiss, she glared at him. 'I cut my toe and Alessandro was helping me.'

Jack glowered at Alessandro as he stood up. 'Yeah, right.'

She could see Alessandro was as put out as she was with Jack, but unlike her, he was trying to hide his feelings. 'You have, er, house shoes?'

She tried to work out what he meant and then it dawned on her. 'Slippers? Yes, I do, but they're enclosed, so I think I'll just put on some flip flops for now. I'll get them and you can put the kettle on if you like.'

'I could do with a cup of tea,' Jack said, walking the three steps to the living room. 'Or a beer, if you have one. I was just coming back from a mate's house when I spotted your lights were on.'

She knew he was only playing for time and wanted to know what was going on between her and Alessandro.

'Yes, well, too bad,' Sacha said. She waited for Alessandro to go into the kitchen. 'Listen, Jack,' she said, lowering her voice and hoping Alessandro couldn't hear. 'Alessandro and I have things to discuss. So, unless you came here to tell me something in particular I suggest you bugger off back to Bella's cottage and get some sleep.'

'I don't understand how he got to be half-naked if all he was doing was fixing your toe?'

She told him about Alessandro using his T-shirt as a make-shift bandage.

Jack seemed a little happier to know this and ruffled her hair. 'You're so grumpy, sometimes.'

'Go, Jack. I'll see you later.'

She watched him leave and listened for the sound of the front door closing behind him. Then, slipping her bound foot carefully into a different pair of flip flops, she returned to the living room. She opened the French doors onto the balcony and breathed in the early morning air. It was going to be a scorcher today, she thought, a little soothed by the realisation.

Alessandro brought in two mugs of tea and placed them on the coffee table and Sacha sat down on the chair opposite the two-seater sofa and waited for him to speak.

He stared at her thoughtfully for a moment. 'I am sorry for what has happened.'

She cleared her throat. 'You must know this changes every-thing between us? I mean, about the gelateria, not before.'

'When we kissed,' he said quietly.

'Yes, well.' She took a deep breath to focus on what she was trying to say. 'Look, do you want me to find you something to put on?' She didn't really want him to cover up his torso, but it was rather distracting having him in front of her looking like the hero in a romantic film.

'No, it is warm. I am fine, thank you.'

'Right, well. Um... I thought we were friends and I can't understand why you didn't tell me about your business plans.' Unintentionally, she added. 'You kissed me, knowing you were going to go behind my back?'

He looked at his hands, holding the mug of steaming tea. 'I did not know that you ran the café when I kissed you.' He hesitated. 'The first time I kissed you. When I came to your café the other day and saw how close it is to the gelateria, I was shocked.'

'So, why didn't you say something?'

'My father, he has been unwell.' She automatically wanted to sympathise, but he continued before she had the chance. 'It is his heart, but he is much better now. I knew he wanted to open a business here for many years.'

She took a tentative sip of her drink. She wasn't going to say anything in case it stopped him from speaking, but looked at him silently.

'I never thought to tell you about my family's businesses in Italy,' he said. 'When we met in Rome, I was coming here to see this island for him and maybe look at a few properties on his behalf with his contact, but this wasn't planned. For once, my father has worked quickly. It only took three weeks to sort out the paperwork before I arrived to set everything up. Until I discovered what you did for a living, I thought I would be coming here to start this business while being able to spend time with a woman I liked, very much.'

She shrugged. 'I did think you seemed to know a lot about gelato, but I thought you just liked the stuff.'

He cleared his throat and put his mug back down on the table. 'Usually, my father takes a long time to make big decisions, but he contacted me the day after we had spoken and told me he had been in contact with an old friend who lived here.

His friend told him about a small shop that was vacant and said he thought it would be perfect for a small gelateria, the kind my father has set up in several towns at home.'

She thought about Mrs Le Breton's shop staying empty for several months, too small to be any use to most businesses, and how she'd dreaded it being taken over and turned into a sandwich bar.

Alessandro carried on explaining. 'His friend emailed the shop details and draft lease over to my father. He agreed to be my father's representative and set everything up for him, but my father wanted me to come to the island and take charge of the work, even though he knew I couldn't run the business for him.'

'Because you don't have a licence to work here?' she asked, aware how difficult it was for people to get the right paperwork to be allowed to work on the island.

'And because I love my work as an archaeologist. I've studied this for many years and even though my father's dream is running his gelaterias, and one day I might take over from him, for now this is what I enjoy doing.' Alessandro shook his head and leant forward, his hands clasped. 'I came here to do this for my father, but I never dreamed that in doing this I would be hurting you.'

'But how did you get permission, and so quickly?'

'My father's friend, Franco, he has power of attorney for my father. He will look after the financial side of the business and I must find and employ a manager to look after the day-to-day running of the gelateria. I can help, but not be employed by the business or earn money doing it. Once everything is in place, I will return to my own work.'

'You couldn't say no,' she said, recalling how difficult she'd found it to argue with her own father on occasion.

'No. My father knows I would not have agreed to this if he'd been feeling better. I am aware he's used being unwell to persuade me to do this for him.' He gave a hint of a smile. 'And I didn't mind, because I hoped to see you. He told me that having an outlet on the island has been a dream of his,' he shrugged. 'That someone ruined his chances back in the sixties when he'd been about to set up his first business. His heart had been broken back then and so he returned to Italy to move on with his life. It's the least I can do for him to help banish those ghosts in his past.' He frowned. 'I am sorry.'

Her toe was throbbing painfully now and so was her head, but how could she be angry with someone who was helping a sick parent?

'I don't suppose there's any way you can change the use of the place to, say, a takeaway for Italian food?' she asked, only half joking.

'No, his business is in gelato and it is what he knows. Good gelato is what he has promoted all his working life. It is not ideal.'

She laughed. 'You're not kidding.' Sacha tried to get comfortable in her chair and yawned.

'You are tired,' Alessandro said, standing up to leave. He checked his watch. 'You should try and sleep for one or two hours. I can speak to your brother when I return to Bella's cottage and ask him to open your café today, if you like? Then you could keep your feet up for the day and rest.'

She yawned again. The thought did appeal to her. She wrote down her mobile number on a piece of notepaper. 'Here, take this, and if Jack has other plans please ask him to call me, or send me a text and I'll go downstairs and help Lucy until Milo arrives.'

'I can help, if you wish?' he said. 'I must meet with shopfitters later this morning, but I can come back afterwards.'

'What?' she said, standing up. 'Let the competition in on my business secrets?' She thought of the sundaes she'd made in front of him. 'Not a chance.'

He looked hurt. 'I will leave you now, but I will return and see how you are later, if that is okay with you?'

'Yes, that's fine,' she said, wishing she hadn't teased him. He might have been the reason she wasn't concentrating when rushing up those steps, but it wasn't his fault she was a clumsy oaf. 'And thank you for doing this,' she pointed to her bandaged foot. 'If you leave the keys there and just drop the latch on the door, that'll be fine.'

'Latch?'

'Lock.'

He bent forward to kiss her cheek then seemed to change his mind and left. She didn't bother tidying up and went into her bedroom and lay down. She closed her eyes but even though she was tired, the pain in her foot and upset at what had happened kept her awake. She touched her lips with the tips of her fingers, remembering how Alessandro's lips had felt on hers. Why was there always a catch? she wondered, reminding herself that whether his father had set up the business or not, there was still the matter of Alessandro's grief for Livia. Sacha turned on her side, staring out at the dawn sky. Why couldn't things in her life ever be simple?

She must have dozed off because she was woken by a buzzing noise. Reaching out, she patted the top of her alarm, but the buzzing kept going. Waking slightly, she recognised the sound of the ringtone on her mobile and grabbed it from her bedside table.

'Yes?' she said, her voice gravelly from sleep.

'Alessandro said I must come and run the café for you today,'

Jack said. 'But I can't find the key you gave me when you went away. I think I must have left it in your flat.'

'Jack,' she shook her head. 'Give me a few minutes and I'll throw the keys down, so you can let yourself in.'

She dragged a hairbrush through her bed hair and found Jack's keys by the small treasured picture of their grandparents. She limped over to the balcony, called for him to catch them, and returned to her bedroom.

'Sorry, Sis,' he said, running up the stairs a short while later. He looked down at her bandaged foot. 'You been to the hospital?'

'No,' she said, glancing down at Alessandro's neat handiwork. 'Alessandro dressed it for me.'

'Proper Florence Nightingale, isn't he?'

'He was very good actually, so don't be sarcastic.' Jack went to argue, but Sacha quickly added. 'I know we were angry with him, but I now know he was in a difficult position with his father and had very little choice but to come here and do what he's done.'

'Yeah, whatever,' Jack said. 'I need to make something to eat before I do anything else. Bella usually does us a breakfast, but I didn't have time to eat there this morning.'

'Help yourself,' Sacha said, relieved he'd changed the subject. Jack never could cope with anything on an empty stomach. She lay back against her pillows and stared out of the window at the blue, cloudless sky. She could hear Jack slamming down pans and stomping around the café. He was obviously still angry with Alessandro. She needed to have another word with her brother and explain everything properly before he saw Alessandro again.

Sacha dozed off, waking a little before noon. Unable to spend any more time doing nothing, she found a pair of sandals she rarely wore because they were a little too loose on her, put them on and went downstairs to help Jack. It was busy in the café and Jack was chatting to a group of elderly ladies sitting at one of the tables. At least this had taken his mind off his annoyance with Alessandro. She said hello to customers, making small talk as she walked between tables to get to the counter where Lucy was busily making up a large strawberry sundae.

'Oh, I didn't see you there,' Lucy said, when she looked up and saw Sacha.

'I didn't like to disturb you,' Sacha said. 'Need any help?'

Lucy looked down at the creation she'd just made and shook her head. 'I'm only making the one, for table three. Do you want me for something?' She placed the large glass on a saucer with a long-handled spoon. 'I'll just go and serve this.'

Sacha stood back to let Lucy past and wiped up the mess she'd left, enjoying the sweet smell of fresh strawberries. She surveyed her café and couldn't help smiling. This really was the best job in the world.

Lucy came back to join her. 'How's your toe? Jack said you'd hurt yourself when you and Alessandro were on the beach in the middle of the night.'

It wasn't quite how she'd have described it and she explained what had happened, leaving out the bit about Alessandro's ice cream parlour being set up a few doors away.

'Ouch, poor you,' Lucy said, frowning. 'I can come in on my day off, if you need me to, I really don't mind.'

Jack hurried over. 'Hi Sis, how's the injury?' He put an arm around her shoulders and gave her a brief hug. 'You really are the clumsiest person I know.'

She was. The amount of times she'd fallen up the stairs and down on the pavement when there was nothing at all to trip her up was embarrassing. 'The injury is fine, thanks, Jack,' she said, pulling a face at him. 'Can I let you know about the extra hours?' she asked Lucy.

'Yes, of course,' Lucy said, giving Jack a quick smile before going into the kitchen.

Jack looked at Sacha, he seemed confused. 'I'm not sure what she means half the time,' he whispered. 'She's always giving me strange little looks. She's nice, so I don't want to risk upsetting her by asking her, so I pretend I get the meaning behind them.'

Sacha rolled her eyes. 'Just be pleasant to her, Jack,' she said, hoping Lucy would soon find another focus for her adoration. 'Don't encourage her if you're going back to Nikki, it wouldn't be fair.'

Jack looked horrified. 'I'm not doing anything of the sort.'

'What? Flirting with Lucy or going back to Nikki?'

'Flirting. I'm not sure about Nikki yet.'

The rest of the day passed quickly. Sacha stayed down at the café, taking over the making of the meals from Jack in the kitchen, so that he could serve in the café until the last of the rush was over.

'Why don't you go and see Bella,' Jack suggested. 'Lucy and I've got it covered here and we don't need three of us now.'

She wasn't used to not being needed in her own café, but liked the idea of confiding in Bella about what Alessandro had told her. 'Okay, but I'll be back in an hour or so and then you can get off and go kayaking or something. It's glorious out there and it would be a shame not to make the most of it.' She pulled him discreetly to one side. 'Have you thought any more about whether you're going to give it a go here, over the summer?'

He sighed, his happy mood slipping. 'Yeah. I told Nikki the other night and she wasn't at all happy. She's sure there's someone else and had a bit of a rant, but I think I finally persuaded her that there wasn't anything going on with anyone else.'

'Good,' Sacha smiled at him. 'You're not that kind of guy, thankfully. Right, I'll get going before you change your mind. See you in a bit.'

'No worries, you take your time.'

Sacha grabbed her spare sunglasses from the drawer by the kitchen door and saying goodbye to the customers she knew, left the café. The heat hit her. She hadn't realised how hot it was and closing her eyes, she pushed her glasses on and breathed in the familiar sea air. 'Perfect,' she said.

'I agree,' said a cheeky teenage boy as he cycled past, giving her a wink.

Sacha laughed as she walked slowly along the pavement, watching the families and youngsters laughing as they enjoyed themselves.

Reaching the once vacant shop with its door closed and workmen busily updating the insides, her mood dipped. She had to give Alessandro credit though, it was summer and the work was being carried out quietly. There'd been very little extra noise intruding on any of the other businesses or homes nearby. She stopped and looked up at his sign now saying that the opening would be in a few days' time. What was she going to do about this? she wondered, peeking inside and walking a little faster when she caught Alessandro's gaze. She wasn't ready to speak to him again yet, not until she'd thought it through a bit more.

'Sacha,' he called, rushing out to join her.

Sacha stopped and turned to face him, a fixed smile on her face.

'Your foot, it is a little better?' he asked, looking down at her neon pink sandals, which didn't go with what she was wearing.

'Yes, it's not throbbing as much,' she said, determined to be polite. 'Thanks for all you did earlier, it was kind.'

He shook his head. 'It was the least I could do, after all that's happened between us.' She started to continue on her way when he began walking next to her. 'We must speak about what is happening with our businesses, Sacha,' he said. 'Maybe we can find a way that helps both of us.'

'I can't see how,' she said, not in the mood to discuss it right now. 'I really should be going. I'm on my way to see Bella about something.'

He smiled, began to walk away, but changed his mind. 'Come in and have a look.' When she faltered, he added. 'One minute only, maybe two.'

It wouldn't hurt, she thought. It wasn't as if Bella was expecting her and she was curious about what was going on inside his new shop.

'Fine. Just briefly, though.'

Alessandro led the way, stopping to open the door and wait for her to walk in. She pushed her sunglasses up onto the top of her head and squinted. It was so bright outside that it took a few seconds for her eyes to get used to the darker room.

The two men working near the counter stopped what they were doing. 'We were going to take a quick break, if you'd like us to leave you in peace for a few minutes,' the older one said.

'Yes, thank you.' Alessandro stepped back, waiting for them to leave, and closed the door behind them. 'It is much smaller than your café,' he said, stating the obvious. She suspected he was hoping to persuade her that his new business wasn't going to take all her customers.

Sacha took in the area. The counter, similar to but smaller than hers, ran along the right-hand side, from the window by the door to the back of the room. Whereas her refrigerated counter held ice cream filled containers without lids, his held round metal things that looked like large, shallow thermos flasks. There was a room behind this area, and what looked like a further small room at the rear, where she assumed his sink, loo and storeroom must be situated. In front of the door was the seating area. She had enough for thirty-five covers, he looked as if he only had enough for a maximum of ten to twelve customers.

'It's tiny,' she whispered to herself, trying to picture how it had looked when Mrs Le Breton ran her wool shop from here.

'It is,' he agreed.

Embarrassed that he'd heard her comment, she added. 'Sorry, I just meant...'

'No, it is okay. This is a very small gelateria. I have permission for two small tables out of the front, but I am happy with this.'

She tried to picture which of her customers might be enticed to come here. Recalling the delicious gelato she and Alessandro had sampled in the tiny gelateria he'd taken her to that first day in Rome, she realised he was copying the concept. Then it dawned on her.

'You're using the same canisters,' she said, pointing to the empty ones in the counter so that he knew what she meant. 'That gelateria you took me to was your fathers?'

'No,' he said. 'It was my uncle's. My father's other brother. He also is in the same business.'

She looked at the ultra-modern interior, so different from her vintage themed café. 'It is very different to my place, and I suppose you'll be serving your home-made Italian ice creams.'

'Si, and you will serve your locally made Jersey ice creams. We will be similar but, I believe, different enough to be able to run businesses in the same area. Do you agree?'

She could see he was trying to convince her. She wanted to be convinced, but wasn't sure that she would be.

'I don't really have much choice, seeing as you look like you're almost ready to open.' She tried to sound jovial, but failed.

He straightened up a table and she wondered if he was trying to give himself time to think of what to say next. 'I will have an opening event on Thursday evening,' he said. 'After your closing time. You will come, I hope?'

She closed at six on a Thursday, only staying open until seven-thirty on Friday and Saturday evenings, so couldn't refuse without being rude. 'Yes, I'll be there.'

'Thank you, Sacha,' he said. 'I understand why this is not easy for you and I would not be opening this gelateria here if I had any choice.'

She pulled her sunglasses back down to rest on her nose. 'It's fine, Alessandro,' she fibbed. 'Sometimes we have to fit in with what our family wants and put their interests before our own.' She walked to the door. 'It looks lovely in here,' she said, wanting him to know that she was impressed with how he'd changed the dingy old-fashioned wool shop into a brighter, more welcoming space. 'I think it's going to do really well.'

He watched in silence as she opened the door. 'Thank you, Sacha,' he said. 'I'm happy you like it. As you can see it is very much in the same design as my uncle's gelateria in Rome. I have not had to think too much about décor.'

She laughed. 'Maybe not, but it does fit in to this area, strangely enough. I wouldn't have thought it would if I'd seen this on paper. Now, I really must get on and get to Bella's.'

He followed her outside and kissed her on both cheeks. 'I will see you soon. Ciao, Sacha.'

'Ciao, Alessandro,' she said.

She heard him go over to the workmen and chat to them as she walked towards Bella's shop. He really had done a fine job with the tiny space and she hoped that it wouldn't detract too much from the appeal of her café. She supposed it would depend on the holidaymakers that visited the beach and what they were looking for. If his idea was going to work then they would have to come up with a clever marketing plan to ensure there would be enough call for ice creams during the summer and winter months for the pair of them to make both ventures work. It wasn't going to be easy, but a bit of hard work had never deterred her before now, why should this be any different?

7

Sacha reached Bella's cottage and opened the shop door, hearing the familiar tinkle of the little brass bell above her. Seeing a couple of customers looking at Bella's selection of vintage compacts, Sacha approached the counter to speak to her friend.

'Have you heard?'

'What? About your stubbed toe, or Alessandro's new business venture?' she asked, raising her perfectly threaded eyebrows.

'The business venture,' Sacha said, disappointed that, yet again, Bella already knew everything that was going on in the village. She sat on the beautiful balloon backed chair next to her.

Bella grinned and came around the counter to join her. 'Yes, I thought you'd meant that.' She punched Sacha's shoulder playfully. 'Don't pout, it's not as attractive as you imagine.'

Sacha stuck her tongue out at her friend. 'Better?'

'Not really.'

'Anyway, how do you know all about it?' Sacha asked. 'Was it Jack, or the instigator, Alessandro?'

'Jack,' she laughed. 'He was raging when I came down this morning. I was going to offer him breakfast, but he went on and on and so I told him I had to be somewhere. He stormed out before I had the chance to say anything else. Bless him, I don't fancy Alessandro's chances if he gets to him.'

Sacha grimaced. 'He already has, but thankfully I think the only things that were exchanged were a few angry words from Jack.'

'That's a relief,' Bella said. 'I like Alessandro and I love Jack, so I'd hate for them to fall out, especially as they're staying here at the cottage.' She groaned. 'This place is far too small for people to have a problem with each other.'

Sacha looked around the small living room. It never ceased to amaze her how Bella managed to fit in so much furniture and stock to sell. She was impressed with how the place felt like you were in someone's home, but still knew that everything was for sale. Bella was the only person she knew who didn't seem attached to objects, despite loving her antiques. She seemed happy enough owning them even for a short time and never worried much about parting with things.

'There really isn't anywhere to hide, is there?' Sacha said, smiling. 'I love this place. I never know how this room is going to look when I come here because it's always changing.'

Bella laughed. 'I know. I want people to feel like they're at home and comfortable enough to look at everything without feeling like they're in a shop.'

'And it works well.'

Bella glanced over at the customers, who were now looking at the underneath of a large pottery vase and inspecting the markings. 'I had to stop those two from going upstairs. They thought that they could rummage around in all the rooms, so I had to explain that this was the shop and the rest of the cottage was my home.'

Sacha covered her mouth so her giggles couldn't be heard. 'You can't blame them, I suppose. You should probably put up a sign so that people know that this is the only room that's incorporated into the shop.'

'I don't like the idea of having signs all over the place. As it is, I have to have that exit sign there so people know the way out.' Bella explained. 'Though if they can't remember coming straight into this room from the pavement, then the sign won't be much good.'

Sacha thought about a solution for her. 'Maybe you should hook up a thick burgundy cord across the entry way to the back of the house. It can be unhooked whenever you, or your lodgers go through, and kept across the doorway the rest of the time so customers know not to go through there.'

Bella thought about what she'd said. 'Like those VIP cordons, you mean?'

'Yes,' Sacha said. 'It's a little different and would go with the eclectic style of the shop.'

'I like it,' Bella said, smiling. 'I'm going to do that.' She tapped Sacha's knee. 'You're so clever sometimes, do you know that?'

The couple decided to buy the vase, and while Bella served them Sacha went to look at the new stock. She especially liked the vintage cocktail hats Bella had recently acquired. She knew it was good for her bank account that her flat was so small, otherwise she'd have a hard time not treating herself to many of the beautiful things she discovered in this little shop. She was about to try one of them on when she heard the little brass bell announcing that the door was being opened, and waited for the customers to close it behind them.

'Good sale?' she asked Bella.

'Yes, I got that for a bargain, but it is a beautiful piece and they've not done too badly either.' She sat back down. 'Right, what were we talking about? Oh yes, your issue with Alessandro.'

'I really like him,' Sacha admitted. 'But however I try to look at it, there's no point in allowing myself to get involved with someone who's opened up an ice cream parlour in direct competition to mine.' Bella went to argue, but Sacha carried on before she had the chance. 'Look, I know he's doing it for his father, so I get that he probably can't really not do it, but it makes things very difficult between us.'

'I can see why,' Bella said, giving Sacha a sympathetic look. 'Does your dad know about all this yet?'

'No,' Sacha said, dreading the prospect of him coming down to the boardwalk and causing a fuss. She loved her dad, but he was a big local character and seemed to believe that he had some sort of entitlement to have a successful business there. She was still surprised that he'd suggested she take over this particular café. It had been the first one he'd set up, years before, with several following whenever he could afford to start them up.

'It's all a bit of a mess and I know he's not going to take the news well. I was hoping you might help me come up with a way to make both businesses work successfully.'

'You just want to find a way to stop him returning to Italy and his life as an archaeologist.' Bella winked at her.

'It's more complicated than that,' Sacha said miserably. She thought of the pictures she'd seen of Alessandro and Livia and explained about his past.

'I thought he looked familiar, but I never thought he was someone I'd recognise from magazines.' Bella stood up. 'Keep an eye on the shop for a second and I'll make us a cup of tea. I think we both need it.'

Sacha agreed and when Bella disappeared into her tiny kitchen, she stared into space for a while. Annoyed at the downturn in her mood, she got up, needing something to take her mind off her problems. She went over to the aqua cocktail hat with a short veil that had taken her fancy earlier. Maybe, she mused, as she picked it up, it wouldn't be too bad if someone took over the gelateria and then Alessandro would be distanced from it. She was being ridiculous. Whether she liked it or not, he was connected to it and she was just going to have to deal with it and work extra hard to be inventive and ensure her business didn't suffer.

She suggested this to Bella, who was making a noise in the kitchen. Bella eventually shouted back, 'You'll make it work, you're determined.'

'I don't really have much choice, do I?' she said, mainly to herself. If she lost the café then she'd have to move out of her flat and not wake up to that view each morning. No, she would simply have to find a way. Feeling a little heartened by her own positivity, she studied the little hat, entranced by how it was made with some form of wiring inside.

She placed it on her head, moving it a little until she was happy. The hat held itself in place without a hat pin or elastic, and standing in front of a fifties-style mirror, Sacha pulled down the fine net veil to cover her eyes.

'Maybe your dad can come up with some ideas, or your mum?'

The thought of her father becoming involved; arguing with Alessandro and ordering her around, was not the answer she'd been hoping for. 'No chance. Maybe your dad might be a good person to ask such a thing, but not mine.'

Sacha wondered if her mum would be helpful. She doubted it, especially as her mother would more than likely agree with her father on any matter. Her mother had worked as hard as he had over the years. Her business acumen had played a big part in his success. Sacha thought back to when she was small, and all the times her mum had left her and Jack with their grandparents, or a willing neighbour. She remembered many occasions when her mum had needed to cover an absent employee at one of the cafés, or had taken Sacha and Jack with her to buy supplies if they couldn't be delivered soon enough. No, her parents pretty much stood together on anything to do with their businesses. Sacha knew it was their united front and support of each other that had helped make them so successful.

'Very pretty,' Bella commented, walking into the room, carrying a small tray with mismatched cups and saucers. 'I've treated us to a custard cream each, too.'

Sacha laughed. 'Lovely, my favourites.' She tilted her head to one side and then the other. 'So, you think I should buy this hat?'

'I do.'

Sacha put her hands on her hips. 'Where would I wear it, though?'

'You don't have to wear it, just have it on display.' Bella thought for a moment. 'Did your mum ever have those polystyrene heads? Mine did, she kept one for wigs and hair pieces. Maybe you could get something like that and display it on there. Put it on your dressing table?'

Sacha vaguely knew what she was talking about. She liked the idea, although she had no idea where she'd find such a thing. It was something to look out for, though.

'Yes, I'll buy it. Can you keep it for me until tomorrow and I'll pay for it then?'

'You can take it now, you don't have to wait,' Bella said, shaking her head.

'No, tomorrow's fine. I don't really know where I'm going to put it until I get that head thing sorted.' She took a sip of her tea.

'Anyway,' Bella said, thoughtfully. 'If Alessandro found someone to take over from him at his place then surely it would mean he'd go back to his archaeological work?'

'He has to find someone to manage the place,' Bella said, chewing her lower lip. 'He's not licenced to work here.'

'No, he isn't,' Bella said, frowning. 'So once he does that, then he'll have no reason to stay.'

'No.' Bella was right, if he didn't have the gelateria keeping him here, then he'd move on. Sacha sighed, miserable at the thought, then decided that if she couldn't ever be with him, then maybe it would be easier if he left once everything was sorted out. It would take her time to get used to him not being around, but it was better than having him here and knowing he was still pining for Livia.

She noticed Bella seemed a little sad. 'Is something bothering you?'

Bella frowned. 'You probably haven't heard about Betty's cottage?'

'No,' Sacha said, forgetting her worries about Alessandro. 'Why? What's happened?'

'She's very private and usually keeps everything close to her chest, as you know,' Bella said. 'But I popped in to see her last night with some apple crumble and found her in tears.'

Sacha gasped. Everyone was fond of the petite stalwart of their village. Betty was well respected and independent despite being ninety-three and rather frail. 'I hope she's okay,' she said.

'I've only seen her from a distance since coming back from my trip. It did occur to me that she hadn't popped in to the café, like she usually does a couple of mornings each week.' Sacha's heart pounded with fright. 'I thought she had other things going on. I hope nothing bad has happened to her.'

'She's fine physically, if that's what you mean,' Bella said. 'No, it's just that she received a letter from some administrator who looks after the company that owns her cottage.'

'But I thought she owned it,' Sacha said, confused. 'Though thinking about it, I only assumed that because she's always been there.'

'I thought so, too,' Bella said miserably. 'She was in such a state that I asked to see the letter she was holding and it turns out that the lease on the cottage is up in a couple of months and she needs to either renew it, pay for an extension of five years, which is something they've offered her, or find somewhere else to live.'

Sacha felt sick. 'But that would kill her. What can we do?'

Bella shrugged. 'I phoned the number on the letter for her and explained that she couldn't afford the extra money. To be fair, the woman I spoke to was very sympathetic. She said they don't usually offer five-year extensions, but are doing this for Betty because they're aware of her age and the fact that she's lived there for the past fifty years.'

'I suppose that's nice of them,' Sacha conceded.

'I could tell she didn't like the situation, but she explained that Betty needs to pay the five thousand pounds for the extension, or they'll have to lease it to someone else. Apparently, there are people desperate to get their hands on any one of the places along this boardwalk.'

'I can see why,' Sacha said. Betty's bad news had put her own issues with Alessandro into perspective. 'She should be cared for after all she's given to this island over the years. We can't let that happen to her. We have to find a way to help.'

'I agree,' Bella said. 'But none of us has the available cash to pay for the extension.'

They sat in silence, each slowly drinking their tea and desperately trying to come up with some way of helping their elderly friend.

'Did you know,' Bella asked, interrupting Sacha's thoughts, 'that all the properties on the boardwalk are owned by the same company?'

Sacha didn't. 'What, all of them?'

Bella nodded. 'Don't you think that's odd? Especially in this day and age?'

'Mmm.' Sacha mulled over this piece of news. 'Maybe we could find the directors of the company and discover who owns everything?'

'And what? Try to persuade them to leave Betty carrying on as she has done, without having to pay for the extension?'

'It's worth a try.'

'It is.'

'Right,' Sacha said. 'The first thing we need to do is look up the company on the local company register.' She watched as Bella opened her laptop and typed in the company name.

'This is all very good, but it only tells us when the company was formed and where the registered office is, and we already know that address because it was on the letter.'

'We can apply for the company papers,' Sacha suggested. 'But first I think we should try and find out who's behind the company by phoning and asking the same woman you spoke to.'

Bella frowned. 'You really think she's allowed to tell us anything? Come on, that's never going to happen.'

'So, should we pay to download the information then?'

'Why not?'

By the time Sacha left, they'd downloaded documents and discovered that the directors of the company were nominee shareholders. 'So, all we've found out is that two companies are the shareholders of the company that owns these properties then?'

They sat in annoyed silence.

'We'll have to go with Plan B then,' Bella said.

'We have one?'

'Nope, not yet.'

'I know,' Sacha shrieked eventually, a delighted grin on her tanned face. 'We can arrange a fête.'

'What?'

'A fête,' Sacha said, satisfied with her suggestion. 'To raise money for Betty's Fund. It'll bring all the people on the board-walk together for one big event and hopefully we can raise enough to pay for her lease.'

Bella's eyes widened. 'You're brilliant,' she said, raising her cup and spilling some on her wooden floor. 'We can also intro-duce Alessandro's ice cream parlour to more people. It'll be a way to show everyone that there's room enough for both your businesses.'

Sacha thought about what her friend was saying. 'I suppose we could promote the differences between the two businesses and maybe encourage people to come to the boardwalk to try both. It would be a way to attract attention to the area for those who live on the island but don't ever think to come down this way.'

Excited by her idea, her mind raced with plans for the event. 'We could invite others from outside the area to set up stalls. I'm pretty sure that when people discover what's happened to Betty they'll want to get involved with their own stalls, and if they don't have anything to sell then they can donate towards the fund. It would make it a little more diverse. We've got my café, Alessandro's ice cream parlour, your antique shop and Jools' second-hand book shop. We could ask that couple with the cider business to set up a stall and those people we saw at the Christmas market with the lavender cushions, oils and other bits and pieces. We could also ask the family who adapted their tomato farming business to make and sell fresh tomato sauces.'

Excited, Bella clapped her hands. 'Yes, and Betty can make her Jersey Wonders. She'd love to be involved. What about the local couple we met a few months ago who make that divine salted caramel sauce? You could use some on your ice creams and maybe some waffles, and if they like it...'

'Which they're bound to because it's heaven in a bottle,' Sacha said, clapping her hands. This was going to be brilliant, she knew it.

'Hell, yes,' Bella giggled. 'Then you could point them in the direction of the stall to buy their own to take home.'

Sacha smiled. 'I knew we could do this, Bella.'

'We could get Lexi to set up a stall with her father's paintings,' Bella added. 'She's always looking for more outlets.'

Sacha contemplated how else they could make the event successful. 'We'll need to arrange a raffle and some events that people have to pay to take part in.'

'The stall holders will pay to rent the spot where their stall is positioned and maybe they could give a small percentage of their takings to the fund for Betty?'

'Good idea,' Sacha said. 'I'm happy to donate all my profits on the day and I can ask Alessandro and Lexi if they'll do the same.'

'I'm happy to,' Bella agreed. 'We also need to make the boardwalk look like we're holding an event.'

'I know, we can hang bunting from the Victorian lampposts across to the shops. It would look wonderfully colourful. What else could we do?'

They thought a bit more and Bella stretched across her counter to reach a notepad and biro. 'We need to write this down,' she said, making hurried notes.

'We have to get everyone together and decide on a date that suits everyone here.'

'No, that won't work,' Bella said.

'Why not?'

'It'll take too long. You know how much they faff about when they have to do anything out of the ordinary.'

She had a point, Sacha agreed.

Bella tapped her notes with the back of her biro. 'You and I can work out the perfect weekend for this. We only need a couple of weeks' notice, because we're already here and the stall holders are used to popping up in different locations all the time. I think we should save time by deciding the date between us and making up leaflets to pop through the other doors along the boardwalk, asking if they want to be involved, and give them till this Sunday to decide. We need to get on with it, if we're going to make the most of any fundraising activities we can come up with.'

It sounded like a good plan to Sacha. 'Hang on a second; we're bound to need permission for this. Do you have a phone book?'

'What for?' Bella reached for the book that Sacha remembered being almost twice the thickness before most people stopped bothering with their landlines and used their mobile phones instead.

'I'm going to give the Parish Hall a call. Hopefully I can speak to a centenier and ask what we need to do.'

A few moments later, Sacha ended the call to one of the voluntary officers who policed the parish. 'He said we need permission from the bailiff and that usually takes three to six months.'

'We can't do it then,' Bella folded her arms across her chest, a sad expression on her face.

'Not necessarily,' Sacha said. 'He said to carry on with our planning, because we don't have enough time to waste, and he'll get back to me tomorrow after speaking to someone at the bailiff's office.'

'I hope we can do this,' Bella said.

Me too, thought Sacha. 'He did say that if all else fails the Parish Hall has a permit and we can hold the event there.'

'That's kind of him, but it won't be the same.'

'At least we know we can hold it to raise money for Betty,' Sacha said. 'That's the main thing.'

Bella agreed. 'We need to get planning.'

'I agree, and we need to put a small advert in the *Gazette* so that anyone we haven't thought of can let us know if they'd like to reserve a pitch.'

'Perfect.' Bella grinned. 'Now all we have to do is sort out that leaflet and decide who is going to do what.'

'I'm sure Jack, Lucy and Milo will be willing to help set up the bunting and stalls. They all have so much energy and love getting involved in new things.'

'Brilliant.' Bella laughed. 'You see, this will sort everything out.'

Watching Bella scribble away on her notepad, absorbed by the prospect of bringing everyone together, Sacha felt a surge of pleasure. It felt good to be doing something positive to help Betty. She realised how long she'd been away from the café and, finishing her cold tea, told Bella she'd better get back to relieve Jack, who must be desperate for a paddle by now.

'I'll see you later on, maybe,' she said, smiling when Bella narrowed her eyes thoughtfully, the end of the biro in her mouth as she concentrated on ideas for the event.

Trailing her fingers along the railings as she crossed the boardwalk, Sacha noticed they felt sticky, and looked a darker colour – as if they'd been painted again overnight. How odd, she thought.

Approaching the café, it dawned on her how she never ceased to be cheered by the happy laughter drifting from the beach. She and Jack had spent a lot of their childhood there, building sandcastles and swimming in the sea. They had been happy days, and she wondered whether she'd be lucky enough raise her own children here, so they could enjoy this glorious place.

'Mummy, I want an ice cream,' she heard a little boy saying. 'Please. You promised.'

Sacha waited for the mother to react. She argued a little with the boy, although Sacha could tell it was in a half-hearted way, and eventually gave in, asking the couple sitting nearby to watch over their belongings. How many places were there where you could still do that? Sacha wondered as she watched the mother and her two sons make their way up the granite steps.

She waved at someone she recognised on the beach and entered the café. As she set about making some ice-cream sundaes, she wondered whether her mother would be happy to get involved with the fête.

It was busy in the café, as it usually was on hot summer days like this one. Milo came out from the kitchen. 'Did you know there's going to be another ice cream place?' he said, his voice barely above a whisper so no one could overhear.

'I did,' she said. 'It'll be fine though,' she added, wondering if maybe he was worried that if they lost business she might not need him any more. Then it occurred to her that maybe he was interested in going to work at the new, exciting Italian gelateria. She waved for him to follow her back to the store area.

Once inside she said. 'He might be wanting staff to work for him.'

Milo blushed. 'I saw an advert in my Mum's *Gazette* last night,' he admitted.

'If you want to apply for the job I'll understand.' She wouldn't like to see him leave, but remembered how it felt to be a teenager, excited by new experiences. 'I would miss you, of course.'

'You want me to go?'

Sacha took him by his shoulders. 'No, of course not, but I don't want you to worry about it if you decide you want to go and work there.'

'Thanks, but I'd rather stay working for you.' He looked at her, hesitating before adding, 'I might want to try out his ice creams though, just once.'

'Me, too,' she said winking at him. 'But don't tell Jack, I don't think he'd understand.'

'He was telling Lucy about Alessandro this morning. I don't think he's very happy with him.'

Sacha grimaced. 'He's not.'

8

'How can my feet be sore from handing out these leaflets?'
Sacha asked Bella, slumping down on her sofa later the
following day. 'I'm used to being on my feet all day.'

'I'm knackered, too,' Bella said, kicking off her trainers.
'Whose bright idea was it to do this anyway?'

'Yours,' Sacha laughed. 'Or was it mine? I forget.'

'I forget how steep those hills are at either end of this
village,' Bella grimaced, flexing her toes and moving her feet
around in circles to loosen up her stiff ankles. 'I've got a few
people who've signed up for a stall. Lexi is a definite and I'm not
sure about Jools as she's still away, but she should be back soon
and is always up for anything exciting.'

'She loves Betty, too, so she's bound to agree to take part,'
Sacha said.

'How about you?' Bella asked. 'Any immediate interest?'

Sacha moved a cushion from under her arm to behind her
back. 'Um, yes, two people. One is the lady who makes the jams
and sloe gin, the other was her friend, who was visiting.' She
thought back to the woman with the elaborate earrings. 'She

makes jewellery and cushions and other things out of old scarves. I'll be visiting her stall if I have a moment. I should think it'll look nice and colourful on the boardwalk.'

'Brilliant,' Bella said, closing her eyes. 'You see, it's coming together already and we've only just started arranging the event.'

'You did remember to take their contact details in case we have to let them know that the venue has changed, if we don't get permission?'

'I did,' Bella said, crossing one leg over the other and rubbing her sore feet.

They sat in exhausted silence for a few moments. This was the best thing about a good friendship, Sacha thought; knowing each other well enough that words weren't always necessary.

'Do you think your mum will agree to make extra cookies and cakes for the day?' Bella asked. 'I'd ask mine, but she's hopeless at anything that doesn't constitute a stew, or beans on toast.'

'Probably,' Sacha mused. 'It'll depend on how busy she is. Since she semi-retired she spends her time golfing, visiting art studios and travelling away to festivals like the one in Hay-on-Wye. Anything that gives her a break from Dad, so he can't make her help out when she'd rather not.'

Sacha didn't blame her mother for making the most of her free time; she'd worked hard enough to deserve all the fun she could have. She suspected her mother would make the space in her diary for the fête, though. She wouldn't be able to resist meeting Alessandro and getting to know him and the plans for his venture.

'I think we can rely on her to be there for at least part of the time,' she said, smiling.

Bella looked at her quizzically for a moment and then

grinned. 'Ah, of course, your mother, the divine Mrs Collins wouldn't be able to resist, would she?'

'Especially if I tell her how good looking he is,' Sacha giggled.

Bella gasped. 'Oh, my God, imagine her dilemma. On the one hand, here's this bloke who's set up in competition with your business, and on the other, he's a delicious guy who she'd probably like to see her daughter with. I wonder which side of her nature will win?'

Sacha laughed. 'You're so right. Poor Mum, she's not going to know what to do.'

Her mother would probably be annoyed with Alessandro, because of his business. She could never understand how her mother, falling in love with her father at nineteen, could be content to be with him her entire adult life. She always insisted that she'd never been interested in other men and had only ever loved Sacha's father.

Sacha suspected that this reciprocated adoration was the reason she and Jack could never find the right partner. Jack was looking for that perfect relationship, albeit unsuccessfully. She couldn't understand why he felt so tied to Nikki, but Jack would have his reasons, whatever they might be. And she, well, she thought she'd found it with her ex, Giles, but it wasn't to be. Anyway, she reminded herself, she didn't want and certainly didn't need a partner to feel fulfilled.

She noticed Bella watching her. She seemed to be waiting for Sacha to answer an unheard question.

'Sorry, I was miles away,' she admitted.

Bella shook her head. 'That was pretty obvious. What I said was, we'll go out again tomorrow and give out more leaflets.' She handed Sacha a batch. 'These are to top up any you haven't given out. I'll visit the rest of the shops and cottages along the boardwalk and suggest they stick at least one in their front window, so hopefully passers-by will read them.'

'Yes,' agreed Sacha. 'We can put these out on our counters and ask other businesses in the area to do the same. I'll contact Mum and see if she'll share them around Dad's other cafés.'

She pulled her mobile out of her shorts pocket and tapped out a text for her mum. Pressing send, she focused her attention back on Bella. 'What else can we do that won't cost a fortune?'

'I'll speak to my friend at the *Gazette*, I'm sure he'll do a quick interview with me, and you, if you like. That should make sure that most of Jersey knows about the fête, even if they decide they don't want to bother coming.'

'Great idea,' Sacha said. Excitement welled up in her chest. 'I'm really looking forward to the day, I think it's going to be brilliant.'

'Only if we organise it properly, and if the weather holds.'

They groaned in unison. The weather, thought Sacha, the bane of all their lives when it came to outdoor events.

'It'll have to,' Sacha said, hopefully. Her phone pinged. 'Mum,' she said, looking at the screen on her mobile. She laughed. 'She said if we pop round now we can join them for a barbecue. She said to bring Jack and Alessandro.'

They looked at each other.

'How does she know about him, already?' Bella laughed. 'Does anything happen on this island that your mum doesn't know about?'

'Not much,' Sacha said, shaking her head. 'Right, I'll go and find Jack.'

Just then the door opened and Alessandro walked in. 'Ciao ladies,' he said. 'I am sorry to interrupt you.'

Bella stood. 'Hang on a sec,' she said. 'We've all been invited to a barbecue at Sacha's parent's place. You've been invited. Coming?'

He looked bewildered for a moment. 'I have time to shower quickly?'

'Yes,' Sacha said, walking over to the door. 'I've got to get hold of Jack. How about we meet outside in half an hour? I'll text Mum and let her know we're coming and we can walk up?'

'Perfect,' Bella said, shooing Alessandro towards the stairs. 'Hurry up, in case Jack wants a shower, too.'

Just at that moment Bella's doorbell rang. 'Anyone in?' asked a deep voice as the door slowly opened.

'Sod it,' Bella whispered. 'I'd forgotten I'd arranged this.'

Sacha knew as soon as she saw the man walk in carrying a large box of wrapped up objects that he had come to do a deal with Bella.

'Don't worry,' she said. Mum will have loads of barbecues this summer and you can come with me to the next one.'

Bella pulled a face, quickly replacing her grimace with a wide smile as she turned to welcome her guest.

Sacha was outside Bella's cottage when Jack arrived. 'I've been looking for you,' he said. 'The Centenier just phoned and said that there's been a meeting at the Parish Hall to approve a special licence to hold the fête. Betty is a local war hero, so the bailiff wants to grant the licence to her by way of a small thank you from the local community.'

Sacha knew the Centenier worked hard to ensure the parishioners were looked after and was glad he had decided to honour her in this way.

* * *

Sacha and Alessandro walked up the steep hill at one side of the bay, Jack slightly ahead of them. She explained about the fête and what they were hoping to achieve.

'Bella can give you some leaflets for your place, and one or two to put in the window. What do you think?' she asked.

'It is a good idea,' Alessandro said. 'I haven't been to a fête before and I look forward to taking part.' He smiled at her. 'What did you think of my gelateria? Is small but good enough, I hope.'

'It's perfect. Especially as you're only doing ice creams.' A thought occurred to her. 'What will you serve in the winter when people aren't interested in eating ice creams, though? Will you only be open during the summer season?'

'I thought so, but my father has insisted we do crêpes in the winter.'

'But they're not Italian, they're French,' she said. 'I thought the whole point of your place was that it was an Italian gelateria?'

Alessandro shrugged. 'They serve crêpes in gelaterias also. They are very popular, too. This is the choice we will have to keep open for the winter.' He walked in silence for a bit. 'If it doesn't work then my father will need to think of an alternative way to do business.'

As they reached the summit of the hill, Alessandro and Sacha were both slightly out of breath and stopped to give their legs a break. He looked back at the bay. Sacha watched his reaction as he looked down on the sea glistening in the sunshine, and listened to the distant screams of excitement from children building sandcastles and playing football on the beach. She wondered if she'd had the same expression of pleasure on her face when she'd seen the exquisite vista of spires, rooftops and sunset that Alessandro had shown her from the Gianicolo.

'It is very lovely,' he said. 'Very like in a black and white English movie, no?'

Sacha laughed. 'I suppose so.' She checked her watch. Her mother hated having to wait for anyone. 'Come along, we'd better get a move on.'

It wasn't much further, only another ten more minutes if they hurried, she thought.

She pointed out the top of the large pine tree that her father had planted as a sapling when they'd first moved into their home. 'We're nearly there.'

Finally, reaching the tall cream gateposts either side of black iron electric gates, she pressed the intercom. 'Mum, we're here, can you open the gates please.'

She wondered where Jack had got to. He must have been walking quickly to arrive so much earlier than they had. Surely he hadn't gone in already?

Her mother called for them to come in. 'We're in the back garden, waiting for you.'

Sacha stifled a giggle. 'I told you she was impatient,' she said, breaking into a jog and leading Alessandro through the gates and between two tall palm trees towards the sound of Jack's voice exclaiming over the steaks their father was no doubt barbecuing.

Sacha and Alessandro turned a corner to see a large wooden garden table laden with salads, garlic bread, and a pile of plates and utensils, waiting for them to help themselves.

'Hi, sorry we're a little late,' Sacha said. 'This is Alessandro.' She hugged her mother and then her father and beckoned Alessandro over. 'He's opening a little gelateria along the boardwalk.' She knew they would be interested and it would save him having to break the news to them later in the evening. Better that everyone knew where they stood straight away.

Her father's heavy grey eyebrows knitted together in a deep frown. 'Yes, I've heard about this,' he said, not bothering to hide his disapproval.

Sacha spotted Jack glowering at Alessandro and hoped he didn't add to their father's anger by adding his thoughts on the matter.

'No arguments tonight, Tom,' her mother said, touching his right cheek lightly with her hand. 'Alessandro is new to the island and he's our guest for the evening.' She turned to Alessandro. 'Welcome, I'm glad you could come. Tom is very proud of his enormous steaks, so I hope you're hungry and ready to eat a lot.'

Alessandro looked over at the meat cooking in front of Tom, who still had a scowl on his face. Sacha hoped he'd do as her mother had asked and be polite to his guest. It wasn't often she asked him to do something and he usually obliged rather than risk upsetting her.

'Fine,' he said, eventually giving in and winking at Sacha. 'I don't know why your mother thinks I'd be anything other than a perfect gentleman,' he whispered. 'Right, I know you're funny when it comes to eating meat.'

'I'm a vegetarian, Dad,' she said, shaking her head. She had been since she was thirteen and could just about get away with it during family meals. She didn't mind handling meat at the café but just didn't enjoy eating it. Sacha couldn't understand why her father still found it strange, when she hadn't eaten meat for sixteen years.

'Yes, whatever,' he pointed to a tray over on a separate small table. 'Your mother made me rush out and buy you some strange soya things. I'll cook them after the meat is ready.'

She peered over at the kebabs and liked the look of the sweet red peppers with carrots and onions, although some were speared together with chunks of chicken fillet and others with beef.

'You needn't have bothered though, Mum always does far too much salad and I can see that she's also made her potato salad.'

The food served, everyone sat down at the table. Sacha noticed Jack positioning himself as far away from Alessandro as possible. Her mother pushed a small pot of Jersey Black Butter towards Alessandro.

'Try that,' she said explaining what it was. 'It's made from cider, apples, a little lemon and spices and it's delicious. Have some with your meat or the cheeses at the end of the meal.'

He thanked her, but Sacha wasn't sure if he was convinced by the dark mixture in the bowl in front of him. She waited, knowing her father would have to find a way to bring up the gelateria. As expected, he waited for her mother to go in the house along with Jack, who carried the plates for her. Once she was out of earshot, he addressed Alessandro.

'Right, son,' he said. 'I'm not happy, not happy at all about this ice cream parlour of yours. I've had a business down that boardwalk for nigh on fifty years now and don't need you muscling your way in and buggering things up for my girl here.'

Here we go, thought Sacha suppressing a groan. 'Dad,' she said, quickly glancing at the house to check her mother wasn't on the way back to join them. 'It's not Alessandro's business, it's his father's. He wanted to set up a gelateria in Jersey.'

'Why?'

'Yes, why?' Jack said, returning from inside the house.

'Why not?' she said, unhelpfully, irritated with her brother for getting involved. 'There's no reason why a little competition won't be a good thing, if it's done the right way.' Satisfied with her quick thinking, she settled back in her chair.

'Which is?' her father asked, putting a dampener on her thoughts.

Alessandro clasped his hands together. 'Mr Collins, I understand your feelings about what I'm doing, and I would feel the same way. My father worked over here many years ago and it has been his dream to come back and set up his own business, but family ties and other restrictions have meant that was impossible.'

Her father took a mouthful of his drink and contemplated Alessandro's words. 'Then surely he should just forget about it.'

'Or you could try to change his mind,' Jack said, ignoring Sacha's glare.

Alessandro shrugged one shoulder. 'What can I say? I will be focusing on an Italian way of making and serving my gelatos and Sacha will continue running her wonderful café. I believe the businesses can work side by side.'

'I'm sure I can make it work without seeing a reduction in takings,' she assured her father. 'I'm going to work on a marketing plan for the café and some new ideas to keep the customers coming in. I believe that you don't know what you're capable of until you're put in a tight corner and have to be inventive.'

'You're right,' her father said proudly. 'I'm sure you can do it, setbacks have never stopped you before now.'

'Thanks, Dad,' she said, smiling at him.

Her father opened his mouth to say something, but her mother's voice, announcing the arrival of her famous summer pudding, put an end to any argument he was about to make.

'That looks delicious,' Sacha said, standing up to help take the dessert from her and place it on the table. 'Now,' she said to Alessandro. 'This is a true British pudding and one I doubt you'll have tasted at home. You have to try some.'

'It looks very nice,' he said, looking as if he was trying to work out exactly what it was.

'Fresh Jersey cream to go with it, of course,' her mother added, as Jack made space on the table for her to put down a pile of plates and large crystal jug of cream.

He watched silently as their mother served Alessandro and placed the bowl in front of him, pushing the jug towards him.

'It's made with slices of white bread,' Sacha said, before Alessandro took a mouthful, so that he'd have an idea of what he was about to eat. 'It's that dark purply colour because inside are redcurrants, blackcurrants and raspberries. All from our garden, aren't they, Mum?'

'Yes, all grown here. There's golden caster sugar too, to sweeten it up. I hope you like it.'

Sacha felt sorry for the poor man as everyone watched silently, first as he poured on the cream, then while he dipped his spoon into the pudding and raised it to his mouth. She caught his eye and smiled as he chewed and swallowed.

'Well?' her mum asked. 'What do you think?'

He closed his eyes briefly. 'Very good. I like this, a lot.'

Sacha believed him, relieved. Her mother looked delighted.

The front gate buzzer cut through their conversation. Her father pressed the remote to speak.

'It's me,' Aunt Rosie's voice came through the speakers. 'Let me in, I've got some fabulous news.'

Everyone looked up expectantly as her little red sports car roared in through the gates.

'It's your aunt, from Rome?' Alessandro asked.

'The very same,' Sacha laughed. 'I wonder what she's been doing now.' She leaned in closer to him and lowered her voice. 'She's always up to something and never ceases to entertain us and irritate my father.'

'Sweeties,' she said, tottering around the side pathway of the house in her achingly high heels. She untied a coloured silk headscarf from under her chin and whipped it off, waving it at everyone in excitement.

Her father frowned. 'I'll get more drinks,' he said, giving Sacha's aunt a curt nod.

'He loves her really,' Sacha added to Alessandro before going up to her aunt and giving her a kiss on each cheek.

Aunt Rosie took Sacha's face in both hands and looked up to her. 'Precious girl, you're looking rather sun-kissed, which is what I like to see.' She looked past her and widened her eyes, glancing at Sacha and smiling. 'Well, if it isn't the very gorgeous Alessandro.' She gave him a kiss on each cheek. 'What a glorious surprise to find you here.'

'Thank you,' he said. 'It is good to see you, also.'

Sacha's mum patted the vacant seat next to her. 'Come and sit,' she said, pulling over an unused glass and pouring a little rosé into it. 'Now, what is this exciting news?'

'I've heard about your lovely fête idea,' she said, tilting her head in Sacha's direction. 'My neighbour was given one of your leaflets by,' she hesitated, 'oh, I forget now. Anyway, I wanted to tell you that earlier today I was out to lunch with a few friends and bumped into one of my childhood sweethearts.'

'This should be interesting,' Sacha's father said, returning to the table and taking his seat.

Rosie glowered at him. 'If I'm boring you, do tell me and I'll shut up.'

'No,' shouted Sacha, desperate to hear more. She gave her dad a pleading look and then smiled at her aunt. 'Go on, we're listening.'

'As I was saying, I was enjoying lunch with a few girlfriends, when George Newton arrived and came over to have a chat.'

Sacha thought she must have heard wrong. 'George Newton, the actor, from *The Rising Moon?* He's your ex-boyfriend?'

'Yes,' her aunt said, confused. 'Why, is there another George Newton I've forgotten about?'

Sacha looked at her mother. 'Mum, did you know about this?'

Her mother refilled her glass. 'What, that Rosie was at lunch with her friends today, or that she used to date George?'

Sacha glared at her mother. 'I think you know what I mean. Why did I not know about this before now?'

Her aunt shook her head and took a sip of her wine. 'Probably because no one thought you'd be interested, maybe?'

Sacha took a deep breath. Her mother and aunt could be infuriating sometimes. They'd seemed to enjoy dropping these nuggets of information on her over the years and she wasn't sure whether it was because they enjoyed doing this sort of thing to her, or whether they simply never thought to mention these things. She suspected the former, because they both shared a devilish sense of humour.

'I remember him,' her father said. 'Full of himself, he was. Used to flounce around by the boardwalk every summer. Kept on telling anyone who'd listen that he was going to be a big movie star,' he said, amused.

'He is though, Dad,' Sacha said, wondering if her family were getting worse, or whether she'd forgotten how infuriating they could be at times like these. 'Go on, Aunt Rosie, what about him?'

Her aunt had lost interest in the conversation and was tearing the end from a slice of garlic bread. 'What? Oh, sorry, darling. Um, oh yes, George said he'd open your fête for you.'

Sacha knew her mouth was open, but was too stunned to close it for a moment. 'George... what?'

'This is very good,' Alessandro said. 'He is very famous in Italy also. Many people will come to the fête if he is there, no?'

'Er,' Sacha couldn't make her brain form cohesive words. She bit back from adding that he was also pretty famous in his homeland. Still stuck on her aunt's unexpected announcement, all she could think of was Bella's reaction. She was a massive George Newton fan – bigger, even, than Sacha. She looked at Alessandro who seemed to be waiting for an answer to something. 'Yes,' she said, hoping it was the right one.

'Do pull yourself together, Sacha,' her aunt said. 'I know he's a bit dishy,' she giggled to herself. 'I could tell you a few things about Georgie.'

'Not at this table, you won't,' Sacha's father said. 'I think we can all imagine what you mean.'

Damn, thought Sacha. She'd love to hear all about her aunt's fling with the movie star. She'd make a plan with Bella to invite her to the cottage or her café to chat more about him.

'So, what did he say?' Sacha asked, regaining some semblance of intelligent speech.

'What?' Her aunt looked bemused, briefly. 'Yes, George said he'll be here for the next couple of weeks, some voiceover work at a studio here, or something. He's based at a hotel in town, but I've invited him to come and stay with me for a few days. The damn paparazzi have already discovered he's here, no doubt because someone has tipped them off for a fee. I hate to see him hounded, so he'll come to stay with me and I'll bring him down to the fête. I thought he could give a little speech, he loves talking about his work.'

'Doesn't he just.' Her dad had a pained expression.

'We'd love to hear about it,' Sacha said, still unable to believe that she was referring to 'the' George Newton, an older, more refined version of Tom Hardy. Although George was over forty and handsome in a classic way, he was brilliant in his latest role, playing a goofy detective who somehow captured the murderer and got the girl in the end. Sacha had watched his latest film with Bella, Lexi and Jools the week before going on holiday with her aunt. 'You do really mean the actor and not a bin man with the same name, don't you?'

'Shut up and listen,' her aunt said. 'I gather you're opening the proceedings at noon, so I'll make sure he's there in good time.'

Sacha pictured the day. 'Hopefully the weather will be good and there'll be people on the beach from early on.'

Her mind raced. She had so much to plan and prepare for and now that there would be a movie star opening the event, she really did need to make sure everything was as organised as possible.

Later, when her mother and aunt were chatting and she'd spotted Jack and her father sneaking into the house to catch the final of the latest Formula One Grand Prix, she exchanged thoughts with Alessandro about their favourite George Newton roles in films. She couldn't help imaging their fête being a huge success.

'I can do a blog post and we must set up an event on Facebook and share it with all our friends,' she said, excitement growing by the minute. 'We'll only have one chance to make this fête the very best it can be,' she added, trying to think of more ways to share this exciting news.

Alessandro sat back in his chair. 'It will be a great success. How can it fail?'

That's what worried her. 'We have to make plans for the weather letting us down, by having umbrellas on all the outside tables, and maybe a marquee at one end of the boardwalk so that if it does rain then we can still serve customers who can't fit in the café or your gelateria. Whatever happens we have to cover every eventuality.'

'You worry too much, Sacha,' he said. 'We will all help each other to make sure everything is perfect, no?'

She forced a smile. 'Yes, you're right. It'll be fine,' she said, wishing she felt as confident as she sounded.

He was silent for a few seconds. 'We must make new leaflets to hand out and put up in the windows,' he said thoughtfully.

'New ones?' The thought of spending time retracing her steps was daunting.

'We have to add a picture of the actor, George. Tell people he will be making a speech. Otherwise how will people know to come and see him?'

He was right. 'Yes, we will. Damn. Mind you, Bella will be only too happy to update the brochure, seeing as it's George's picture she'll be adding.'

She had her work cut out for her over the next few days, but if the fête was as good as she hoped then it would all be worth it, but first, she had to speak to Bella about the leaflets.

She chatted with everyone for a bit longer and then told them she had to leave.

'I'll drive you down to the boardwalk, if you like?' her aunt said. 'I must get going, I promised to spend some time with George this afternoon.'

'That doesn't sound like much of a hardship,' she said.

'It isn't,' Aunt Rosie said. 'He has a lot of endearing qualities.'

'Really, Rosie,' her mother said. 'Stop being so coarse.'

Aunt Rosie pulled her scarf from the back of her chair before placing it carefully over her immaculately groomed hair and tying it neatly under her chin. She reapplied her pillar box red lipstick and stood up. 'I don't recall saying anything unto-ward,' she said.

Sacha tried not to let her mother see how amused she was by her aunt's comment. She lowered her sunglasses to cover her eyes and straightened her T-shirt as she stifled a giggle. Aunt Rosie obviously knew George Newton well and couldn't under-stand why no one had mentioned her relationship with him before now.

'Can you elaborate, Aunt Rosie?'

'About what, darling?' her aunt asked, a mischievous twinkle in her eye.

Her mother grimaced. 'Please, don't get her started about George. He's her... What is it you call him, Rosie?'

'My occasional treat to myself.'

'You see?' her mother said. 'Coarse.'

Sacha was intrigued. 'How did you meet him and what is going on between you?'

Aunt Rosie sighed loudly. 'We met as teenagers.'

'You are older than he is by a good few years,' her mother scolded.

'Five or six, nothing much.'

'Ten, at least,' her mother argued.

'Please, carry on with the story, I'm dying to know,' Sacha said, aware she should get a move on.

'I'll tell you another time,' Rosie whispered.'

Disappointed, Sacha asked. 'Do you think George would mind meeting Bella and I before the day of the fête?' Her stomach fluttered in excited anticipation at the prospect. 'She's a massive fan of his and I don't want her obsessing about him when she'll need to help run everything.'

'Yes, of course,' her aunt gave Sacha's mum a kiss on the cheek. 'Where have Jack and Thomas gone?'

Her mother seemed to notice their absence for the first time and scowled. 'Inside to watch the racing I should think. Very rude of them when we have guests.'

Laughter came from the house as Jack and her father walked back out to join them.

'You're going, Rosie?' her father asked sarcastically. 'So soon?'

Rosie glared at him. 'You know something? You're not nearly as amusing as you assume.'

Sacha gave her aunt a hug before they descended into a row and ruined everyone's day. 'We are grateful about you arranging for George to open the fête, truly.'

Rosie smiled. 'Do you want that lift? It's only a couple of minutes out of my way and on a glorious evening like this one, I'm happy to take the long way around and make the most of having the roof down on my little car.'

Everyone looked over at the red sports car.

'We're tempted,' Sacha said, 'But it is a lovely evening and I'm sure Alessandro won't mind walking back down to the village.'

'Whatever you wish,' he said quickly.

She spoke to her mother about making cookies for her proposed stall. 'And a few cakes, if you have the time?'

Her mother agreed. 'I'd be happy to,' she said.

They said goodbye to her parents, and Jack who had decided to stay on and enjoy a few more drinks with his dad, and walked her aunt over to her car.

Alessandro opened the door for Aunt Rosie and waited for her to get settled before closing it.

'Such a gorgeous young man,' she said, reaching up and placing her palm against his cheek. 'You rather remind me of George when he and I first met.' She waved for Sacha to come closer and lowered her voice. 'Your mother was right, George is about ten years younger than me which is why I never married him when he asked me. The thought of being older than him when he's surrounded by all those exquisite actresses was too much for my ego. But we meet up every so often and spend a blissful few days together. Makes it all more fun than any marriage, I can tell you.'

Sacha had to concentrate on closing her mouth. 'Good for you, Aunt Rosie,' she said. 'You have more balls than any other woman I know.'

Her aunt gave her a wink. 'Now you two go off and make the most of the time you have together.' She lowered her voice to a whisper. 'I wouldn't let this one go too quickly if I was you darling, he's worth keeping.'

Sacha kissed her aunt on the cheek and stepped back from the car. 'I'll try to remember,' she said, smiling as her aunt started the engine and the car roared off out of the driveway.

Sacha and Alessandro smiled at each other as the sound of her aunt's sports car disappeared through the lanes.

'She's quite incredible,' Sacha said.

'So is her niece,' he said, taking her hand as they began the walk back to the village. The low banks either side of the narrow lane from her parent's home gave them a perfect vista of the bay below. The navy sea had risen almost to high tide now, hiding the caves that became visible twice a day when the tide was low enough for people to reach them via a short swim around the headland.

Sacha breathed in the warm summer air and relished being back. 'I've been home for two years,' she said, aware he already knew this. 'And still I can't help feeling like I'm on holiday every day. It's a treat to wake up to all this.' She picked a piece of dried grass from the bank as they walked.

'You are lucky to live in such a place,' he agreed. 'I feel much as you do, and would like to be able to remain here.'

The thought of him leaving saddened Sacha. She regretted that he had to move on, and sooner than she'd expected.

'Is there no way you can stay longer?' she asked.

He shook his head and gave her a sad smile. 'Unfortunately, no. Under Jersey employment laws I'm told I need to be here for five years to be able to run the business.'

He took her hand in his and pulled her gently to a stop. 'I will miss seeing you each day,' he said, lifting her chin and kissing her before she had time to respond.

Sacha put her arms around his neck as he took her in his arms and, forgetting their differences, kissed him back, wanting to make the most of what little time she might have left in his company.

A car beeped behind her, giving them a shock. They jumped apart and Alessandro grabbed Sacha to pull her back out of the way, so the vehicle could pass by.

The driver stopped. 'Hello there, Sach.' It was a distant neighbour she hadn't seen for a few weeks. 'I thought it was you.' He gave her a wide grin. 'Welcoming the newbies to the area, are you?'

She bit back a retort and forced a smile. 'I thought it was the least I could do,' she said, glimpsing his smile slip a little. 'Have a nice evening.'

He waved and, scowl on his face, drove away a little faster than was safe on the narrow lane.

'He was a bit; how do you say...' Alessandro frowned thoughtfully, trying to find the word he was looking for.

'Annoying?' Sacha suggested.

He laughed. 'Yes, annoying.' He took her hand and gave it a gentle squeeze before continuing with their walk.

She liked the sensation of her hand in his and calmed down. 'That's the one thing about living here that can be frustrating, knowing almost everyone, and some of them believing they are entitled to have an opinion about you and that you should abide by it.'

'It is the same in the town where I come from,' he said. 'All small communities are like that, I believe.'

He was probably right, she decided. 'I went to school with him, and went out with him for three weeks when I was seventeen. I finished with him because he was a bit too serious and I didn't want to get involved in something I wasn't ready for.'

'And he's never forgiven you?'

'Something like that. I can't tell him to bugger off because this is a small community and I don't want any ill feeling with anyone living here. I need all the business I can get, especially now that...' She remembered who she was talking to and reddened. 'Sorry, I just meant, well, you know.'

'I do,' he said, giving her hand another comforting squeeze. 'Let us focus on the fête and raising money for Betty.'

'Good idea, and on that note, I need to let Bella know what my aunt is hopefully arranging for the grand opening.'

They walked a little faster to get home, each lost in their thoughts, when it dawned on Sacha that they didn't have a Plan B if they failed to save Betty's home.

9

As it turned out, Sacha was right about Bella's reaction to George opening the fête.

'It is very good, no?' Alessandro asked.

'What? You're serious?' Bella's eyes widened as she placed her hands on her cheeks. Sacha knew that in a matter of seconds her friend would react to the exciting news and covered her ears in anticipation of Bella's delighted high-pitched scream. This was a typical Bella reaction when she was surprised and happy.

Alessandro looked startled. 'You are okay?'

'She's fine,' Sacha said, holding back a smile while remembering how Alessandro had kissed her at the top of the hill, and again, just before they arrived at the boardwalk. She sighed happily. Things were coming together.

Bella noticed. Narrowing her eyes, she asked, 'Have a nice meal with your family?'

Sacha shot her a warning glare. Bella knew her well enough to correctly guess the reason behind her happy sigh and she didn't need her mentioning it, not while Alessandro was still here. She'd hate him to think that she'd share what had happened between them with her friend, who also happened to be his landlady. A thought occurred to her.

'Will you be moving above the gelateria, now that it's almost ready to be opened?'

'No, I have to stay here,' he said. 'I will need to keep the rooms for the new manager.'

'Any idea who that'll be yet?' Bella asked.

'I placed an advertisement in the *Gazette* and have met a few people.'

She was intrigued. 'Anyone you're happy with?'

He nodded, thoughtfully. 'I have employed a man called Finn. He was born here, but has been away travelling for a couple of years. Maybe you know him.'

Sacha immediately suspected who he meant. 'Finn Gallichan?' she asked, picturing the lanky boy she'd been at school with.

Alessandro smiled. 'You know Finn?'

'Yes, we went to the same school, but I haven't seen him for years. He's nice, and practically grew up helping at his parent's café in town. So, will he be moving in soon?'

'Yes, the morning of the opening. I will be glad of his help at the party.'

'Finn's a good bloke,' Bella said, walking to the kitchen to get them some drinks. 'I'm not surprised you found someone only too pleased to move here. Who wouldn't want to open the curtains to that view each morning?' she called, while opening the fridge and retrieving three bottles of lager.

She came back out to join them and handed one each to Sacha and Alessandro. 'You're welcome to stay here as long as you like,' she said to him. 'I've enjoyed having you and Jack living here,' She winked. 'Despite your spats about the ice cream trade.'

'I'm enjoying it too,' Alessandro said.

She turned her attention to Sacha. 'So, when are we going to meet George Newton?'

'I'm not sure yet, but soon,' she said waiting for her friend's reaction.

Bella squealed. 'I'm so excited, I can't believe I'm actually going to be in the same room as him.' She thought for a moment. 'I'm going to make the most of meeting him and think of something I can talk to him about.' She fanned herself with her hand. 'I think I need to sit down and take this in for a bit.'

Sacha shared her friend's excitement and would have been as panicky about meeting him if Alessandro's earlier kiss hadn't taken her mind off it. He was the first man she'd kissed since her relationship with Giles had ended, and it had been memorable to say the least.

'... leaflets,' she heard Alessandro say, reminding her of all they still had to do if this event was going to be the success she hoped it would be.

'Yes, that's true,' she said, not quite sure of his entire sentence, but trying to focus on the matter in hand.

Bella frowned. 'What, all of them? To all the same houses we've already covered? Why?'

'Because if we don't, they won't know about George Newton, and they might not bother to turn up, and we'd lose the opportunity to raise more money.'

They sat contemplating this thought and drank their lager.

'What about asking the local news station to come and interview him?' Bella asked. 'They could also interview us and a few of the other business owners and stall holders.'

Sacha mulled this idea over. 'It would have to be just before the event, for Betty to benefit financially,' she said.

Bella and Alessandro agreed.

'I'll ask my aunt if George will agree to a television interview as well as one with the *Gazette*,' Sacha said, her excitement growing at the thought of how well it could go. 'We might even attract more stall holders.'

'We can use it to entice them to sign up.' Bella added.

Sacha checked her watch. 'Do you think Aunt Rosie's had time to speak to him yet?'

'There's no harm in giving her a call and asking her,' Bella said, handing Sacha her mobile.

Sacha took it, amused that Bella had noticed she didn't have her own phone with her again. She hated the thing and since returning to the island used it as little as possible. Recalling her aunt's number, she keyed it into the phone. It was engaged the first three times she tried to get through and she hoped this was a sign that her aunt was on the phone to George.

Finally, Rosie answered. 'Who is this?' she snapped.

Sacha cleared her throat. 'Sorry, Aunt Rosie, it's me, Sacha. I was wondering if you'd spoken to George Newton yet, about meeting us before the fête?'

There was a momentary silence. She could hear her aunt being distracted by someone in the background.

'Sorry, about that,' Aunt Rosie said. 'Just pouring myself a drink.

Sacha wasn't sure if this was a good sign or a bad one.

'No problem,' Sacha said, as calmly as she could manage while supressing her impatience. 'So, have you spoken to him?'

'I have, in fact he's just leaving now.'

When she didn't elaborate, Sacha added. 'Did he say he'd meet us before the fête?'

'Stop worrying, darling. You always worry too much, I was only saying so to your mother the other day.'

'Aunt Rosie,' Sacha said, interrupting her aunt's ramblings.

'Yes?'

'Did he agree?'

There was a momentary pause and then her aunt said, 'Can you imagine anyone telling me I can't have something I want?'

No, she couldn't, but she needed to hear the words confirmed. 'No?'

'No. Exactly. Of course, he's agreed to meet you. I need to go and lie down for a bit, I'm shattered. Why don't you go ahead and print those leaflets you were talking about earlier?'

Sacha gave the thumbs up to Bella, who grabbed Alessandro and forced him to do a little dance around the tiny space in front of the counter.

'When can we meet him?' Sacha added quickly, before her aunt rang off. 'Oh, and we're hoping he'll agree to be interviewed by the *Gazette* and the local news station. Do you think he will?'

'Yes, yes, now I need to get on. I'll let you know when you can meet up with him.'

Sacha didn't like to remind her aunt that they had very little time left to finalise all the arrangements and not wishing to annoy her, said goodbye.

'This is going to be brilliant,' Bella said, after Sacha had repeated her aunt's words.

Bella carried on dancing, wriggling her hips and waving her hands in the air. Alessandro looked on and smiled.

Sacha giggled at her friend's antics. 'I think it might be,' she said, hoping they were right.

Settling down, Bella sat and, taking her notepad and pen, began adding to her list. 'Printers, we need to get there first thing tomorrow,' she said. 'Then you can rope in Milo and with the three of us, and Jack, we should be able to deliver all the leaflets in a couple of hours after work tomorrow.'

'Can't we print off the leaflets here, or on my printer?' Sacha asked, thinking of the time and money they'd save.

'No,' Bella shook her head. 'They won't be as clear and I want them to look as professional as possible.'

'Thank heavens you're on such good terms with the bloke at the printers,' Sacha teased. 'One of these days you're actually going to have to go out for a drink with him, he's done you so many favours recently.'

'I will happily do so, if this works out as well as I'm hoping it does.'

* * *

The following evening, they delivered their leaflets, meeting up later for a catch up in the café. Lucy had agreed to stay late and make them all something to eat and drink, and the five of them relaxed and recovered from all the uphill walking they'd done.

Sacha glanced at the pile of leaflets she'd placed at the end of her counter. She'd also pinned a couple on her cork notice-board and stuck two up in the window. 'I think we're doing all we can,' she said. 'We can meet here again tomorrow and go through the list of stallholders wishing to participate, check they've paid for their spot and what it is they'll be selling and then we'll have a better picture of how it's all going to look.'

Alessandro thanked Lucy as she placed a large plate of crab salad in front of him. 'Grazie, this looks very good.'

'Thanks,' she said, looking across the table at Jack to see if he'd noticed her exchange with Alessandro.

Sacha spotted him scowling at Alessandro. She hoped Lucy

didn't think this was because Jack was jealous. She could tell her twin was still angry with Alessandro and was probably oblivious to Lucy looking at him. Sacha suspected there was something else on Jack's mind. She wondered whether he needed to pay Nikki a visit. He'd been keeping himself very much to himself over the past week. Maybe he'd been arguing with his girlfriend. If that was the case, then Sacha supposed he wasn't confiding in her in case she worried about him leaving her short-handed at the café. She decided to have a chat with him alone when the opportunity arose. She needed to know his plans, but didn't want him making a decision that would affect his happiness.

There was a knock on the café door. Everyone looked up to see Lexi doing a strange little dance and waving impatiently for them to let her in. 'Hurry,' she mouthed.

Sacha couldn't tell if her friend needed to race to the loo, or if something exciting had happened. She leapt up and ran to unlock the door. 'You okay?' she asked, concerned.

Lexi took a deep calming breath and pushed her messy hair back from her face. 'You'll never guess who's booked into one of my holiday cottages,' she said.

The others looked at each other and back at Lexi. 'You'll have to give us a bit of a clue,' Bella said, clearly trying not to laugh.

'George bloody Newton, that's who,' Lexi raised a finger and tapped the side of her nose. 'I'm not supposed to tell anyone, but I'm only telling you, um, five. So, you have to swear you won't tell a soul.' She watched them until each had nodded their agreement.

'Go on,' Sacha said, wondering why he'd chosen not to stay with her aunt after all.

'Your Aunt Rosie contacted me earlier today and said he

needed somewhere quiet and unassuming to stay.' She raised an eyebrow. 'I'm not sure if that was a compliment... anyway, I said yes immediately and he's moved in.'

Sacha's heart pounded with excitement. 'We need to meet him,' she said, trying not to sound too desperate. 'My aunt has promised us that he's going to open the fête and we need to find out exactly what he's willing to do.'

'Yes,' Bella said. 'I'm a bit concerned that he doesn't realise that this is just a little event compared to what he's used to.'

Lexi thought for a moment. 'Look, don't come up to the cottages until you hear from me. I'll have a quiet word with him and ask if he'll chat to you and then let you know. Is that okay?'

'Sounds good to me,' Sacha said, relieved to be getting somewhere.

Alessandro stood up and offered Lexi his chair. She sat and he pulled over another one for himself.

'Someone said this was all in aid of Betty's lease on her cottage,' Lexi said, her voice lowered.

Sacha brought her up to date with the situation. 'We don't mind the locals being aware, as long as it's kept quiet. You know how private Betty is, don't forget she kept what she'd done in the war a secret for over twenty years until someone else announced her bravery. She desperately doesn't want to leave the boardwalk though, it's been her home since her husband died and she moved here in the sixties.'

'But I thought Betty owned that cottage,' Lexi said. 'She's been there as long as anyone can remember.'

'We thought so too,' Bella said. 'But this wouldn't be an issue if she did, poor thing. We're determined to help her and all the funds raised will go towards paying for the lease extension. The only issue, is will we raise enough?'

'We have to, somehow,' Sacha continued. 'We must make

sure this event is a success, and I need to be certain George Newton knows why it matters so much, so that he doesn't let us down.'

Lexi stood up. 'Leave it with me. I'll speak to him and heaven help him if he doesn't do the right thing.'

They laughed. Lexi was only five feet tall and petite, and might look sweet, but could be more determined and feisty than any of them.

'Thanks, Lexi,' Sacha said, showing her out. She joined the others back at the table. 'Right, it looks like this really could be going ahead. You all look like you've nearly finished eating, so I'm going to get some paper and we can make up the plan for the stalls and any other bits.'

She left them and went to the bunker at the back of the café, looking for some A3 paper, which she'd used for notices a few months before. Grabbing a few sheets and some highlighter pens, she returned to see Jack and Lucy clearing away the plates and wiping the table. Alessandro was making a space in front of where Sacha had been sitting for the plan.

'Right,' we need to know how many stalls we've all managed to sign up so far,' she said. 'Lucy, please pass your notepad to Alessandro, he can note down the amounts that have been promised, or paid, for those stalls.

An hour and a half and several coffees later, they'd drawn up a plan, a list of expected funds raised, and a further list of who would be arranging and locating other necessary items for the event.

Sacha sat back and stifled a yawn. 'I think we're getting somewhere, finally.' She pictured the scene. 'I know my dad and mum will come down to help on the day. That should leave me free to give any extra help to anyone who needs it. Is there anything else we need to cover tonight?' She waited for them to have a think.

'I think that's it,' Jack said. 'Now, I don't know about you lot, but I need to get some shut eye and I think you should be getting home, Lucy.'

Lucy beamed at Jack and immediately stood up and went to get her tiny rucksack. 'See you in the morning,' she said, leaving with a wave.

Sacha hugged Bella and Alessandro. 'Thanks for staying tonight, I think we've made great headway.'

'It will be a successful day,' Alessandro said, kissing her on both cheeks, before escorting Bella home.

Sacha stopped Jack. 'Can I have a word before you go?'

'Sure,' he said, leaning against the wall as Sacha closed the door. 'What's bothering you? If it's what I said yesterday about you forgiving Alessandro easily, then I'm sorry, but I'm still angry with him on your behalf.'

'It's not that,' she said, not wishing to get into their disagreement again. She explained about Lucy. 'I'm sure she's got a bit of a crush on you and I know how oblivious you can be sometimes. I just thought I should tip you off so that you're careful how you speak to her.'

He rubbed his eyes. 'I can't say I've noticed. If anything, I think it might be Alessandro she's trying to make jealous by flirting with me. If you think I should be a bit careful though, I will be.' He thought about it for a few seconds, before adding. 'She was no different while you were away to how she is now.'

Sacha thought about what he'd said. Who wouldn't be attracted to Alessandro? Sacha was, after all. Poor Lucy, she hoped she didn't fancy him, especially as he would be returning to Italy soon.

'Yes, well, as I said, you can be a bit oblivious to women's feelings about you sometimes. Talking of which, how's it going with Nikki?'

His mood changed. 'She's still phoning me all the time. Despite what I told her about us taking a break, she still goes on about wanting me to go back and carry on where we left off. She doesn't know what I'm doing here, playing waiter, as she calls it.'

'What a cheek. Don't let her boss you around,' Sacha said, offended by Nikki's comment. 'You go back if you want to, but only if it's the right thing for you.'

He ruffled her hair. 'Always so bossy,' he said. 'Anyone would think you were the eldest.'

'I am.'

He bent his head closer to hers and whispered, 'Only by seven minutes, so it doesn't really count.'

'It does to me,' she said, playfully punching his arm. 'Now go away and let me get to bed.'

He put an arm around her shoulders and hugged her quickly. ''Nite, Sis.'

'And Jack?'

'What?'

'Please don't give Alessandro a hard time, we should be concentrating on Betty right now, at least there's a chance we can do something to help her.'

'Fine,' he said, scowling as he walked out of the café.

Sacha locked the door behind her brother. Then, straightening the chairs, she wiped the table once again before switching off the lights and going up to her flat.

She had only just dried herself off after her shower and dressed in her worn T-shirt and bed shorts when her phone pinged, alerting her to a new text.

She picked it up and looked at the screen. It was from Lexi:

Too upset about Betty's cottage to wait. Spoke to George (so hot!).
G says to pop round at ten thirty tomorrow morning. Sweet
dreams. Lx

She replied, thanking Lexi and sent a text letting Bella know
she'd need to find cover for her shop in the morning.

Things really were coming together.

10

Sacha couldn't tell who was more nervous about meeting George Newton, her or Bella. For once, Bella was silent as they walked up the short hill from the boardwalk to the three fisherman's cottages above the village. She had rehearsed what she was going to say and hoped to sound encouraging and grateful that he had agreed to take part in their special day, without sounding like the fan she truly was.

They reached Lexi's cottage at the end of the row that had historically housed local fishermen, who'd taken their boats from the little harbour down the hill, out into the channel to fish for their daily catch.

'I could just picture that gorgeous widowed fisherman living here with his kids,' Bella said.

Sacha looked at Bella. 'I suppose so.' She wasn't sure where that comment had come from but assumed her friend was just nervous. 'Ready?'

'Just about.'

Sacha was glad she hadn't had much notice for this meeting today. Although she'd still had time to spend the night fretting about what to say to her favourite actor without making him change his mind about opening the fête. She'd taken a little more effort to tame her wavy hair this morning and put on a newish summer skirt with a T-shirt and hoped that was enough. Taking a deep breath, she knocked at Lexi's door.

It opened almost immediately. 'Don't look so terrified,' Lexi giggled. 'He's not going to bite you.' She stepped outside and led them to the front door of the cottage at the other end of the small terrace. Lowering her voice to a whisper, she added. 'Honestly, calm down, he's quite nice.'

Lexi knocked on the door, which opened moments later to reveal George Newton, in person. Sacha and Bella stared at him in silence. There was a quiet confidence about him that she'd expected and he was wearing faded denims with a pale blue cashmere V-necked sweater that showed off his dark tan to perfection. She heard Bella whimper quietly behind her and cleared her throat to cover up the sound.

'Sorry, George,' Lexi said, waving them both inside. 'Hurry up, you two, he hasn't got all day.'

Sacha couldn't believe he could be any better looking in the flesh, but he was, remarkably so. She had to take a moment to look at him; take in his broad shoulders, those blue-grey eyes, and that perfect mouth that her aunt had kissed. The thought threw her. She didn't doubt her aunt had told the truth about her connection to him, not for a second. The notion still seemed a little surreal though, or, Sacha wondered, could it simply be that she was a tiny bit envious.

She thought of her recent kiss with Alessandro and couldn't imagine any other kisses being that perfect, not even George Newton's. No, she decided, he might be super impressive and very famous, and he was perfect to look at and to watch on screen, but he wasn't Alessandro. Her stomach contracted at the thought of the handsome Italian she'd been thinking about more and more often. Refusing to ruin her mood she pushed away all thoughts of him.

George reached out to shake their hands, bringing Sacha's thoughts back to the present and reminding her why they were there. He led them into the tiny cottage and motioned for them to take a seat on the two-seater sofa at the end of the small room. No one spoke for a few seconds.

Clearing his throat, he said. 'Your aunt,' he narrowed his eyes and pointed at Bella. She shook her head. He turned his attention to Sacha. 'Sorry, your aunt has asked me to open your fête in a couple of weeks' time and I gather you want me to confirm that I'm happy to do so.' He smiled, showing off his Hollywood white teeth. 'I am. I think both of you know how difficult it is to refuse Rosie anything.'

Sacha certainly did. She relaxed slightly, George was such a nice man. 'We really are incredibly grateful.'

'I've told him about Betty,' Lexi sat on the arm of the nearest chair and folded her arms. 'So, you don't have to go over everything again.'

'Would you all like something to drink?' George asked. He was the most relaxed person in the room, which wasn't entirely surprising. Sacha was usually confident with people, but he was super smooth and very likeable. She realised he was still speaking so focused on what he was saying. 'Lexi stocked up my fridge and I think she's ensured that I have most juices and several selections of teas and coffees to hand.'

Sacha was amused to discover that Lexi was more impressed with her guest than she was letting on. It made her own reaction to him feel a little less ridiculous.

'No, thank you.' She waited for Bella to shake her head before adding. 'If Lexi's told you our reasons for the fête then you'll know why this is so important to us all. We have to raise as much money for Betty's cause as possible, and you agreeing to open the fête is an unexpected bonus.'

'That's very kind of you to say so.' He stared at her for a moment. 'Your aunt and I go way back and I'd do anything for her. I grew up hearing about Betty's heroics and I'm only too pleased to be able to help a lady who did such a brave thing during the Occupation.'

'Yes, Dad told me that if she'd been caught she could have been sent to Ravensbrück concentration camp like Louisa Gould or executed up at the manor like Francois Scornet in 1941.' It was hard to imagine these days, a lady being arrested and a twenty-one-year-old being executed up the hill from the boardwalk, especially on such a peaceful summer's day.

'I suppose you'll want me to make a brief speech before declaring the fête open?' he said, interrupting her thoughts.

'Please,' Sacha said, relaxing further. If the day itself went this well then there was little chance of them not succeeding.

'Fine, I'm happy to do that. I've put the date in my diary. Time?'

'We thought midday?' Bella said, finally speaking.

He smiled at her. 'Great, midday it is then.'

Delighted, Sacha and Bella thanked him once again, and not wishing to outstay their welcome, left with Lexi.

'See?' Lexi said as they walked down the path to the road. 'I told you he was nice. Everything will be fine.'

Sacha thanked her and began walking back down the hill with Bella. 'I think I can stop panicking now,' she said. 'It does seem like everything has fallen into place. If the weather is perfect, then there should be no reason the fête won't be a massive success.' She watched her friend out of the corner of her eye. 'I've never known you to be that quiet.' Sacha giggled at the thought of her friend sitting in wide-eyed silence at Lexi's cottage.

'I still can't believe we've met him.' She walked on in a daze. 'He really is incredibly hot.'

He was.

Sacha arranged to meet Bella later for a glass of wine on the beach after they'd both closed their businesses for the day. Then, as she walked slowly back to the café, she stopped to stare out across the channel to where the sun was shining on the distant island of Sark. She hoped she'd have enough time while Alessandro was here to be able to take him on one of her friend's boats to visit Guernsey, Sark, Herm and Alderney, some of the other exquisite Channel Islands.

She arrived back in time to help Jack and Milo with a large group of people who were on a coach tour of the island for the day. She loved it when the coaches brought people down to the boardwalk because they never failed to be excited by the nostalgic charm of the place and they always enjoyed the refreshments at her café.

Thirty-two tea cakes, eight rounds of cabbage loaf toast with fresh local jam and fifteen sundaes later, Sacha and Milo had waved them off and were helping Jack clear up.

'They were fun, weren't they?' Milo said, noticing a camera that one of them had left behind and racing out of the café to go and find the owner.

Sacha carried a pile of plates into the kitchen, returning to serve another two tables that had recently been taken up by new arrivals.

By the end of the day she was exhausted. 'I love the height of summer,' Sacha said, wiping down the counter after tidying away the cones and flakes into the back storeroom. 'But it is shattering when there isn't time to take much of a break.'

'At least you had a break when you went up to meet the actor bloke at Lexi's place. Do you think you can stop worrying so much about this event for Betty now?' Jack asked as they both sat down with a coffee after Milo had left.

'Yes,' she said, picking up her glass cup and blowing on the drink in a vain attempt to cool it slightly. 'I was only nervous because it matters so much for Betty that we do this right.'

'I know, Sis.'

There was a knock on the door, and they looked over and saw Alessandro waving at them.

'It's alright, I'm not going to upset you and give him a hard time. I've spoken to Bella and she insists he isn't such a bad bloke. I've decided, after a lot of nagging from your friend that I'm going to give him a chance to prove it,' Jack whispered as he went over to unlock the door. 'Although I think we still need a bit of a quiet talk, him and me.'

Sacha went to argue, but Jack just smiled.

'Come in, mate. How's it going at your place?'

Alessandro beamed at them, his tanned face contrasting with his perfect white smile. 'I am here to ask if you would like to try some of the gelato I've prepared. Both of you.'

'I can't,' Jack said. 'I've got to be somewhere, but I'm sure Sacha can be persuaded. She can compare it to hers.' He pulled a scared face and Alessandro, unsure, looked to Sacha to see her reaction. When she stuck her tongue out at Jack, Alessandro laughed.

'We have to know what secrets the competition holds,' Jack said.

'I'd love to,' Sacha responded, honestly. 'But I've promised Bella...' She trailed off mid-sentence as Bella ran up to the door.

'No, it's fine,' Bella waved at her frantically. 'I've already told Alessandro you'll be free. We can drink wine on the beach any old night. You can't turn down an offer like this, you know, one that mixes business and pleasure.'

Sacha noticed her friend's emphasis on the word 'pleasure' and widened her eyes slightly at her, hoping her brother and Alessandro wouldn't notice.

'That would be lovely,' she said, turning to address Alessandro. 'Give me a few minutes and I'll meet you at, what's it called again?'

'Gelateria di Isola,' he said proudly. 'It means of the island. I will see you soon.'

He left and Jack and Bella stared at her for a moment.

'What?' she asked, irritated with them both. She didn't need to be teased about something that could never happen.

'Seriously?' Bella said. 'You think we haven't noticed.' She held up her hand to stop Sacha from arguing. 'We were saying only this morning, weren't we, Jack?'

Jack gave her a fierce look. '*You* were saying,' he corrected. 'I'm not so sure I like the idea that Sach has the hots for anyone. It's all a little bit gross.'

Sacha was used to her brother behaving like a teenager when it came to her and boyfriends. Her twin always found any reference to her having intimacy with a man unsavoury. She understood where he was coming from, as she'd never really liked to know much about his relationships.

'You've both got the wrong idea,' Sacha insisted. 'I can't tell you about it now because I need to freshen up, but you can take it from me that even if I did like him, Alessandro is too hung up about his ex-girlfriend to get serious about someone like me.'

Jack looked hurt. 'What do you mean, someone like you?'

'Yeah,' Bella frowned at her. 'I remember seeing his ex,' she lowered her voice even though there were only the three of them left in the café. 'I looked her up. She was gorgeous, wasn't she?'

'Yes, she was,' Sacha said.

Bella hugged her. 'But so are you.'

Sacha could feel the irritation rising in her, not wishing to have to hear about how she should be more confident about her looks. 'Livia was stunning, that's true, but she was also sophisticated and there was something ethereal about her. Now,' she said, tucking a loose strand of sun streaked hair behind her ear, 'I appreciate you being nice to me, but there is no way in any of my wildest dreams that I could ever be described as sophisticated or ethereal.'

Both stared at her in silence. She could see they were trying to think of some way to disagree with her.

'Fine,' Jack said eventually. 'You might not be all that sophisticated, and I'm not exactly sure what ethereal is, but you're more of a... um... beach bum.'

'Beach bum!' He was supposed to be cheering her up, not insulting her. She glared at him.

'No, not a beach bum,' Bella said, trying not to giggle. 'I think your stupid brother is trying to say you're more of a beach babe. Yes, that's it. Or, or maybe a mermaid.'

'Right, you two can go now. Thanks for trying, I think I appreciate it, but seeing as you've dropped me into accepting an evening tasting Alessandro's gelato, I think I'd better get a move on, don't you?'

Bella linked her arm through Jack's. 'I think that's our cue to leave.' She winked at Sacha. 'Go and freshen up before his gelato melts, and you,' she said to Jack, 'stop winding up your sister and come with me. If you've got something to do, then do it and if not, you can join me for the glass of wine I was going to enjoy on the beach with your sister, before she got a better offer.'

He glanced at Sacha and opened his mouth to say something. She folded her arms and he changed his mind and let Bella lead him out of the café.

Stopping just outside the door, Bella turned to point at Sacha. 'Stop frowning, it'll give you wrinkles.'

Sacha waved her friend away, locked the café door and ran upstairs to her flat to shower and change. Through the open windows, she could hear them chatting as they walked along the boardwalk.

'Beach bum,' she murmured, amused by her brother's attempt to compliment her.

Five minutes later, she hurried down the stairs, tucking a damp strand of hair behind her ear. At the bottom, she dropped the flip flops she was carrying and had slipped one on, careful to ensure she didn't jab her tender toe, when she heard a noise.

Turning, and nearly toppling over, she spotted a movement through the opening to the kitchen. Heart pounding, she pushed her other foot into her flip flop and crept through, grabbing a spatula on the way. She caught Lucy bending down in front of one of the store cupboards in the bunker at the back of the building.

'What are you doing?' she asked, jumping back when Lucy leapt up and screamed.

'I didn't see you there!' Lucy's face reddened. 'I thought you were upstairs.'

Sacha couldn't see how that excused her from sneaking around, so asked again. 'Why are you here, Lucy? You left an hour ago.'

Lucy chewed the inside of her lip. 'I was, er...'

Was she stealing something? Sacha looked past Lucy, at the

open cupboard. 'Is there something you need?' Sacha couldn't help feeling guilty for giving Lucy such a fright.

'I, um...' Her blush deepened, but she seemed embarrassed to be caught rather than disingenuous. 'I worry that if I leave my rucksack out someone might steal it when I'm busy.'

'Why put it in here, though? It's where we keep the boxes of cones for the soft ice creams.'

Confused, Sacha closed the cupboard door. 'I'm sorry, I have to dash off.'

She motioned for Lucy to go with her to the front door. Grabbing her keys on the way, she wondered if Jack had left the door unlocked, for Lucy to have got in without her noticing.

'If you're that worried, then of course you can keep your rucksack in a cupboard, but not one where we keep the supplies,' she said, waiting for Lucy to step outside. She seemed to be hanging back. 'Are you sure everything's alright?'

'No, no, it's all good,' Lucy said, giving Sacha a smile that didn't quite meet her eyes.

Sacha studied her. 'You can keep your stuff in one of the cupboards towards the little door at the back. We'll work something out tomorrow, okay?'

'Thank you, that'll be amazing,' Lucy said, relief flooding across her drawn face.

'Maybe though,' Sacha added gently. 'You should leave any valuables at home, if you're worried about them being misplaced.'

Lucy looked horrified by this suggestion. 'No. No, I can't do that.'

Sacha moved slightly closer to Lucy and lowered her voice, checking first that there wasn't anyone in earshot to hear what she was about to say. 'If there's anything you need to talk to me about, Lucy, I hope you'd feel you could confide in me. Do you?'

Lucy thought about this and nodded her head several times. Sacha didn't believe her though, and it troubled her to think that Lucy might have problems that were causing her distress. Maybe that was why she was picking up strange vibes. Sacha decided to keep an eye open for any further signs that something could be wrong.

'I'd want to help you if you ever needed me to.'

Lucy studied her feet for a moment and then looked at Sacha and gave her another beaming smile. Far too forced to be accepted as real.

'Thanks, Sacha,' Lucy said, pulling her rucksack up over her shoulder and turning to walk away. 'I appreciate your kindness, I really do.'

Sacha returned the wave Lucy gave her as she walked away along the boardwalk towards the bus stop, unable to shake off the troubled feeling their exchange had given her. Then, remembering that she was already late to meet Alessandro, she locked the café door, turned and ran to his gelateria as fast as her flip flops and sore toe would allow her to.

She arrived at his door and spotted him tidying up inside. She knocked.

'Ciao, Sacha,' he called, waving her inside.

She walked in, inhaling the heady scent of fresh strawberries. 'It smells heavenly in here,' she smiled, sitting down at the counter on the cushioned stool he indicated.

She saw several delicious looking sundaes in front of her. 'They look extraordinarily tempting,' she said, desperate to taste one.

'This one is a Strawberry Meringata,' he said, handing her a long-handled spoon. 'Please, try.' He waited while she dipped her spoon deep into the tall glass and slowly drew out a spoonful, lifting it to her mouth and savouring it.

The sensation of fresh strawberries, vanilla gelato, and broken meringue made her close her eyes and groan. 'Now, that really is heaven in a glass.' She pushed her spoon into the mixture again and had another taste. 'You've given me the best sundae first, you can't possibly beat that,' she said, hopefully. If he was her competition then she was going to have to up her game, and how. 'Tell me, what's in it?'

He raised an eyebrow. 'You expect me to share secrets with my competition?'

Sacha spooned out some ice cream and pointed it at him. 'Don't think I won't flick this at you,' she teased. 'Tell me your secrets, now.'

Alessandro grabbed her hand, forced the spoon up to his mouth and licked off the ice cream she'd threatened him with.

'You might be a tough Jersey lady,' he laughed, letting go of her wrist. 'But I am also determined.'

Changing tactics, she pursed her lips. 'Please. I told you how I made my sundaes.'

'You did,' he conceded. 'Okay, as you know, in Italy the gelato must have at least three and a half per cent butterfat. This is made with my father's exclusive recipe of crema gelato, made with fresh Madagascan vanilla pods.'

She loved vanilla and presumed using these pods, as well as the butterfat, was what must make such a difference to the taste and texture. 'It is truly delicious.' She went to have another mouthful but he lifted up another gelato sundae from the refrigerated counter and placed it in front of her with a clean spoon. 'I just finished making this when you arrived,' he said with satisfaction. 'If you would try this sample first?'

Again, there was that blissful creamy sensation on her tongue. 'I wish you'd set up this business somewhere else,' she admitted. 'These are far too good, I'm not sure I can compete.'

He came around the counter and sat on the stool next to her. Picking up a spoon, he took a mouthful of the meringue sundae. 'I disagree,' he said. 'You offer so many other options.'

She thought of the pancakes that were becoming more popular each week. 'Maybe.'

'Your café is very English. It's how I imagine English cafés used to be in the sixties when my father first came to this island. I saw you also cater for beach picnics, with those clever...' he struggled to find the word.

'Jam jars?' she suggested, having noticed his surprise when she'd served a smoothie and a sundae to a couple of teenagers a few days before, which they'd taken outside to enjoy.

He was making sense and she began to relax slightly. 'I suppose you're right.'

'We could set up a stall at the fête serving both our specialities,' he said. 'That way, people can try both and I promise you some will like what you have to offer and others will prefer mine. There is room for both of our produces here, Sacha. I really believe that is true.'

'I hope you're right,' she said, beginning to believe that maybe he had a point. 'I know that when Bella and I go out anywhere, or when my aunt and I went away, that we both chose different things from the menus, wherever we went. We can emphasise that we cater for all tastes, both local and familiar, or new and from overseas.'

'The contrast might help boost our sales rather than hurt them,' he said.

She could see he was willing her to agree with him. 'We may as well give it our best shot,' she said. 'If we publicise our differences and promote them with a positive twist, I think it will add a layer of interest that would otherwise not be there.'

'Yes. That is exactly what I was hoping you would say. So, we work together on this and make everyone happy.'

They smiled at each other and he leant forward and kissed her, then dipped his spoon into the cream on the top of his sundae and dabbed some on her nose.

'Hey,' she said, laughing at the unexpected coldness.

Alessandro kissed her nose and removed the cream. 'All gone now,' he said, making her laugh.

'Why did you kiss me?' The question was out of her mouth almost as soon as it had registered in her brain. She grimaced as he stared at her, a confused expression on his face.

'It was wrong?'

Embarrassed, she took a deep breath, trying to find the words to explain how she felt. 'Well, no, not wrong, but not exactly fair.'

His posture stiffened. He looked angry, or maybe hurt.

Not wishing to ruin the mood, although fearing that she'd already gone a long way towards doing that, she repeated, 'Not wrong, no. It's just that, well, we're following different paths, so it probably isn't a good idea.'

'I do not understand.'

Neither do I, Sacha thought, but was too embarrassed to bring up the subject of Livia again. She didn't want to upset him, but he was obviously far freer with his kisses than she was. Was she just assuming Alessandro was still in love with Livia? She couldn't imagine he was ready to move on after losing his fiancée. Or maybe she just thought that way because it had taken her so long to get over Giles and what he'd done to her.

'I was thinking about our dads,' she said changing the subject to safer matters.

After staring at her quizzically for a moment, Alessandro said. 'We must introduce your father to mine and hope they agree with our suggestions about our businesses. Do you think they will?'

Sacha's mood dipped further. 'My father's very traditional and set in his ways, so probably not.'

'Mine will be the same, I think.' Alessandro shrugged, 'No matter, we will have to persuade them to think again.'

A thought niggled in Sacha's brain. She mulled it over for a bit before sharing it with Alessandro. 'You don't think they could have known each other when they were younger and working over here as waiters, do you?'

'I do not know,' he thought for a moment. 'It is possible, of course. We should ask them.'

Relieved to have some sort of plan in mind, or at least the first step to making one, Sacha took another mouthful of the delicious concoction in front of her. 'This is too tasty for my liking,' she said, smiling at him.

'No tastier than those that you make,' he said.

She wasn't sure he was right, but had to hope that each of their products had strengths that would appeal to different tastes.

11

Through her bedroom window, Sacha could hear laughter, the buzz of friendly conversation and the sound of glasses clinking. It was Alessandro's launch night. She put down her hair straighteners and leant out to see what was going on. Bella and Jack were laughing with Lexi and her artist father outside the gelateria.

Sacha smiled. It was a perfect evening for the party, she decided, standing back and pulling open her wardrobe door. Noticing that her blonde hair had already returned to its wavy self, she switched off her straighteners. Sacha could not think what to wear. She wasn't going to try to compete with Bella and Lexi who were dressed in their finery.

She might not be sophisticated, but she could do casual. Sacha scanned the dresses and skirts hanging in her small white wardrobe. She hadn't had the time or the inclination to go shopping for new clothes since taking over the café, so it had been a relief when her aunt had treated her to a couple of summer dresses for their cruise. Sacha lifted out a yellow one with daisies printed all over it. This was perfect. She would just have to make the best of what she had and if that was the casual beach look, then so be it.

Quickly shrugging off her thin dressing gown, she stepped into her summer dress and pulled the shoestring straps over her tanned shoulders.

'Shoes,' she murmured, spotting a pair of pale blue flip flops. These would do. No one at the party would expect her to wear anything else, and it was summer after all.

She bent down in front of her dressing table mirror and brushed her hair, then quickly applied a little lip gloss. Grabbing her keys, she hurried downstairs to join the party.

'Here she comes,' Jack shouted, spotting her as she left the café. 'Always in a rush, yet never on time.'

'Cheeky sod,' she said, hurrying to join her friends. She gave him a playful punch to the shoulder which, she soon realised, hurt her more than him.

'I'll let you and Bella have a catch up and fetch you drinks,' he said, laughing at her discomfort.

'Don't worry.' Sacha breathed in the smell of the cool English lager being served nearby. 'I need to see Alessandro and wish him good luck, first.'

'Not too much good luck, though,' Jack teased.

'No, not too much.'

For a small place, there were a lot of people. Sacha didn't recognise some of them and wondered where they'd come from. Alessandro only really knew the people in the village, he hadn't had time to meet anyone else, so she assumed some of them must be associates of his father's and the people who'd worked on getting the gelateria ready.

She heard a tinkly laugh and standing on tiptoe, spotted her aunt's dark hair piled up on her head in a topknot. Aunt Rosie saw her at the same time and held up her hand to stop Sacha coming into the room. Waving her back, her aunt mouthed that she would join her outside.

Sacha made her way back out to the cooler boardwalk and waited.

'You weren't very long,' Jack said.

'And you haven't got our drinks,' Bella winked at him. 'This is supposed to be a party you know, one where we toast Alessandro's new business. We can't do that empty-handed.'

'Yes, Jack, you did say you'd get them for us.' Sacha inched past a red-faced man laughing at his own joke. 'I thought I'd know everyone here.'

'Me, too,' her aunt said, finally reaching her. 'Good grief, it's bedlam in there. That poor boy is run off his feet.'

Sacha looked over and saw Alessandro smiling and chatting to a group of people. 'I think he's enjoying himself. As long as it's a success, I'm sure he won't mind how busy it gets,' she said, wondering if she'd have a chance to catch up with Finn, the new manager.

'That looks like Salva, his father,' her aunt said, looking inside the gelateria. 'I didn't expect to see him here, I thought he was unwell.'

Sacha peered over her aunt's shoulder through the crowd of people and spotted a silver-haired man, only slightly shorter than Alessandro. 'He must have recovered,' she said, wondering how ill he'd been. 'He's like an older version of Alessandro,' she added, assuming that's probably how Alessandro would look when he reached his father's age. 'You never told me his father was so handsome,' she teased.

'Do be quiet, darling,' her aunt said, raising an eyebrow. 'I have to admit I have a penchant for Italian men and can fully appreciate why you're attracted to young Alessandro.'

Jack worked his way inside and fetched a glass of wine for

Sacha. She stayed outside, enjoying the warm summer evening, glad of the slight sea breeze and relieved not to be stuck inside the gelateria with all those people.

Eventually, Alessandro came out to join them, his breath tickling her shoulder as he bent his head to say hello. Sacha turned and came face to face with Alessandro's father.

'Mr Salvatore,' she said, reaching to shake his proffered hand. 'It's lovely to meet you.'

'Is good to meet with you,' he said, his accent much thicker than Alessandro's. 'My Alessandro, he tells me you sell the ice creams.' He pointed in the direction of her café.

Sacha hadn't expected Alessandro to tell his father about her café so soon after his arrival. 'Yes, I'm afraid we're competitors.'

The older man gave Alessandro a quizzical look and said something to him in Italian. Alessandro thought for a moment. 'Ah, si,' before coming out with another flurry of words in his musical accent and then explaining to Sacha. 'I told him we have very different businesses and that there is room enough for both of us here on the boardwalk.'

He seemed to be waiting for her to confirm this assertion, so she smiled at his father and said, 'That's right. We will both be successful.'

She wished she believed it as much as Alessandro seemed to. Her aunt came over to join them and Sacha relaxed a little, grateful to have some of the attention taken from her. When her aunt suggested Mr Salvatore accompany her down to the sea, she relaxed a little more.

'I'm glad Aunt Rosie is here,' Sacha said to Alessandro as they watched his father and her aunt walk away down to the beach. 'She always knows the right thing to say, whereas I worry that I say the wrong thing, especially when I'm nervous.'

'You mustn't worry,' he said, discreetly taking hold of her hand and giving it a brief squeeze. 'Remember, they've known each other for several years and will have much to talk about.'

She smiled up at him. 'This evening is going well. It's a great success,' she said. 'Who are all these people though?'

He puffed out his cheeks. 'I am not certain. I believe I invited some of them when I gave out leaflets and others are contractors who worked hard to make this place ready for opening so quickly.'

'They did work very hard,' she agreed. 'I'm glad they're enjoying themselves. Will you be serving any ice cream?' She hesitated and laughed. 'Sorry, gelato.'

'I like the way you say gelato,' he said. 'Sorry. When my father returns, I will give a short speech and invite everyone to try a few of the flavours I made up this morning especially for the party.'

'I'm sure they'll want to come back for more very soon, then,' she said.

'That is what I am hoping they will do.' Someone was calling for him. 'Thank you for being my good friend, Sacha,' he whispered. 'I have met so many people through your friendship.' His name was called once again. 'I must go and speak to people but I will see you a little later when it is quieter, no?'

'Of course,' she said. 'Don't be too long serving that gelato, it's hot out here and I'm sure it must be baking inside your place.'

'Backing?'

'No,' she laughed. 'Baking. Hot, with all those people standing around chatting.'

'Ah, yes, it is very baking.'

'I was thinking,' Bella said, when Jack had moved away to chat to two friends but still watched them discreetly from a distance. 'When Jools gets back to the book shop after her trip, I'll pop in to see her and arrange for us to get together for a good night out with you, me and Lexi.'

Sacha agreed. 'It'll have to probably wait until high season ends, maybe mid-September?'

Bella grimaced. 'This grown-up life, running businesses, is a bit stifling sometimes, I find.'

Sacha shook her head. 'I love it,' she said, glancing in the direction of her café. 'We do well during the summer, so we shouldn't complain.'

'I suppose not.'

Jack walked back towards them. She noticed he was looking unusually smart in his beige chinos and blue linen shirt. 'All this business about the fête has got me thinking about Betty and what she did. It's hard to imagine now, isn't it?'

She tried to picture the frail lady with her walking stick standing up to the Nazis and her enormous respect of her increased a hundred-fold. 'It's hard to imagine this island being taken over by Nazis.' She couldn't picture Betty living anywhere other than here. She was the stalwart of the boardwalk and it seemed like she'd always been here.

'It is. Alessandro was telling me that in Italy the older people remember how it was when the Nazis occupied their towns. It was a dark time for so many people,' Jack said. 'We all live with the remnants of that time every day and barely notice them.'

'Like what?' she asked, intrigued.

'Like your storeroom,' he said. 'It's made up of two small bunker-like rooms, which were built during the Occupation, weren't they?'

'They were.'

Bella interrupted their conversation by nudging Sacha and

pointing over to the end house by Betty's home. 'Look, another one of those symbols. Has anyone figured out what they mean yet?'

'No.' Sacha wished they could discover who was responsible for them.

'Weird,' Jack said. 'Right, Aunt Rosie and Alessandro's dad will be here in a sec, I'd better go and tip Alessandro off, so that he and Finn can start getting ready to serve the gelato.'

It occurred to Sacha that she hadn't seen Finn anywhere yet and wondered where he could be. She scanned the party-goers, but it was no use.

'What are you doing?' her aunt said, joining her. 'Am I missing something?'

Sacha watched Alessandro's father smile at her aunt before disappearing into the crowd. She turned back to Rosie. 'No, I was just...' She stopped mid flow as someone tapped her on the shoulder with very cold fingers. Sacha looked up to see Finn smiling down at them. Lost for words momentarily, she eventually managed to speak. 'I'd never have recognised you.'

'Nor me,' Bella said, reaching up to kiss his cheek.

Sacha did the same, still stunned by the change in the skinny, pale boy who used to sometimes catch the same bus as her. 'You look, well, amazing.' She didn't care that she was gushing. It was good to see Finn, tanned and smart, wearing long black trousers and a crisp black shirt with Gelateria di Isola embroidered on the pocket. He still had that lazy smile but seemed much more confident than she remembered. 'Alessandro told me that you were moving down to the village to run his gelateria for him.'

Finn looked towards the counter. 'I must go, we're very busy tonight. Maybe I'll catch up with you both tomorrow?'

'Come for breakfast at the café,' Sacha said. 'The one over

there. I'll be inviting Alessandro and his father and we can catch up then.'

He nodded. 'I'll be there. Nine thirty?'

'Perfect,' she said, watching the tall, tanned man go back inside.

'Who'd have thought Finn Gallichan would end up with muscles and look so hot?' Bella said, craning her neck to see him.

'I was thinking the same thing,' Sacha admitted.

Alessandro, Finn and Salva handed out small plates with little china tubs on them, filled with flavours of gelato for all the guests to sample. Sacha picked a strawberry one and Jack and Bella chose chocolate. Her aunt took vanilla from Alessandro's father.

They each dug their spoons into their tubs and took a mouthful, closing their eyes to savour the flavours.

'Bloody hell, Sach,' Jack said after his second spoonful. 'You've got your work cut out beating this lot.'

She didn't need reminding, especially as she could taste the luxury in the bowl she was sampling. 'We've decided to play on our differences, rather than worry about competing in the ice cream stakes,' she said, with a little more confidence than she felt.

Alessandro clapped his hands and called for everyone's attention. Sacha watched as he spoke, trying but failing to take in his words. She heard his deep lilting voice, saw his perfect mouth moving as he welcomed everyone, introducing Finn to those who didn't know him before explaining what they were trying to achieve at Gelateria di Isola.

Her stomach contracted as his smile reached his grey-blue eyes with their thick dark lashes. It seemed his work here was done and there would be little reason for him to stay on the island. Sadness coursed through her. She hadn't been looking for a relationship when she'd accompanied her aunt to Rome, but now that she'd spent time with Alessandro, it upset her to think she wouldn't be able to see him here, or at Bella's.

These summer weeks had been fun so far, more fun than she'd expected, or even wished for. It occurred to her how strange it was to not realise you wanted something until it came to you, in the form of a beautiful, sweet Italian man, and to feel bereft at the knowledge that his leaving would dull the rest of her summer days. She wasn't looking forward to having to say goodbye to him and decided that she needed to put aside any worries about their businesses, and even the fête, and take some time out to be with him. She would look up more archaeological sites on the island to take him to. They could go at sunrise or even just before the sun set on these long sunny evenings. Either way, she was going to make time for him before he had to leave.

Jack and Lucy could look after the café for her, and now that Alessandro had Finn working for him, he could surely afford to do the same.

The evening passed quickly, and she managed to catch a brief moment with Alessandro and his father to invite them to breakfast the following morning. She didn't mention to his father that she mainly wanted to take the opportunity to demonstrate how different the Summer Sundaes Café was to the gelateria. She was delighted when they accepted and agreed to be there at 9.30, with Finn.

* * *

'Good morning,' she said, looking up as they walked in through the café door. 'Please take a seat.' She indicated the table she'd reserved for them next to the window, before turning to Milo and handing him three menus. 'Please can you take these to table three and take their order, I'll be over as soon as I've finished serving these customers.'

'You mean one could order the full English, another the pancake with blueberries, that sort of thing.'

'That would be perfect,' she said, thinking how naturally this work came to the young lad. She could picture him having his own business when he was older, he certainly worked hard enough and always picked up new things the first time he was shown. 'Thanks, Milo.'

She served two customers, noticing how Mr Salvatore was checking out her décor and the people eating in the café. She washed her hands and went over to join them.

'Hi,' she said. 'Thank you for coming this morning.'

'Thank you for asking us,' Mr Salvatore said. 'Alessandro, he tells me how good your food is here and that I must eat your bacon and the eggs.'

Alessandro smiled at her, his eyes twinkling mischievously. 'My father was saying how different our establishments are.'

'Yes,' she agreed, focusing her attention on his father, relieved Alessandro had already begun this line of conversation. 'In my café, people come to relax over a meal, some spending an hour or so enjoying their food and chatting. In Alessandro's, they might sit for a while to savour one of his delicious sundaes, but usually they'll buy what they've ordered and eat it on the beach.'

'It's true,' Alessandro added. 'There isn't the space for many people to sit at tables or even at the counter at Gelateria di Isola. We cater for customers in different moods.'

Jack arrived, followed by her aunt. 'Bella won't be able to join us this morning,' he said. 'She's a bit busy at the shop.'

'That's fine, I wasn't expecting her,' Sacha said. 'Good morning, Aunt Rosie,' she added, giving her aunt a brief hug. 'Please, sit down next to Mr Salvatore.'

She wondered if Alessandro's father was aware of them trying to make his breakfast as enjoyable as possible. She glanced at him and could see a twinkle in his blue-grey eyes similar to the one she'd just noticed in his son's, and suspected he knew full well what was going on. It heartened her to think he might be accepting their rivalries as friendly, in a way that could benefit both their businesses.

They ordered a range of dishes from the menu and Mr Salvatore seemed to be suitably impressed. She waited for him to finish devouring his breakfast and when he'd set his knife and fork down on his plate asked, 'How was that, Mr Salvatore? Did you like it?'

He nodded. 'It was very good. I wish I was staying here a little longer, I would come back for another of your full English breakfasts tomorrow.'

She relaxed a little and smiled at Alessandro, suspecting he had encouraged his father to be open to judgement.

'You see, Salva?' Aunt Rosie finished her fruit salad and smoothie. 'British breakfasts are delicious.'

Alessandro glanced at her half empty bowl and up at Sacha. 'These pancakes were very good, too,' he said.

Her laughter was cut short by everyone's attention turning to someone standing behind her. It was her father, scowling at Mr Salvatore.

'Well, if it isn't Salva. I never thought I'd see you again,' he said.

'Papa?' Alessandro looked concerned. 'You know Mr Collins?'

She noticed any amusement on Mr Salvatore's face

vanishing instantly as he glared up at her father. So they did know each other. It didn't bode well.

'Thomas,' he said, wiping his mouth on his napkin. 'So, you kept this café?'

'It is my daughter's business now,' her father said, with suppressed anger.

Sacha studied his expression and then Mr Salvatore's. The men were still glaring at each other. 'How do you know each other?' she asked. She could see the other customers trying not to look interested in the tense exchange.

'I don't wish to discuss it,' her father said. Sacha was used to him being headstrong, but never rude.

Aunt Rosie cleared her throat and patted the table with her fingers. 'Gentlemen, I think now is not the time to rake over your grievances with each other.'

'Dad?' Sacha touched his arm to get his attention.

Her father forced a smile. 'A young man's battle,' he said. 'Nothing to worry about.'

He lowered his face towards Mr Salvatore and said, 'I think we need to speak away from here. There are a few things I have to get off my chest.'

'Dad,' Sacha said, forcing a smile. 'Can I show you something in one of the storerooms?'

'What?' he frowned, and then seeing her expression, nodded. 'Yes, of course. Let's go now.'

She walked past the tables, smiling and exchanging comments with her regulars, until she and her father reached the counter. 'Please look after everyone, I won't be long,' she said to Lucy, who was standing wide-eyed at the unexpected excitement.

'Dad?' she said, waiting for him to join her in the furthest storeroom.

'Before you say anything,' he said, his voice low. 'There are some things you don't know.'

She stared at him, trying to imagine what they could be. When nothing further was forthcoming, she asked. 'And these things would be?'

'It's not for me to say, not now, anyway.'

Sacha took a deep breath. 'Dad, it's difficult enough trying to make things work without you and Alessandro's father falling out about something that happened years ago. Please can you speak to him and smooth things over before he goes back to Italy?'

He took a deep breath. 'I can't believe Salva is young Alessandro's father. I liked the boy, too.'

She had no idea what he meant and had to concentrate on not letting the panic she was feeling overtake her. 'Dad, what's this is all about?'

'Not today.' He breathed heavily for a moment, his face reddening. 'It's typical of your aunt to be sitting there with him, after everything that happened.'

Perplexed by her father's anger, Sacha hugged him. 'Dad, please calm down, I'm sure whatever it is can be sorted out.' She hoped she was right. She needed to find a way to calm things down between the two men, and watched anxiously as her father paced back and forth. 'Why don't you go out the back?' she said, pointing to the door they rarely used. 'I'll have a word with Alessandro and maybe we can arrange for you and his dad to meet up and talk. It would have to be today though,' she said, sorry that she wouldn't have time to placate him further, or maybe talk to her mother and persuade her to do the same. 'We could meet at the house.'

His face puce with fury, he glared at her. 'I have nothing to say to that... that...'

'Dad, please lower your voice.'

'That man is not coming to my home, Sacha,' he murmured through gritted teeth.

She watched him storm off out of the café and up the road, hoping that the walk up the hill to the house would give him time to calm down.

Returning to the table, she sat down. 'Dad's had to leave, but I think it's probably a good idea if the two of you meet up and talk things through.'

Mr Salvatore straightened his watch on his wrist. 'It seems to me that Thomas has not changed very much over these past decades. Still the hot-headed man I used to know.'

'Papa,' Alessandro groaned. 'Any ill feeling between you two is not Sacha's fault, or mine.'

Not wanting the relationship between her and Alessandro to sour, Sacha thought quickly. 'You could have a chat somewhere neutral, away from the café,' she said. 'I can speak to my dad and sort something out, if you like? I'll send you a message if he agrees to meet you today, and we can decide on a time. What do you think, Mr Salvatore?'

'I think it's an excellent idea,' Aunt Rosie said, patting Mr Salvatore's arm.

He still didn't look entirely convinced, Sacha thought. She gave Alessandro a pleading look. He said something quickly in Italian. His father replied and it looked as if he was arguing with Alessandro, but a short while later, Alessandro smiled.

'He agrees with me that matters can't be left this way and he will meet with your father.' Alessandro and his father stood up. 'I will take him back to the gelateria, there are some matters we need to discuss. Maybe you could let me know when your father is happy to meet?'

She was relieved that Alessandro was also doing his best to

calm the awkward situation. 'That will be wonderful,' she said. 'I'll go and find him now and let you know as soon as I can.'

Alessandro took a deep breath, and kissed her on the cheek. 'Don't worry.'

'I do not think we can resolve this,' she heard Mr Salvatore say, almost under his breath, as he wiped his mouth on his napkin.

'We will try, Papa,' Alessandro said, his hand resting on his father's arm.

'Yes,' her aunt said. 'We've all been expected not to mention Salva's name in front of Thomas for too long now. Male pride can be such a ridiculous thing for others to deal with. It's not fair on these youngsters for you two to carry on with things that happened decades ago.'

'It does not feel so long ago,' Mr Salvatore said, his voice gentler than before. 'But, I know you are right, Rosie.' He looked lovingly at Alessandro and then at Sacha. 'History, it repeats itself sometimes, I think.' He shrugged.

Sacha's head ached. 'I'm still a little busy here for the next hour or so, but I think it's a good idea if Alessandro and I are there when you and Dad meet up. Shall we say eleven-thirty, up on the headland?' She looked at Alessandro. 'It's where we stopped to look at the view after the barbecue,' she said, hoping her face didn't redden at the thought of their kiss.

'I will be there with my father, but now I would like to talk with him about a few things.'

'Thank you for coming for breakfast, Mr Salvatore, I'll see you a bit later.'

He stood up, and placed a hand on her shoulder. 'It is good to meet you, Sacha. Thank you for inviting us here this morning. You run a good business.'

Alessandro kissed her cheeks as he waited for his father to

say goodbye to her aunt and Jack. 'I'm sorry about this morning,' he said. 'I do not know what happened between our fathers, but will try to ensure my father makes amends with yours.'

She wasn't so confident. Her father was stubborn, but she could only try. 'We'll do our best to sort them out.'

As soon as they'd left, she glanced at the clock on the wall. All she had to do now was try and persuade her father to meet Mr Salvatore. She didn't hold out much hope that he'd oblige, but she had to try. She doubted her father would have reached home yet and quickly went out to the back to call her mother. Her mother's stunned silence at the other end told Sacha that there was much more to this fall-out than either she or Alessandro could possibly imagine.

'Mum, are you okay?' she asked, nervously.

'Your father's just walking in through the front gates,' she said. 'I'll have to go, but you can leave this to me. Thanks for the warning.'

What did her mother mean, 'warning'? Sacha's heart pounded. Just what had gone on between the two older men? Pushing her concerns away, she hurried back into the café to help Lucy and Milo.

Thankfully, the next two hours flew by. It was soon time for her to go with her father to meet Alessandro and Mr Salvatore. She could see him pacing back and forth, smoothing his thinning hair down with the palms of his hands as she arrived at the house.

'Dad, I'm relieved Mum persuaded you to come,' she panted, having run part of the way up the hill.

'She can be a very persuasive woman,' he grumbled. He kicked the grass with the toe of his sandal. She noticed several strands stuck to his feet, but he seemed oblivious. Whatever had gone on between the two men, it had been serious enough to cause a lasting antagonism.

Sacha put her arm around her dad's waist. 'Please tell me what happened between you two before the others arrive.'

Her father hugged her, holding her tight for a little longer than usual, which made her feel more uneasy than she had before. 'Quick, tell me.'

He bent to pull the strands of grass from his sandal. 'Stupid shoes, your mother insisted I bought these.' He mumbled something to himself and then added, 'You never know people as well as you think.'

'Dad, quickly.'

He took a deep breath. Whatever it was had hurt him, deeply. She'd never seen him acting like this.

'It was back in the sixties,' he said, eventually. 'Salva came over to work on the island as a waiter and we worked at the same restaurant. He was my best friend,' he said quietly, going silent as he mused over this memory.

'And what happened?'

'He knew I was in love with your mother, because I told him. I'd been on a few dates with her and thought things were going well between us. Then Salva and I had a misunderstanding and fell out. Rather than doing the decent thing like most friends, that snake asked your mother on a date and to annoy me, she accepted.'

Sacha held back her surprised reaction, not wishing to distract her father from continuing. It was hard to imagine her mother ever doing anything to upset her father. She'd always adored him and hated for him to be angry with anyone, let alone her.

'I can't believe Mum would do such a thing,' she said, unable to hide her disbelief.

'Well, she did,' her father said, scowling.

Sacha realised there was more to this than met the eye. She also knew her father wouldn't leave things without reacting to them.

'You paid him back somehow, didn't you?'

He stared at her briefly. He opened his mouth to continue, but didn't get the chance.

'He took the café from me,' Mr Salvatore said, coming up behind them, panting from the exertion of walking up the hill from the village.

Sacha jumped when she heard his voice. 'Summer Sundaes was yours?'

'It was never yours,' her father snapped.

'It should have been,' Mr Salvatore said to Sacha. 'You took it as your first café, didn't you, Thomas?' He turned to glare at her father.

'Papa, please,' Alessandro pleaded, his voice quiet.

He reacted by folding his arms in front of his chest. 'Yes, it was my first café,' he said, looking satisfied with what he had done.

'You took the café from him, how?' Sacha was upset by the thought of her father purposely hurting anyone.

'It wasn't his,' her father said, then hesitating, added. 'Not at the time.'

Mr Salvatore stepped closer to her father. 'It was about to be. I showed you details of the lease and shared my costings with you. You knew how long I'd worked to get an opportunity like that and then you took it from me.'

'You tried to take my wife from me,' her father shouted, finally giving in to his building temper.

'She wasn't your wife then, Thomas,' Mr Salvatore retaliated.

'Papa,' Alessandro said, stepping in between the two men before one landed a punch on the other. He said something in Italian and his father looked a little shame-faced and stepped back. 'The way I see it,' Alessandro said, 'these actions are not something either of you should be proud of, but if you, Papa, hadn't lost the café to Mr Collins, you wouldn't have returned to Italy, met Mama and built your gelateria business. You, Mr Collins, wouldn't have been able to pass on the Summer Sundaes Café to Sacha.'

'So, Mr Salvatore did you a favour then, Dad?' Sacha said, relieved. She stepped up and linked her arm through her father's so that he was forced to lower his hands and relax a little. 'It wasn't very nice, of either of you, to be honest. But you were young and, by the sounds of things, hot-headed. It appears that everything worked out all right in the end, for both families. Don't you think?' She looked from one to the other.

Her father frowned. 'Not intentionally.'

'Dad?'

'I suppose you have a point, but—'

'No buts, Dad.'

Alessandro nudged his father lightly. 'Papa? Remember what I said earlier.'

Mr Salvatore closed his eyes, briefly. 'Yes, I agree to, how you say, move on.'

'Good,' Alessandro said. He looked tired. 'I will come to see you this afternoon,' he whispered as he walked past Sacha.

'That'll be lovely,' she said.

He hurried after his father who was already striding away.

Sacha ran after her father who was making his way up the hill to the house. 'Dad,' she called, when he didn't stop. 'Wait. I'm glad you two have resolved this, even if it was for me and Alessandro.' Catching up, she kissed her dad's florid cheek.

'He'll be returning to his job as soon as he finds a dig some-where.' Her heart sank at the thought. 'Now he's taken on Finn to run the gelateria there isn't any reason for him to stay on the island,' she went on. 'I'd rather there wasn't any aggro between us while he's still here.'

Her father grunted. 'At least I can tell your mother we've sorted things between us,' he said grudgingly, looking at the worn tar on the lane as they continued walking. 'She always thought I'd been a bit harsh by taking the café from under his nose, but what did he expect?' He looked at Sacha, as if she had the answer. 'Age hasn't improved him, I noticed.'

'He probably thinks the same about you,' she said, giving him a smile to soften her reply. 'I can't believe this has been dragging on since the sixties, that's way too long to bear a grudge, for either of you.'

They arrived at the house and Sacha went in with him. She wanted to hear what he told her mother.

'So, how did it go?' her mother asked, wiping her hands on a towel by the sink in the kitchen. 'Tom? Did you manage to make up? Please tell me you did. This is so childish.'

'Yes, Marion, I did as you asked,' he said looking, Sacha thought, a bit like a churlish schoolboy.

Her mother gave him a quick peck on the lips. 'You see, it wasn't that difficult after all. I can't see why it's taken the two of you fifty years to sort this out.' She shook her head and winked at Sacha.

'I'd better get going,' Sacha said, kissing her parents and leaving the house. As she strolled back to the village she amused herself by reflecting how much her father liked to believe that he made all the family decisions, when in reality it was her mother who managed to persuade him round to her way of thinking, every time.

She reached the boardwalk and ran to the gelateria to look for Alessandro.

'He's not here,' Finn said, serving three holidaymakers. 'You could try Bella's, they were popping in there for a quick coffee before she gave him and his dad a lift to the airport.'

She thanked him and hurried to Bella's cottage, arriving just as the three of them walked out of the cottage. Alessandro raised his eyebrows in surprise to see her there.

'Look,' Bella said, pointing to the largest rock on the beach. 'One of those annoying symbols again.'

'I can't quite make it out?' Sacha asked, intrigued. She peered over at the arrangement of shells displayed on the rock.

'It is not clear,' Alessandro said. 'Maybe it is someone playing a game.'

'Or leaving a message for someone else,' Sacha said.

'It could be some sort of love token, maybe?' Bella murmured.

'Whatever it is, the shells will go when the next tide comes or some children take them away,' Sacha said, hoping that Bella was right.

Relieved that the marking wasn't permanent, she remembered why she was here. 'I just wanted to catch you quickly,' she said to him as he lifted his father's suitcase into the boot of Bella's battered Fiat while his father got into the passenger seat.

'I'll see you when I get back.'

'I'd like that,' she said, looking forward to it.

Glancing at the mysterious symbol again, she returned to the café and called the Parish Hall to speak to the Centenier. She explained about the symbols and small changes being made to the boardwalk and asked if he knew anything about it.

'You're the fifth person to call me this week,' he said, the irritation in his voice unmissable. 'We've no idea what those ridiculous symbols are. They take me back to those peace ones we kept finding through the sixties and seventies, but we don't even know what these stand for. Nothing, probably.'

'And the painting of the railings?'

'No idea, but we're doing our best to find out. And find out we will, I can assure you.'

'They are positive changes,' she reminded him. 'But it's a little strange that someone is doing this without being open about it. It must be costing them a lot of money.'

'Never mind the cost, young Sacha, what annoys me is that they're doing it without requesting permission first.'

She thanked him and rang off, none the wiser. There was a lot going on and she wondered why she had ever imagined this was a peaceful place to live.

12

Sacha hurried back to the café to give Lucy and Milo a break. She walked inside and saw Jack regaling them with one of his stories. Milo was doubled up with laughter and Lucy had tears rolling down her tanned cheeks. There were several customers, all of whom seemed equally amused by her brother's tale.

'Nice to see you working hard, Jack,' she teased, picking up three sundae glasses from a table behind him. 'If you would like to take your lunch breaks now, I can look after everything here.' She lowered her voice and turning to Jack, said, 'If it's okay with you, I'll be going out somewhere with Alessandro this afternoon. We've got a few things to discuss.'

'I'm sure you have,' he said. 'Mum sent me a text explaining what had happened between Dad and Mr Salvatore. Honestly, I knew Dad was a stubborn sod, but to hold a grudge for nearly fifty years is barking.'

'I agree.' She took the glasses to the kitchen and Jack followed, carrying several plates and dirty napkins. 'I think it's some sort of macho thing.'

He yawned. 'Probably. Oh, and Nikki's coming over.'

'No, when?' She watched his amusement disappear and could see he wasn't looking forward to her visit.

'She wanted me to go back to the mainland this weekend and when I said I needed more time to think, she sent me an email with her flight details and said she was coming whether I liked it or not. She wanted to stay with me at Bella's but I told her the cottage wasn't licenced to have three adults staying there.'

Sacha pulled a face. 'But that's not true.'

'I know,' he said. 'But I've booked her into the Prince of Wales up the road, she'll be comfortable there, and at least I can go and chat to her away from the cottage. It's cosy and the view is great, and she can walk down to find me whenever she likes.'

'Makes sense,' Sacha said. 'Hopefully you can finally sort out any differences between you and make your mind up about whether to stay.'

'Maybe,' he said, loading plates into the dishwasher and running water for the sundae glasses. 'Also, I didn't want to give her the wrong idea. If she stays with me at the cottage, then I can't exactly tell her I won't be going back with her. It wouldn't be fair.'

'No, it wouldn't.' She returned to the café and took orders from Mrs Joliff and two of her friends. 'All ready for the fête?' she said. 'I know people are looking forward to your Jersey Wonders again, Mrs Joliff.'

'I do wish you'd call me Rosemary,' she said, patting Sacha's hand. 'In fact, I was wondering if you might want a few to sell here at the café. I could bake you a batch in no time.'

Sacha wasn't sure why she hadn't thought of this herself. She loved Mrs Joliff's Jersey Wonder doughnuts. 'I'd love you to,' she said. 'Thank you very much.'

Lucy came through from the kitchen followed by Milo, both

carrying plates of sandwiches and a smoothie each. Sacha watched them take a seat at a table at the back of the café. Lucy took a sip from her smoothie and looked up at Jack, giving him a half smile.

Jack smiled back, glancing guiltily at Sacha. She still didn't know what it was about Lucy, but something didn't seem right. Sacha was sure of it, but had no idea what it could be. Jack was always kind to her and Sacha hoped Lucy wasn't misreading his friendliness. She wondered if it was this sort of obliviousness about women that concerned Nikki, and why she was so in his face every time she wanted something from him.

A teenage couple came in. 'Could we have a couple of strawberry Eton Mess sundaes to eat outside?'

'Of course,' Sacha said. 'Go and take a seat.'

She made the sundaes and took them out, and Jack emerged to chat to a school friend he'd seen walking past. When she went back inside, Lucy had finished her lunch and Sacha gave her some cash and asked her to pop down to the local shop for a few bits.

Sacha watched as she walked slowly past Jack and his friend, smiling at them both as she went. Jack, as was typical, smiled back, but Sacha could see the flirtation was one-sided and felt sorry for Lucy.

Moments later, Jack came back in and Sacha waved him over, making sure Milo was out at the back sorting dishes and couldn't overhear what she was about to say. 'I think Lucy's got a crush on you.'

'Will you stop being so soft,' he said, seeming bemused at the notion. 'She's just a friendly girl, that's all.'

'Jack,' she said, making sure to keep her voice low. 'I'm sure I'm right. I'd hate her to get hurt, so please be careful not to encourage her in any way.'

'But...' Jack looked hurt at the thought of doing such a thing.

'I know,' she said, placing a hand on his arm. 'You wouldn't do it on purpose, but I just need you to be aware, that's all.'

'I think you'll find she's the same with Alessandro,' he said. 'It's not just me she smiles at. Shall I have a word with her?'

'No,' she said, horrified. 'I don't want her to be embarrassed. Only say something if you have no choice. Maybe mention something about probably going back to Nikki, or that your relationship hasn't quite finished. I don't know, but just be sensitive to her feelings when you do it.'

'I think she's just a bit lonely and doesn't know how to express herself maybe,' he said.

'I'm not sure. There's something bothering her though, I'm sure of it.'

'Then speak to her about it.'

'I will.' He gave her a bear hug, holding her tightly for a little longer than she liked, making her struggle and push him away. 'Get off, you big oaf.'

'You're so easy to wind up,' he laughed, nudging her gently.

'Never mind that,' she said, grimacing at him. 'We've got to get this place ready for a kid's ice cream party in an hour and I need you to help me set up the tables.'

She was used to catering for these parties and encouraged the parents who visited the café to book their children's birthday bashes via a mailing list she'd set up soon after taking over.

She was walking back into the café after checking the twelve party bags the mum had brought in earlier when she'd dropped off the cake, when she heard Jack roar for someone to slow down.

'Your table is over there,' he said, pointing to the long table at the back of the café, laden with plates of chocolate, cakes and long sundae spoons. 'Find your places and we'll come and take your orders.'

'They're noisy little devils, aren't they?' he laughed, walking up to Sacha at the counter. 'Poor mother must be knackered chasing after that lot.' Just at that moment the mother and two of her friends followed the boys inside, each laden with bags of clothes and towels and looking flustered. Jack rushed over, closely followed by Sacha.

'Here,' she said, relieving two of the women of some of their load. 'We'll look after these until you leave.' She pointed to a table next to where the boys were seated. 'I've reserved this one for you.'

'Drinks?' Jack suggested, holding up his pen and notepad and giving them his best cheeky grin.

Sacha caught their reaction over his shoulder as she took the boys' bags round the back of the café.

He took their order and moved behind the counter to make up some fruit smoothies. 'Those poor women looking after all those kids,' he said, appearing impressed.

'You could charm the fairies out the trees,' she said, wiping the top of the counter. 'What?' she said, confused when he frowned at her.

'I think it's birds, rather than fairies.'

There was a loud cheer and the decibel levels in the café rose. Sacha noticed the frantic expression on the mothers' faces and looked at Jack. 'I think this is going to be a long couple of hours.'

She picked up twelve speciality menus and walked over to the boys' table. 'Right guys, here are a few menus. Have a look and decide which sundae you'd like, and let me know.'

'Yayyyyyy,' they cheered. One slapped the birthday boy over the head with the laminated menu and others followed. He looked as if he was about to cry, so Sacha held up her hands. 'Any more of that and I'll give you a half sundae rather than the full size one.'

Twelve faces stared at her in silence at the thought of having a smaller sundae than their friends. They studied the menus, some whispering with others about what choice to make. It didn't take long for them to decide, although a couple changed their minds a few times while the others voiced their orders.

'Okay, now which toppings?' she asked, smiling as their eyes widened. 'We don't do nuts for younger children in case there is anyone with allergies, but we have chocolate sprinkles, flakes and chunks, toffee and fudge chunks, hundreds and thousands, and if you like something a little healthier and still sweet, we have fresh strawberries, raspberries and blueberries. We also have chocolate, fudge and strawberry sauces. Have a think and Jack will bring over a selection, and you can add them yourself.'

It was a little frantic to have so many excitable children wanting sundaes at the same time, but Sacha enjoyed the chaos and fun of it all. She remembered only too well her and Jack's birthdays when their parents had hosted sundae parties for them and their friends. As it had been a double celebration, they'd taken over the entire café and it really had been mayhem, but the best fun, and had created wonderful memories they still joked about now.

Jack took the smoothies to the wilting mother and her two friends who, Sacha noticed, were beginning to perk up a bit now they were sitting in the cool café.

'It's a relief for someone else to take over for a bit,' the birthday boy's mum said. 'I never imagined twelve little five-year-olds could take so much looking after. I'll bring them straight here next time and forget about trying to entertain them on the beach.'

'You do that,' Jack said. 'How about I bring you a cake each, or maybe you'd like one of Sacha's over-the-top sundaes?'

'I'm fine with this, thanks,' the mother said. Her friends agreed.

Jack went to set up a tray with the toppings and sauces. 'Want some help?' he asked Sacha as she created her third sundae.

'No, you're okay. Just take these to the boys, will you?' She indicated the one with a large candy number five stuck in the top, next to the cherry. 'That's for the birthday boy, and then work your way round clockwise.'

As soon as the last boy was served, Jack carried over the toppings. 'Starting with the birthday boy, who wants what out of this lot?' he asked.

Sacha cleared up the mess she'd made, refilled the strawberry and chocolate tubs with fresh ice cream and stocked up with more wafers and spoons, before going over to the party table to help Jack.

'Hey guys, slow down a little,' he was saying. 'You've got all the time you need to finish those off, no need to hurry.' He took away a couple of empty glasses as the boys teased each other and exchanged a few playful punches. 'The joys of hosting children's parties,' Jack whispered to Sacha.

As each boy left, Sacha gave out a party bag and finally, the last guest was collected and the mother thanked Sacha and Jack and left with her son and her two exhausted friends.

'That went well,' Jack said. 'For the most part, anyway.' He waved at someone outside and the door opened and Alessandro walked in. 'Hi, have you come to take her away from all this mess?' Jack asked, indicating the table strewn with toppings, napkins and party hats.

'It looks like I've timed this well.' Alessandro looked around at the chaos. 'You need me to help you clean this?'

'No, he doesn't,' Sacha said. 'Jack has offered to do it, haven't you Jack?'

'Looks like I might have done,' he said, grimacing as he opened a bin bag and dropped several ice-cream smeared napkins into it. 'Lucy will be here soon and can help me. I can see she wants to chat with you,' he said to Alessandro, 'so why don't you two go off somewhere and make the most of this incredible weather?'

'You don't have to tell me twice,' Sacha teased, grabbing her car keys. 'Call me if you need me.'

Lucy arrived and seemed to perk up a bit, seeing Sacha walking with Alessandro towards the door. 'Have a lovely time,' she said.

'Thanks,' Sacha said, wondering if Lucy had got over whatever it was that had been bothering her. 'I'll see you in the morning.' The door closed behind them and she breathed in the warm summer air. 'I need to dip my flip flops in the sea,' she said, lifting her foot and displaying the sticky coating of various toppings and syrups. 'Those little kids were like whirlwinds in there today.'

'I can wait while you change them in your flat, if you would rather.'

'No, I need to get out of here before Jack finds a reason for me to stay. I haven't been outside for hours and want to feel the sand between my toes.'

They walked along the boardwalk to the steps, which Sacha noticed had been smartened up. 'All these little changes being made to the boardwalk,' she said, trying to work out who could be behind them. 'They're improving the place, but no one seems to know who's doing it and it isn't the parish arranging it because I gave them a call yesterday and asked.' Reaching the soft sand, the sensation of the tiny grains between her toes was soothing and she pushed away all thoughts of mysterious changes and symbols. They weren't hurting anyone and someone surely would discover who was behind it all. 'This is bliss,' she said.

'First, I need to do this.' Alessandro kicked off his sandals and picked them up. Taking hold of Sacha's hand, he began to walk, and then run towards the sea, pulling her behind him.

Sacha shrieked with excitement at the freedom of running down the sandy beach. This was her favourite place in the entire world and today the weather was perfect. They reached the sea and ran into the waves and she wriggled her toes in the cool water, staring out to the row of small islands on the horizon.

'Where shall we go to?' Alessandro asked.

Sacha closed her eyes, relishing the warmth of the late after-noon sunshine on her face. 'I really don't mind. You tell me what you'd like to see and I'll find it for you.'

'I read that on the north coast of the island there are cliff walks. Maybe we could do one of those?'

'There are pathways we can take all round the island, but the ones on the north coast are probably the most dramatic and rugged. Do you want to go now?' she asked.

'When you are ready. There is no rush,' he said. 'I don't have to be anywhere else.'

She realised that neither did she and the thought cheered her.

'I thought we could eat out somewhere later. Spend some time alone to talk.'

She opened her eyes and looked at him. He was staring out at the channel, but rather than looking happy, as she'd expected him to, he seemed to be troubled by something. Sensing he wanted to talk to her privately, she tugged on his hand.

'Come along, let's get going then.'

They walked, hand in hand, up the beach, onto the promenade and to the car park where she was relieved to see that her car was in the shade of one of the large pine trees. Like other trees on the island, the tree's branches grew on one side only as if a strong wind was pushing the leaves in one direction.

She unlocked her car and let the heat escape as she wound down the windows. 'It's amazing how hot it gets in here, despite being in the shade.'

'You have air conditioning in your car?' he asked doubtfully.

'Sorry, it's an old model and there's nothing that fancy in this banger.' She loved her Fiat 500, despite wishing she could afford one of the newer, more glamorous versions. It was the only one she'd ever owned and had saved for it for several years. She'd been thrilled when her father had kept it at his house while she was away, starting it every so often so that the battery always worked when she came home on holiday. She loved the freedom it gave her and knew that one day she'd have to replace it with a newer model. For now, though, it was perfect, apart from the heat inside.

She drove them through the lanes to the north coast. The warm summer air cooled the interior of the car very slightly, and made it less uncomfortable. Both were silent, lost in their own thoughts. Sacha wondered if he had suggested their walk to be able to tell her that he was leaving the island. She dreaded him giving her an actual date for his departure, making it real.

She decided to take him the scenic route through the lanes in St Mary, along the coast at St John and along Les Platons.

'Where are we going?' he asked, looking around.

'We're in Trinity, now,' she said, 'and I'm taking you to Egypt.'

He looked at her, confused. 'Egypt?'

Sacha laughed. She'd expected this reaction. Few people who visited the island were aware of Egypt.

'There are some nice walks near there,' she said. 'It was actually Egypt Farm. I've seen some pictures and it looked lovely, with a big granite house and outbuildings. Unfortunately, the place was taken over by the Nazis in the Second World War when they occupied the island from 1940 to when the islanders were liberated on the ninth of May 1945.' She could see he was fascinated, and added. 'You missed Liberation Day, but the ninth of May each year is taken as a Bank Holiday on the island.'

'Bank Holiday?'

'Yes, the whole island has a day off from work.'

'Ah, si.'

'Most people celebrate the occasion by raising flags and having parties. There's a big presentation in town near to the Pomme d'Or Hotel where the soldiers who liberated the island raised the British flag.'

'I like the sound of this.'

She smiled, recalling times she and her family had celebrated with barbecues at home or on the beach near their home. 'It's still a very recent memory to some of the older people here and I grew up hearing all about it, too.'

'This Egypt, what happened?'

'There's nothing much left, it's all very sad. If you're interested in the Second World War there's so much I can show you here. Many old bunkers and even strange little pillbox type ones built on the side of roads. All sorts.'

'I would love to learn more.'

'There was a commando raid down near Egypt but one of the men stepped on a mine and died a short while after.' She thought back to her grandmother telling her tales of things that had happened to her friends and their families during the Occupation.

They used the place to train their soldiers for combat training and target practice. There's very little left now, which is a shame. The family live in South Africa, I think, and although they've tried to get planning permission to rebuild the site, they haven't been successful.'

'That is very sad,' he said, frowning.

'I think so, too. There's another farm further down, called Little Egypt and it's all very secluded.

'There is much history on this island,' Alessandro said. 'It is a fascinating place, especially for somewhere so small.'

'Actually, I'm going to park at Bouley Bay,' she said. 'There's a café just above the beach there, which sells really good burgers, if you want to stop and eat one. I thought we could buy a drink and begin our walk; it's only three to four miles, but very beautiful along the coastal pathways. The walk goes between two bays and we'll pass by Egypt Woods and end up at Bonne Nuit, where we can stop for a quick bite to eat and then make our way back to the car at Bouley Bay. What do you think?'

'I like this idea.'

She had wondered if maybe they were starting their walk a little late, especially as the sun set in the west of the island on the other side of the hills, but she could always give her brother a call to come and fetch them if necessary.

After parking her car at Bouley Bay, she pointed down a pathway to their right.

'There's the café, would you like something?'

'A cool drink, maybe?'

She needed one too. They bought their drinks and she changed into the sensible walking boots she hadn't worn since her last time travelling with friends. She put a peaked cap on, tucking strands of her hair behind her ears.

'Ready, let's get going then.'

They walked a short way up the hill on the side of the road until they came to a wooden sign, indicating the path for their cliff walk. She'd forgotten the initial part of the walk was uphill but reasoned that the beauty of the area was well worth the effort. She walked in front of Alessandro, stopping every so often so each of them could take photos of the fields, and as they made their way upwards they spotted the small ruin near the brow of the hill. Taking a few selfies with the view of the bay below them in the background, Sacha sighed, happy to be spending some quiet time alone with Alessandro.

'Beautiful, isn't it?' she asked.

'It is incredible,' he said, stepping back to let a woman and her Labrador pass. Sacha took him by the hand and began walking again.

'I must stop thinking about my dad's annoying ways, or I'll get cross,' she said. 'Let's carry on with this beautiful walk.'

They strolled along the path for a while, until Alessandro said, 'I am glad to be seeing this side of the island before I leave.'

Sacha's heart plummeted. She stopped walking, snatching her hand away and turned to him, not caring that she wasn't bothering to hide her shock. 'Leaving, when?'

Another two walkers passed them.

'We should keep going.'

Sacha preferred him not to see the tears that were welling up in her eyes, so did as he suggested. 'So, you're leaving,' she said over her shoulder. 'Have you got an actual date?'

'I didn't want to go before the fête,' he said. 'I want to help everyone on the boardwalk to secure Betty's home for her. I have enjoyed feeling part of this community and hate to leave, but I cannot stay much longer, I need to work again, Sacha.'

'I wish you didn't have to,' she said, staring out to sea, concentrating on not giving in to the tears that were threatening to make an appearance.

'I would like to, probably more than you realise. I've enjoyed getting to know everyone, especially your friends and family. I cannot be employed here, not unless I am given a special licence which I can only be granted if I am doing a job no one else here is qualified to do, or if I'm married to someone who is entitled to live here.'

She stopped and looked up at him, kissing him on his smooth, tanned cheek.

'I know. It's good of you to stay this long,' she said, relieved to still have a few days with him around and not having to pull everything together without his help. 'I'm sad you have to go, but I understand,' she admitted, reluctantly. 'If only there was a job you could apply for here.'

'I would like to find something, but am not hopeful,' he said, his voice quiet. 'There aren't many archaeological programmes in this area, and I need to go where the work is.'

'Of course, you do,' she said, swallowing the lump constricting her throat. It had been an unexpectedly exciting summer and she'd willed it not to end, but as was so typical, real life was going to get in the way. 'I'll miss you,' she said, immediately thinking that maybe his going was a blessing in disguise. Falling in love with a man who lived elsewhere really wasn't a good idea.

'You will miss me?'

She tried to backtrack. 'I might do,' she teased, thinking

back to his arrival only a couple of weeks before. 'I wish we hadn't wasted time battling over your plans for the gelateria.'

He laughed. 'We have made up now, mostly.'

They continued to walk in silence for a bit.

Sacha stopped when they reached a bench. 'Shall we sit for a moment?'

He sat next to her. 'I have enjoyed getting to know you, Sacha,' he said, leaning forward and kissing her.

Sacha leapt to her feet. 'Stop it,' she shouted, taken aback by the harshness of her words.

Alessandro's mouth fell open. 'Sacha,' he took hold of her hand. 'What have I done?'

'You shouldn't keep kissing me,' she snapped, pulling her hand from his and walking on to the nearby vantage point.

He came up behind her. 'I'm sorry. I misjudged the moment.'

Embarrassed by her over-reaction, she forced a smile. 'Look, it's fine. Let's go back to the car. I think I misjudged the time it took to walk here,' she said, when he opened his mouth to say something further. 'Look, the sun is going to set very soon.'

Without waiting for him to agree, she marched off along the pathway, swallowing the lump forming in her throat, desperate not to give in to the misery that was threatening to overwhelm her. Why was she in love with him, of all people? She heard him catch up with her.

'Sacha,' he said, his voice strained. 'Please slow down, the pathway is narrow and uneven and you should be careful not to fall.'

He was right. Her toe had only just healed and the last thing she needed was to damage herself again, especially when there was so much she needed to do.

'Why don't you go ahead,' she said, stopping to let him pass.

'Then at least if I trip I can grab hold of you to break my fall.'
She knew she was wasting her time trying to make light of the
moment, but she felt compelled to try.

He walked ahead of her in the direction of the road. The
view in front and to the side of her was stunning, but not quite
as attractive as his rear view. From his broad shoulders to his
narrower waist and tight bottom, it was all rather gorgeous. She
couldn't help staring at his firm bottom, encased in faded jeans,
and sighed. Why was life so unfair, sometimes?

Alessandro suddenly stopped and turned sideways to look
at her. 'You should walk in front of me,' he said. 'It is getting
darker now the sun has almost set and I would rather walk
behind you.'

She was about to tell him that she was more than capable of
looking after herself, but didn't wish to antagonise him further.
It wasn't his fault he'd been in love with someone before they'd
even met, and she'd already given him a difficult enough time.
She did as he asked.

As they walked, her mood dipped further. Sacha thought
back to how content she'd been before meeting Alessandro, and
wondered briefly whether life would have been easier if she
hadn't met him in Rome.

'Everything is done, I think,' he said, as they concentrated
on the rugged stony pathway. It took her a moment to realise
what he was talking about. 'The stallholders have booked their
spots along the boardwalk. Bella, she tells me a friend has
arranged for a small band to play. The actor is coming to open
the event and I think all we need to do is put up tables for the
stalls, hang up the, um...'

She tried to picture what he meant. 'Bunting?'

'A strange word. Yes, that must be put up, but it has been
collected by some ladies in the village.'

'The WI?'

'Yes, I think that is what they said. Now we only need to be sure we have enough supplies for our businesses so that we don't run out if many people come along.'

They reached the road.

'Look,' he said pointing out to the rolling waves. 'Is very beautiful, calming. I wish I didn't have to leave you.'

They stared silently out at the sea in front of them. She tried to imprint the smell of his clean skin into her brain, so that she wouldn't ever forget it. She couldn't help wondering how good they could have been as a couple. She would miss him more than he knew, even more than she'd realised until he'd told her for certain that he would be leaving.

He put his arm around her shoulders and kissed the top of her head. 'I will miss you very much, Sacha,' he said. 'My beautiful friend.'

There it was again. His friend. 'Come along,' she said. 'It's getting too dark to be out here.'

13

Sacha parked the car. It had been an awkward drive back with both of them deep in thought. They walked along the boardwalk, stopping in front of the café. The smell from a nearby beach barbecue filled the warm summer evening. Alessandro looked around before bending down to kiss Sacha's cheeks. She wished the place wasn't so busy, but on perfect evenings like this one, they always were. She thought ahead to the grey days only a few months away and how she wouldn't be able to share them with Alessandro.

'Are you angry with me kissing you?' he asked quietly, after looking around to check that no one could overhear him.

'No,' she said miserably. 'If the circumstances were different, I'd be happy for you to kiss me again,' she said, forgetting her embarrassment for a moment and being honest with him about her feelings.

'Hi, Sis,' Jack said, as he walked out of the café. 'Have a fun afternoon?'

Sacha stepped back from Alessandro and cleared her throat.

She wasn't sure if she was grateful for Jack's intrusion or irritated by it and decided in this instance it was the former.

'It was fun,' she said. 'Right, I'd better go. I'll see you sometime tomorrow, no doubt,'

He frowned. 'We need to be up early to begin—' His words were cut off by a sudden commotion as Jack returned to the café just as people came outside carrying tables, chairs and filled bags. It was as if someone had sounded an alarm Sacha and Alessandro couldn't hear.

'What the hell?' She looked around and gasped when her café door sprung open and Jack's excited chatter could be heard coming from inside. She followed his voice. 'What's going on?'

'I was about to tell you, but you were acting a little weird.'

'Jack?' She narrowed her eyes at him, hoping he would tell her what was happening.

He widened his eyes and gave Alessandro a sympathetic glance. 'Lexi phoned earlier. There's a reporter from the local news station coming to interview George Newton first thing tomorrow, so we're getting ready.'

'That's brilliant.' A bubble of excitement built up in Sacha's stomach. It was a relief to have something other than her relationship with Alessandro to focus on. 'What about an interview with the *Gazette*?'

Jack moved the table slightly. 'A journalist spoke to him up at the cottage,' he said, standing back and checking it was positioned correctly before moving it a little to the left. 'They were delighted when Aunt Rosie tipped them off that George was here. He agreed to discuss his latest film project, as long as they mentioned the fête.'

'When will it be published?'

Jack laughed. 'That was Aunt Rosie's other bargaining point.

They had to publish it in tomorrow's edition. It'll be out around
11 a.m.'

'So there'll be plenty of time for people to read it and come
along.'

'Grab the end of this,' Jack said, pointing to a long trestle
table she hadn't noticed behind him. He must have collected it
from their parent's home. 'Finn is getting stuff together at your
place,' he said to Alessandro. It was his cue to leave and he
took it.

'I'll go and help him,' he said, giving Sacha a fleeting smile
before hurrying off in the direction of his gelateria.

'You really are away with the fairies, aren't you?' Jack gave
her an affectionate smile. 'You knew the fête was tomorrow,
when did you think we were going to do this?'

She had no idea. Her mind had been filled with so many
conflicting things, she'd somehow lost track of what was
happening.

'Stop being so bossy,' Sacha said, lifting the other end of the
table and walking backwards out to the boardwalk.

Her sadness at Alessandro's news about his departure less-
ened as the excitement of everyone on the boardwalk became
infectious. Sacha couldn't help smiling as she noticed Bella
holding a ladder for Lexi who was tying the end of a string of
bunting to one of the lampposts. She waved at Jools, delighted
to see her back from her holiday in Ireland. Finn was pointing
up at the shutters on one of the houses and explaining something to her, but she seemed more interested in looking at him,
rather than listening to what he was saying. Even the two
elderly statesmen that met in her café several times a week to
argue over local politics, were putting up a temporary pergola at
the other end of the row of stalls. Betty was nearby, leaning on
her walking stick and giving directions.

'Everyone's so organised,' she said when they'd placed their table opposite their café window.

They walked back to collect a small row of bunting to hang across the front of their table.

'We all knew what jobs we had to do,' Jack said.

Sacha looked around. The buzz was building and she finally believed that they could make the event the success it needed to be. 'It's exciting, isn't it?'

He nodded and pointed to Mrs Joliff, setting up a stall opposite one of the cottages. 'Mrs Joliff is selling Jersey Wonders, which she and Betty will be making, the next one along is selling salted caramel and chocolate smoothies, that one there,' he pointed to the next stall being set up. 'They'll be bringing veggies from their farm and there's another one further along selling produce from several allotments in Gorey.'

Sacha's heart swelled with pride that they'd managed to pull this together at such short notice. 'I just hope we end up raising enough money,' she said, wondering if she should approach Betty to ask her about the Occupation and her part in it, which the Centenier had seemed so impressed about. She didn't want to risk upsetting her before the fête, so decided that if she didn't manage to speak to her parents about it then she'd approach Betty cautiously afterwards. 'At least the weather forecast is good,' she said, aware Jack was waiting for her to say something.

'We're taking it in turns to keep an eye on the stalls overnight,' he said. 'Just in case our mysterious artist decided to pop down here and change things. One of us one end and another at the other end, so no chancers coming across this set up will be able to take advantage and mess everything up.'

'I can help, if you need me to,' she said.

'You can, if you like, but I thought you'd want to make up

extra batches of smoothies for our stall.' Jack began erecting the makeshift pergola. 'What's he doing down there?'

She looked in the direction Jack was indicating and spotted two women chatting excitedly with Alessandro outside his gelateria. One handed him a notepad and pen and Sacha watched, wondering what he could be writing down for them.

'I've no idea,' she said, as Alessandro continued to speak with the two excitable young women. He couldn't be giving directions. He barely knew his way around. He looked rather awkward but still beamed at their cameras as each took turns standing next to him for selfies. It dawned on Sacha that the girls must have recognised Alessandro from his modelling days.

She turned to help Jack with one side of the pergola when Alessandro waved goodbye to the women and looked in their direction. She didn't want him to think she was spying on him, but was intrigued.

She peeked up through her lashes to see him going back inside the gelateria.

'Anyone would think they'd mistaken him for a pop star, or something,' Jack laughed.

'Oh yes, did you know, he used to be a model?'

'So, he's gone from posing for a living, to digging holes?'

'I wouldn't put it quite that way,' Sacha said, wondering if her brother and Alessandro would ever be friends.

It took a few hours but by ten in the evening everything that their neighbours could set up was completed. Sacha returned to her café and made some smoothies. She usually made them as customers waited, but needed some stock made up and refrigerated, ready for the following day.

She fell into bed just after midnight, tired but satisfied that they'd done everything they could.

A commotion outside her bedroom window woke her. She rubbed her eyes to try and come around and realised it was daylight. Had she overslept? She squinted at her bedside clock. *Nine-thirty!* She'd never slept this late. She leapt out of bed and pulled the curtains open, peering down in the direction of voices below.

A camera crew was there, filming George Newton. She scanned the people congregating round the interviewer as she spoke to the actor, but couldn't see her aunt. Running through to her bathroom, she quickly showered and dressed, wetting her hairbrush to dampen down her bed hair before hurrying down to the café.

'Good morning,' Lucy said, smiling as she placed two plates of toasted cabbage loaf down in front of the fisherman and his children. 'Jack asked me to wake you about an hour ago but I've been too busy to leave the café, I hope that's okay?'

Sacha frowned. She couldn't argue, but couldn't imagine not having a moment to run up the stairs to bang on her bedroom door. 'It's fine. Um, Lucy, can I have a quick word?' she said, lowering her voice so the customers couldn't hear her as she led the young girl through to the kitchen.

'Is it something I've done?' Lucy's eyes widened.

'No, but I've been meaning to have a quiet word with you.' Sacha reached out and patted her forearm. 'Don't worry, I only wanted to check that everything is alright. You know you can always confide in me if you need to?'

Lucy stared at the floor for a few seconds. 'I'm fine. Thank you.'

'If you're certain?' she asked, aware that she needed to get outside. Lucy nodded. 'Can you manage here for a bit longer?'

'I'm fine. Milo's here.'

Sacha didn't bother to ask why Lucy hadn't asked Milo to keep an eye on the café while she came to wake her – after all, she'd been the one to oversleep, not the other way around. 'Thanks for looking after things,' she said. 'I'm not sure why I didn't wake at the usual time.'

She ran out of the café and hurried to join the others to watch George being interviewed. He was dressed smartly in a two-piece suit, holding forth about his upcoming role as a spy in a new film. He looked so well-groomed that his appearance seemed slightly at odds with the casually turned out people grouped around him. As he answered questions, she scanned the boardwalk to check if everything was still in place from the night before. She spotted Mrs Joliff and Betty arranging napkins and plates on their stall, and another stallholder unpacking a box of jars of Jersey Black Butter, which reminded her that she was running low and must buy a couple of jars for the café.

'He's so hot,' said a female voice.

Sacha looked over, expecting the girl to be referring to George but was surprised to notice that she was looking the other way. Following her line of vision, she spotted Alessandro chatting to Bella near her cottage.

'Go and ask him for his autograph,' one of the girls said to the other.

She nudged her friend, saying,' No, you go. I pointed him out to you.'

They giggled and whispered something to each other. 'Fine,' said the taller of the two. 'We'll both go.'

Sacha watched them run over to Alessandro and start chatting to him. By the look on Bella's face, she wasn't pleased to have her conversation interrupted and went back into her cottage.

Alessandro spotted her as one of the girls took a photo of

him with her friend. He smiled at her and she nodded her acknowledgement before turning back to George who was wrapping up the interview. As soon as it was over, she went over to him.

'Thanks very much, George,' she said. 'We really appreciate your help. I'm sure you must have lots of people vying for your attention and it can't be easy finding time for yourself.'

'It's fine,' he said, putting his arm around her shoulders and walking with her towards the café. 'I'm happy to do anything to help a good cause and when Rosie told me about Betty I thought it was the least I could do.'

'Can I offer you breakfast at the café?'

'That would be wonderful. I've been meaning to come down here to sample some of your food but haven't had the time to actually do so.'

Sacha led him inside, and the buzz of chatter died away. Sacha guessed it must happen whenever George Newton made an appearance, and felt a bit sorry for him. She spotted a couple paying at the counter and showed him to the table they'd vacated.

'If you sit here I'll ask Milo to clear the table. I'll be back to join you in a few seconds.'

She hurried to the kitchen 'Milo, can you clear that table over there,' she said. 'It's George Newton. I don't want to leave him on his own, or people will start pestering him.'

Returning to the table she handed George a menu and sat opposite him. He read it and placed it down on the table, smiling as he looked around the café.

Milo came over to take their order, notepad and pen in hand, calm and relaxed, unlike the customers who were craning their necks to get a good look at the handsome actor.

'I'll have the fried eggs on toasted cabbage loaf,' George said. 'With a mixed fruit smoothie.'

'Me too,' Sacha said. 'Thanks, Milo.'

'I love any place that serves toasted cabbage loaf, you just can't beat it.'

'Untoasted?' she teased.

George laughed. 'Maybe.' He smiled at one or two people. 'I love this place,' he said. 'I used to come here when I was a teenager.' He thought for a moment. 'In fact, I think this was where I had my first holiday job. Yes, it was.'

Sacha tried to imagine a teenage George serving in the café. 'I can imagine it was full of teenagers on the days you worked here,' she laughed.

He leant forward and lowered his voice. 'You know, I was a lousy waiter and I think your dad only employed me to keep the youngsters coming in. He used to tell me off for flirting with the girls.'

She could imagine her father being none too impressed with George wasting time when he should have been working.

'I didn't realise young Alessandro was famous,' he said. 'I thought I recognised him, but it was only when Rosie pointed out a couple of pictures of him online with his fiancée that I remembered him. I think I met her a few times, she was nice, but kind of distant.'

They ate their breakfast and Sacha couldn't help feeling guilty for not helping with the stalls outside. 'I'd better get going,' she said, after he'd finished eating. 'Do you need me to give you a lift up to the cottage?'

'No thanks, I love the walk and it isn't far. The uphill walk will do me good after eating this delicious meal.'

'It's my pleasure. Please come again, any time.'

She saw him out and then helped Lucy and Milo with the breakfast rush, and made up three more large flasks of smoothies for the stall.

'Right, I'd better get ready,' she said, going into the storeroom and loading a large hamper with low calorie chocolate brownies, several cabbage loaves, and a few jars of black butter. 'I'll take a couple of menus to fix to the side of the stall,' she said to Milo, taking them from him. 'Are you sure you'll be okay to stay here and help Lucy, or would you rather help on the stall?'

'I can do a bit of both, if you like?'

'Thanks.' She pointed to the plastic plates she'd taken out of the store cupboard. 'If you bring those and the flasks, I'll take these hampers and we can get set up.'

Just before noon, Jack came running up to Sacha's stall. 'Have you seen George?'

'No. Why?' Panic coursed through her. She couldn't imagine her aunt would let him be late for his opening speech. 'Haven't you?'

'I was chatting to him about ten minutes ago, but no one can find him now.' Jack raked his hands through his long hair. 'Damn, what are we going to do if he doesn't appear?'

It dawned on Sacha that she hadn't seen George since breakfast. She searched the crowds milling around the stalls, but only managed to spot another symbol on the wall near the bottom of the door on the cottage next door to her café. What the hell did those symbols mean? She assumed that whoever was doing them had a point to make, or a message to give to someone. Now wasn't the time to get caught up in that mystery though. She waved Milo over.

'Please stay here and wait to serve anyone, I'm going to look for George.'

She ran into the café and almost bumped into Lucy holding a tray in one hand as she kicked closed one of the cupboard doors in the storeroom. 'Have you seen George?'

Lucy shook her head.

Sacha was about to carry on searching when she noticed Lucy reddening as she glanced back at the cupboard. It dawned on Sacha that maybe Lucy was trying to hide her belongings. She didn't look as groomed as usual, and there were black shadows under her eyes.

'Lucy, do you need a place to stay?'

Lucy's eyes widened. 'I know I need an address for a job,' she said, confusing Sacha. 'I promise I'll find somewhere soon.' She looked as if she was about to cry and Sacha gently took the tray from the girl's hands and placed it on the worktop.

'Where've you been sleeping if not at home?'

'I was staying with my aunt, but she's moved back to Ireland,' Lucy said, tears spilling over and rolling down her cheeks. 'I told her I was staying with a friend and she believed me.'

'So, where have you been sleeping?'

'Here,' Lucy said, her voice barely above a whisper.

Confused, Sacha looked around. 'Where?'

When Lucy didn't reply, Sacha took her by the shoulders and smiled at her reassuringly, hoping she would confide in her.

'I waited on the beach until I saw your bedroom light go off and then crept through the back door and slept in one of the storerooms.'

Sacha had to concentrate on not showing her horror. 'But it must have been horrible in there. Why didn't you tell me?'

Lucy hesitated and sniffed.

Sacha pulled some kitchen paper from the roll nearby and

handed it to her. 'It's fine. Look, you can't possibly spend another night in there. You can sleep on my sofa tonight, but it isn't really big enough. Leave it with me and I'll speak to someone,' she said. 'My friend, Jools, might have a room you can rent. Would you mind me asking to her?' She hoped Jools wouldn't mind. It might even work well, Sacha thought. Jools was always worried about leaving her mother alone and Lucy needed to feel like she belonged somewhere, so it could be the answer to all their needs.

Lucy blew her nose and shook her head. 'No, of course I don't mind. Thank you, Sacha.'

Sacha gave her a hug, swamped by guilt that the girl had been sleeping rough in her storeroom and she hadn't noticed. 'It's fine, but if ever you have another problem I'd rather you come to me and we find a way to resolve it. Okay?'

'I promise.'

'Good,' she said. It was difficult at times, having to deal with family issues – like Jack's relationship with Nikki and her father's reaction to anything that didn't work as he expected it to, but she preferred being part of an awkward family than being lonely like poor Lucy. Sacha was happy to think that she was making things better for the young girl, then, remembering why she was there in the first place, panicked. 'I need to find George Newton.'

'Good luck.'

She shot back outside to see if George had made an appearance. Hearing the crackle of a tannoy that Finn had helped Alessandro set up the afternoon before, she jumped when she heard George's voice welcoming everyone. Breathing a sigh of relief, she watched as he proceeded to give a short speech and open the fête.

As the afternoon wore on, Sacha didn't have time to think further than serving the next person at the stall, hurrying to the café to collect more supplies and make more fruit smoothies, leaving the stall in Milo and Jack's capable hands. Every so often she emptied the cash tin and took the money to the café to lock away until later. By the time she'd checked on the other stall holders, to see if anyone needed any help or change, it was almost five o'clock and her feet were beginning to ache.

She noticed Betty leaning against the railings, looking a little pale, and took a chair over to her.

'Here, I think you need to sit down for a bit,' she said. 'I hope you haven't been standing all afternoon.'

'No, she hasn't.' Mrs Joliff frowned as she handed a brown paper bag containing some freshly baked Jersey Wonders to a customer. 'Alessandro accompanied Betty home for a rest about an hour and a half ago, so she's not too bad.'

Betty waved at them. 'I am here, you know, so stop fussing. If I get tired I only live over there.' She laughed. 'I could do with one of those to perk me up though.'

Sacha smiled fondly at her friend and willed the attendees of the fête to spend enough money that they could pay off the extension to her lease. 'Do you want me to go and make you a latte at the café, or would you like a cool drink?'

'I'm fine, my love, stop your worrying.'

Sacha hugged Betty and offered Mrs Joliff a drink. 'No, you're all right, love, I have a bottle of water here. Go and get on with what you're doing, you're looking pretty shattered yourself.'

Sacha tidied up her hair, which was probably a little wild by now. It was hot and she hadn't stopped for hours, but like the rest of her friends who were working so hard, now wasn't the time to stop and think.

She passed the gelateria and waved at Alessandro who hurried out to speak to her. 'It's going well, no?'

'Yes, I think so,' she said, realising that the apron she was wearing over her T-shirt and shorts was tucked up on one side in her pocket. 'We'll have to wait until later and hope that we've done enough.'

'Sacha,' he said, taking her hand and leading her away from the gelateria. 'I must speak with you about something.'

She knew he was leaving and that he saw her as a friend, what could there possibly be for them to discuss? Nothing she wanted to hear, she was sure of that. 'Sorry, I can't stop now,' she said, taking her hand from his. 'I have to get back to the stall, but we can talk later if you like.'

'Okay.'

He looked a little crestfallen, but she pushed away the guilty feeling inside and hurried back to the stall to help Jack and Milo.

By the end of the day, all the stallholders had helped each other load cars, carry trestle tables back to a van to be taken to the Parish Hall, and return what little stock they had left to their homes and back to the café. Sacha stopped for a moment, leaning her hands on the metal railings and breathed in the warm sea air. They'd done it. Now they just needed to count out the money and hope that they'd made enough.

'Come on dilly daydream,' her mother called from the café. Sacha was glad she'd been able to come down and help Lucy run the café while Sacha had been working at the fête.

She spotted Jools returning with her mum to their cottage and remembered her promise to Lucy to ask her about letting a room. 'I'll be a couple of minutes, Mum,' she said, running off to speak to them.

'Sorry,' she said, reaching their cottage and standing in the open doorway as Jools settled her mother in her favourite chair. 'I hope you don't mind me asking, but Lucy who works at the café has had to move out of her digs and needs somewhere to stay for now. I was wondering if you'd consider renting her your spare room.'

Jools looked at her mum, who nodded straight away. 'We were only talking about letting out the room just this morning,' Jools said. 'Lucy's a lovely girl, she'll be perfect, won't she, Mum?'

'Yes, she will.' She smiled up at Sacha. 'We'd love her to move in here. She can come tonight, if she likes, there's no reason to wait.'

Sacha thanked them, grateful the issue had been resolved so easily. She ran back to the café to let her know, and afterwards, helped Lucy serve cool drinks to Jack, Alessandro, Bella and a few others as they sat and counted the money. Tapping her foot as she tidied up in the kitchen, she anxiously waited for them to work out if they'd made enough money to cover the lease extension.

Hearing a commotion and lots of excited chatter, Sacha went back to join them, stunned to see that it wasn't excitement at all, but shock that was causing the outburst.

'Well?' she asked, unable to stand it a moment longer.

'It's not enough.' Jack stood up and raked his hands through his messy hair. 'How can it not be enough? I thought today had gone well.'

'We all did,' Sacha said. 'How much are we short by? Maybe we can raise it ourselves.'

He looked at his calculations. 'Just over a thousand pounds,' he said.

Alessandro glanced at her and she wondered whether he looked so uncomfortable because they still hadn't spoken about whatever was troubling him, or whether he wanted to say some-thing about the money.

'Please, I would like to donate the money to Betty's Fund,' he said, quietly.

'No.' Jack scowled at him. 'It's not for you to do that. We'll think of something.'

To divert an argument, Sacha went over and took hold of Alessandro's arm. 'You wanted to speak to me about something.'

He frowned as if trying to recall what he'd wanted to say and then slowly stood up. 'Yes, I will come with you. To the beach?'

Relieved to be able to leave Jack to mull over what they were going to do next, she agreed. 'Fine.'

They left the café and as they walked along the boardwalk to the steps, Alessandro said, 'I would very much like to help Betty. I do not see why Jack doesn't want me to.'

She explained that it was Jack's pride and his fierce ideas about the locals looking after each other.

Alessandro shrugged. 'I understand loyalty,' he said. They walked down the granite steps, taking off their shoes and carrying them. 'Which is why I must speak with you now.'

Here it is, thought Sacha. She really didn't want to speak about him kissing her, or Livia and his loss, but if she didn't want him going back inside to argue with Jack then this is what she'd have to do until they both cooled down a bit.

They walked to the water's edge, dropped their shoes on the sand and paddled. 'I have some news,' he said looking at her. 'I have been accepted to join a dig that will begin here in two months.'

Relief coursed through Sacha. 'But that's wonderful,' she said. She stared at him for a moment. 'You should be happy, but you don't look it.'

He walked a little deeper into the sea and she followed him, enjoying the coolness of the water up to her knees.

'You were angry with me for kissing you.'

Here it came, she thought, holding back a groan. 'Yes, because I know how much you were in love with Livia and how you must miss her and as much as I love you,' horror at what she'd said shot through her. 'I mean, as a friend, of course. Um. Well.' She struggled to think where to go next with what she was saying. 'Yes, well, as much as you're my friend and I'm glad you're staying here, as least for the time being, I think that if we're friends, which we are, then we should act like friends.'

'And friends don't kiss?'

She saw the twinkle in his eyes and it made her angry. 'No, not in my book they don't.'

'Your book?'

'Shut up, you know what I mean.' She could see that he did and turned away from him.

They paddled in silence for a few minutes, then Alessandro broke their silence by saying, 'I was in love with Livia, but things between us hadn't been good for a while. Days before she died I discovered that she'd been having an affair with one of the photographers on a shoot and I was furious with her for betraying me and intended ending our relationship as soon as she returned home after her most recent trip away.'

Sacha turned to face him, saddened by the sorrow etched on his handsome, tanned face. 'Go on,' she said quietly, taking hold of his hand.

He cleared his throat. 'She died in an accident the day before she was due to come home, so I never told her I knew. This is why to everyone we were still engaged, because I had not been able to finish things with her. I didn't think it was anyone's business and did not wish to sully her name to speak about our troubles to anyone, in case someone sold the story to the newspapers.'

'I don't blame you,' she said. 'It's no one's business but your own.'

He took each of her hands in his and pulled her gently to him. 'I was upset when she died.'

'That's understandable.'

Ignoring what she'd said, he continued. 'We were happy for a long time and she shouldn't have died so young. It was tragic, and for a long time I was devastated, my anger with her forgotten.' He stared at her in silence for a moment his thumbs lightly grazing the top of her hands. 'I only tell you this because I want you to know that when I kissed you it wasn't because I saw you as my friend, but because I was attracted to you. I want to be with you, Sacha. You are beautiful, but also real, not pretending. I love you, Sacha.'

'I...' She looked down at his hands holding hers, trying to unscramble her brain and respond to his unexpected declaration.

Alessandro let go of one of her hands and, bringing his fingertips to her chin raised it gently, kissing her lightly.

Her thoughts raced. He'd been going to finish with Livia, who had betrayed him, and now Alessandro loved Sacha. Loved her? Her mouth drew back into a wide smile and she stood on tiptoe and kissed him back.

'Do you think you can love me too?' he asked.

'I think I can just about manage it,' she said, kissing him again. 'If I try hard enough.'

'You are joking?' he asked.

'I am.'

Alessandro grabbed her waist and swung her round, placing

her feet back into the sea and, pulling her to him, kissed her hard.

After a while, Sacha thought of Jack at the café. 'We'd better get back and see what's happening.'

They returned to find that everyone apart from Jack and Bella had gone home. Bella stared at Sacha, as if trying to fathom out what she and Alessandro had been talking about.

'We've decided that Betty's had a long tiring day today,' Jack said. 'It might be best to leave speaking to her about the money until tomorrow morning.'

Alessandro looked like he wanted to argue, but Sacha took his hand and smiled up at him. 'That's a good idea. Bella and I will speak to her in the morning. I think everyone needs to relax and get some sleep, now, it's been a long few days.'

'We'll leave you two to chat,' Bella said, taking Jack by the arm and pulling him away.

'You'd better go with them,' Sacha said to Alessandro. 'I'll come and see you in the morning. I need to speak to Jools about something.'

'Jools has been here,' Bella said. 'She collected Lucy and her things and said there's no need for you to worry about anything. So, there's no need for Alessandro to come with us just yet.'

Sacha watched Bella and Jack leave. Jack glanced at Sacha and Alessandro over his shoulder and opened his mouth to speak, but Bella dragged him away, making him laugh by whispering something into his ear.

Alessandro bent to kiss Sacha and stood by the open door. 'You wish me to go now?' he asked.

She wanted to say no, but wrestled with her conscience. What was wrong with her? She was twenty-nine years old, single, and in love with this gorgeous man. But what if he stayed and she made a fool of herself? She could see he was waiting for her to reply, but couldn't form the words to ask him to stay.

'Good night, Sacha.' He turned to leave.

'I want you to stay,' she said, embarrassed to have to say it.

'You are sure?'

He looked so concerned and, she noticed, almost as awkward as she felt. The realisation boosted her confidence a little. She walked past him and closed the door, locking it.

'Come upstairs,' she said, taking his hand. 'I think we both need a drink. It's been a long day.'

She let go of his hand outside the kitchen. 'Go and make yourself comfortable,' she said, going into the kitchen to take a bottle of wine from her cupboard, and grabbing two glasses before joining him in the living room.

Sitting next to him, she put the bottle and glasses on the table and poured them both a glass of the dark red liquid.

Taking a sip, she closed her eyes and let the smooth flavours soothe her as she swallowed. 'Thank you for offering to pay the difference for Betty, it was very generous of you.'

Without saying anything, he took her glass from her hand and placed it on the table. Then, putting one hand behind her head he leaned forward and kissed her. 'You are very beautiful, Sacha.'

Unable to speak, she savoured his mouth on hers as he kissed her again, pulling her towards him. Only vaguely aware of anything other than Alessandro's mouth on her lips and various parts of her body, Sacha gave in to the sensations his touch was igniting.

She moved her hands down over his hard chest and, irritated to find cotton between her fingers and his skin, tried to pull off his top and got it tangled.

'Let me help,' he said, pulling it off in one movement and

dropping it onto the floor. He kissed her again and then stopped and looked at her. 'Your top?'

Impatiently, she took off her clothes, fumbling with the clip on her bra. 'Damn thing,' she said, desperate to carry on where they'd left off.

He put his hands behind her back and released the catch, taking the straps from each of her shoulders and letting it fall from his hands as he looked at her naked breasts. He pulled her against him, kissing her neck and sending shivers across her skin.

'You are certain you wish for this?'

Sacha didn't want to be unladylike so resisted from answering and simply nodded. She put her arms around his neck, kissing it as he lifted her and carried her into the bedroom.

* * *

Sacha lay awake for several hours staring out at the black sky, stars shining brightly as they did on clear nights like this. She thought back over the evening, of making love with Alessandro several times, and how each time became less urgent and more familiar. It felt strangely relaxing lying here next to him.

Trying not to wake him, she inched herself up onto one elbow to look down at him. The moonlight shone on his chest as it rose and fell in a slow rhythm, his tousled hair framing his face as he slept. It seemed so natural to be with him in this tiny flat, yet a few weeks ago she hadn't known he existed. She thought back to earlier in the evening, being on the beach with him and what he'd said about being accepted to join a dig on the island. She wouldn't have to say goodbye to him as soon as she'd expected.

She smiled, and closed her eyes for a few seconds. Now all they needed to do was find a way to pay for Betty's lease extension.

Alessandro moved his leg, bending it at the knee, and went to turn over, coming round and opening his eyes. Reaching up, he touched her cheek lightly. 'Sacha, I dreamt I was here with you,' he said, pulling her down and kissing her.

* * *

Later that morning, Sacha woke again, physically tired but happy. She turned her head to say something to Alessandro only to find he wasn't there. Disappointed, she showered and dressed. She needed to go to Bella's cottage, so that they could go together and break the bad news to Betty. The door opened before she had time to ring the bell and Bella stepped outside to join her. She expected a cheeky comment from her friend about Alessandro not coming home the night before, but she didn't say anything. Maybe she hadn't noticed, Sacha thought.

'I'm so nervous about speaking to her,' Bella said, as they walked the short distance to Betty's house. 'I was hoping we'd have good news to give her.'

They found the old lady sitting on a chair just outside her front door, holding a biscuit in one hand and a cup of tea in the other. Sacha forced a smile onto her face.

'We have to put on a positive front for her,' she said, not sure how they were supposed to do this. 'We'll simply have to find a way to sort this out, but we must persuade Betty not to worry about the money.'

Sacha opened her mouth to repeat her rehearsed speech, when Betty held up her hand to stop her.

'I know what you're going to say, ma love,' she said. 'If it had been good news then one of you would have rushed here to tell me last night, so that I didn't fret.'

'I'm so sorry,' Sacha said, close to tears.

'No, no,' Betty soothed, patting Sacha's hand. 'It's fine, love. I had a visit from someone this morning, letting me know they've paid the shortfall. So, it's all done and I can stay here, for the next five years, anyway.'

'Who was it?' Bella shrieked, nudging Sacha out of the way.

'I promised I wouldn't say,' Betty said, shaking her head.

'So, you can stay in your home?' Sacha was barely able to take it in.

'I just told you, it's all sorted,' Betty said. 'You young ones can stop panicking about me and can get on with your own lives again.'

'I wonder who it was?' She studied Betty's lined face for a clue. Not getting one, Sacha bent down to give her neighbour a hug. 'I'm so relieved.'

'You and me both, love,' Betty said, as a seagull swooped down and tried to take the biscuit she was holding in her hand. 'And I'm very grateful for all the trouble everyone here has gone to. Thanks to your efforts, and the anonymous donor, I'll be staying.'

Sacha heard giggling coming from the direction of the gelateria and spotted Alessandro chatting to the two teenage girls who seemed to visit the café more often since his arrival on the boardwalk.

'Look, there's Alessandro,' Bella whispered. 'He looks very relaxed and happy this morning, don't you think?'

Sacha went to answer, but glimpsed Betty winking at him as she gave him a secretive little wave. She glanced at Alessandro in time to see him put a finger up to his mouth and smile at

Betty, and knew then that he'd been the one to pay the difference.

'Well?' Betty asked, interrupting her thoughts.

'I don't know what to say,' Sacha murmured, relieved and happier than she had been in years.

'You could offer to make us all breakfast,' Bella said, oblivious to what had just happened. 'I'm famished.'

'Me, too,' Betty said, handing her cup to Sacha. 'You can help me up and take me to that café of yours. We can celebrate my good fortune over one of your delicious breakfasts.'

ACKNOWLEDGMENTS

Thanks my wonderful editor Tara Loder, to Rose Fox for her proofs and to the entire team at Boldwood Books for being so amazing.

To Rebecca Baudains who entered a competition to name one of the characters in this book. My character, Milo was named after her son, Milo Ray Baudains and Mrs Joliff's name was borrowed from Rebecca's mum.

To Fee Roberts and Natalie Pallot Smith for their delicious recipes that you'll find at the back of the book – there are a few more in a free download when you sign up to my newsletter

To Tess Jackson, Kirsty Greenwood, Karen Clarke and Rachael Troy, for being beta readers for this book and for their suggestions for Summer Sundaes, and my friend Sacha Coppell, whose first name I borrowed for my heroine, Sacha Collins.

Love and thanks to my husband, Rob, who encourages me to leave my writing studio each day to go with him and our three dogs, Jarvis, Claude and Rudi for our beach walk.

To my darling children, James and Saskia for being so thoughtful and fun.

And to the wonderful bloggers, readers, and my many friends on social media for their reviews and for sharing news about my books, I couldn't do this without you.

A LETTER FROM THE AUTHOR

Dear Reader,

I hope you enjoyed spending time at Golden Sands Bay and getting to know the characters who live there.

Georgina x

Here is one of Sacha's sundaes and a few local recipes served
by her at the Summer Sundaes Café

STRAWBERRY MERINGATA
THIS IS SACHA'S FAVOURITE SUMMER SUNDAES SUNDAE

Find a retro Sundae glass and fill with rich crema gelato,
Fresh strawberry sauce (or if you have your own strawberries
wiz them up),
Fresh strawberries,
Mini-meringue pieces, or simply buy a meringue and break it
up in your fingers,
Mix in freshly whipped (Jersey, if you have it) cream,
Pop in two (or three, if you're feeling extravagant) crispy, curly
wafers,
Top with a strawberry,
Et voila! A Strawberry Meringata. Delicious.

NATALIE PALLOT SMITH'S' JERSEY WONDERS
THIS IS THE PALLOT RECIPE FOR DELICIOUS JERSEY WONDERS,
'DES MERVELLES'

These are basically doughnuts, but are shaped and don't have
sugar on them or any filling. Although these are Natalie's Jersey
Wonders, in the book they belong to Mrs Joliff and Betty who
make them for the Summer Sundaes Café. Traditionally, Jersey
housewives cooked their Wonders as the tide went out. If they
cooked them on an incoming tide, the fat in which the Wonders
were cooked would invariably overflow the pan!
The following quantities will make approx. 80 – 100 Wonders,
but this can be halved or quartered if a smaller batch is

required. Jersey Wonders keep well in an airtight container for several days and they also freeze very well.

Ingredients:

3lbs or 1.5kg self-raising flour,
8oz or 250grams block margarine or butter (we use Stork margarine),
1lb or 500 grams caster sugar,
10 -12 medium eggs (beaten),
Cooking oil for deep frying,

Method:

Rub the margarine into the flour until breadcrumbs are resembled. Stir in the sugar. Add beaten eggs to form a soft dough then knead thoroughly until smooth. Roll some of the dough into a long 'sausage', cut into pieces then shape each into balls about the size of a large walnut. Roll into ovals approx. ¼ inch thick. Make a slit in the middle and twist one end through. (There are several traditional ways of slitting and turning). Deep fry in hot oil, turning over once, until golden brown. Drain on absorbent kitchen paper. Enjoy.

FEE ROBERT'S SPECIAL CHOCOLATE BROWNIES
THESE BROWNIES ARE LUCY'S FAVOURITE AND SHE USUALLY HAS ONE WITH HER TEA BREAK IN THE MORNING AT THE SUMMER SUNDAES CAFÉ

Ingredients: (Makes 12 brownies)

Calorie controlled cooking spray,
300g butternut squash (say, what?),
100g half milk/half dark chocolate (no nibbling now),
4 eggs,
200g golden caster sugar,
50g cocoa powder,
75g plain flour,
2 tsp baking power,
1 tsp vanilla essence,
Pinch salt and a pinch of cinnamon,
Icing sugar for dusting,

Method:

Preheat oven 180°C normal oven, 160°C fan oven. Line a 20cm x 20cm baking tin.
Put the squash in a heatproof bowl and cover with that wonderful straitjacket cling film. Microwave for 10 – 12 mins. Can be cooked in the conventional way in pan. Very little water needed. Once cooked, puree with a hand blender or potato masher. Now the magic... put the chocolate into the mix to melt – wait... it will melt. Chop the chocolate into small pieces to assist... (No nibbling!)
Beat the eggs with the vanilla essence and sugar in a bowl until pale and interesting – yes, makes a difference – pale and interesting! Add the cocoa, flour, baking powder, cinnamon and salt. Add the two mixes together – mix well. Place in the prepared tin. Cook for 25 – 30 mins and test with a skewer.
Now the patience bit – leave for an hour. (Yes, a whole hour!).

Dust with the icing sugar and cut into squares. Resist the taste test a little longer until it cools, if you can...

JERSEY CABBAGE LOAF (DU PAIN SUS EUNE FIELLE DE CHOUR)

When my son was at university his girlfriend was amused when he went into a Greggs and asked for a Cabbage Loaf. What he didn't realise was that this is something we can easily buy in Jersey, but it's not available in the UK – if it is, please let me know. The unusual thing about this loaf is that it's wrapped in cabbage leaves before baking. It tastes heavenly and smells delicious, too.

Ingredients:

1 lb strong plain flour,
½ oz fresh yeast,
½ oz pint liquid (half water, half milk),
1 tsp sugar,
1 oz margarine,
Pinch salt,
2 large cabbage leaves,

Method:

Sieve the flour into a warmed mixing bowl. Cream the yeast and sugar in a small basin and add a quarter of the liquid. Make a well in the centre of the flour and add the yeast. Sprinkle over a little flour, cover with a cloth and leave in a warm place until the yeast ferments. Then add the remainder of the liquid, fat and salt and knead into a smooth dough. Return to the basin, cover with a cloth and leave in a warm place until it has doubled in size. Remove from the bowl and give a further kneading. Then mould into a large round loaf, cover with a cloth and leave in a warm place to 'prove' until doubled in size. Finally, wrap the loaf in the large cabbage leaves which have been lightly greased on the inside, tie lightly, and bake in a hot oven, gas mark 6, 200° C (400° F) for approximately 15 minutes.

If you bake this loaf, please contact me and let me know what you think of the taste.

* * *

Sacha sells jars of Jersey Black Butter at the café. **Black Butter (Du Nier Beurre)** is a traditional preserve made in huge quantities, usually during the month of November. There is still a tradition of a few groups of people in the island getting together to peel hundreds of pounds of apples to make the black butter over a period of almost two days. Perfect for spreading on toast, or how about some toasted cabbage loaf, or as a condiment for meat.

* * *

We also have a local recipe called **Jersey Bean Crock,** a traditional recipe that was so popular that apparently most farmhouses had bundles of drying French beans hanging from the rafters waiting to be shelled during the long winter evenings. Town residents would hang their beans in the garages. Another hearty meal and maybe one you might be interested to try out.

MORE FROM GEORGINA TROY

We hope you enjoyed reading *Summer Sundaes at Golden Sands Bay*. If you did, please leave a review.

If you'd like to gift a copy, this book is also available as an ebook, digital audio download and audiobook CD.

Sign up to Georgina Troy's mailing list for news, competitions and updates on future books.

https://bit.ly/GeorginaTroyNews

Explore more wonderful escapist fiction from Georgina Troy:

ABOUT THE AUTHOR

Georgina Troy writes bestselling uplifting romantic escapes and sets her novels on the island of Jersey, where she was born and has lived for most of her life. She has done a twelve-book deal with Boldwood, including backlist titles, and the first book in her Sunshine Island series was published in May 2022.

Visit Georgina's website: https://deborahcarr.org/my-books/georgina-troy-books/

Follow Georgina on social media here:

f facebook.com/GeorginaTroyAuthor
X x.com/GeorginaTroy
instagram.com/ajerseywriter
BB bookbub.com/authors/georgina-troy

Boldw**oo**d

Boldwood Books is an award-winning fiction publishing company seeking out the best stories from around the world.

Find out more at www.boldwoodbooks.com

Join our reader community for brilliant books, competitions and offers!

Follow us
@BoldwoodBooks
@TheBoldBookClub

Sign up to our weekly deals newsletter

https://bit.ly/BoldwoodBNewsletter

Milton Keynes UK
Ingram Content Group UK Ltd.
UKHW041053120424
441054UK00054B/748